"You don't hav
conquer everythi
It's okay to nee
Penny said.

Jonas looked into Penny Castlerock's serious blue eyes and wanted to believe her words. He really did. But his life experiences had taught him to believe otherwise. He had to be strong enough to take care of himself, of his family, on his own.

It wasn't safe to depend on others, especially not rich socialites.

Except…

Penny had begun by watching his daughter Breanna and then she'd sewn shirts for his whole family. Then she helped drive the hay wagon.

And she'd brought light to his home. Laughter that hadn't been there before her arrival at Walt's place.

She'd even given the boys advice on romance.

What if he *did* have a chance at winning her heart?

Books by Lacy Williams

Love Inspired Historical

Marrying Miss Marshal
The Homesteader's Sweetheart

LACY WILLIAMS

is a wife and mom from Oklahoma. Her first novel won ACFW's Genesis Award while it was still unpublished. She has loved romance books and movies from a young age and promises readers *happy endings guaranteed* in all her stories. Lacy combines her love of dogs with her passion for literacy by volunteering with her therapy dog, Mr. Bingley, in a local Kids Reading to Dogs program.

Lacy loves to hear from readers. You can email her at lacyjwilliams@gmail.com. She also posts short stories and does giveaways at her website, www.lacywilliams.net, and you can follow her on social media at www.facebook.com/lacywilliamsbooks or twitter.com/lacy_williams.

The
Homesteader's
Sweetheart

LACY
WILLIAMS

Love Inspired

Recycling programs
for this product may
not exist in your area.

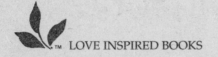

LOVE INSPIRED BOOKS

ISBN-13: 978-0-373-82917-0

THE HOMESTEADER'S SWEETHEART

Copyright © 2012 by Lacy Williams

www.LoveInspiredBooks.com

Printed in U.S.A.

A man's life
does not consist in the abundance of his possessions.
—*Luke* 12:15b

ACKNOWLEDGMENTS

A special thank-you to Luke for his support and encouragement in making this book happen.

Thanks also to…

My parents and in-laws, Sean & Megan, and Haley for their help and support.

My critique partners, Regina Jennings and Mischelle Creager for their excellent insights.

My local writers' groups for their prayers and encouragement.

My editor, Emily Rodmell, for her help making this manuscript the best it could be.

My agent, Sandra Bishop, for sealing the deal.

Chapter One

Wyoming Territory, summer 1890

Hadn't he promised himself not to get into a situation like this again?

Jonas White stood on the dusty street in his Sunday suit, letter clutched in his hand, gazing up at the fine house. It seemed too much of a coincidence that his neighbor and closest friend—although they were two generations apart in age—was related to a wealthy banker when Jonas desperately needed a loan. And the letter Jonas had promised to deliver for his friend would grant him access to the banker he'd been trying to see all day.

But Jonas had stopped questioning the Lord's hand in things once he'd met his neighbors, the Nelsons, just over five years ago.

Staring at the light spilling from the glass-paned windows onto the large, well-kept yard reminded Jonas of another place and time, and how as a child he'd often looked in on some of Philadelphia's wealthy families. Like those stately town houses, this house was ostentatious. Two-story and much larger than the other homes on the street. Or in the whole town of Calvin, Wyoming, for that matter.

Jonas resolutely pushed the painful memories to the back of his mind. His daughter needed him to do this, and he couldn't fail her.

Sounds of voices and tinkling china trickled out from the wide-open front door. Was the banker hosting a party? If so, this might not be the best time to call, but Jonas needed to take care of business before the woman who was watching Breanna for him left town on the next Eastbound train.

He brushed at some dust on his jacket sleeve and took a deep breath, reminding himself that his loan was a reasonable request. If only he felt more comfortable interacting with high-society people like the banker, but his upbringing didn't exactly lend itself to that.

Trudging up the steps before he could change his mind, Jonas entered the elegant home. The entry hall was empty, but voices drew him to a parlor packed with people.

One or two of them shook his hand, welcoming him as he moved through the crowded room. Most ignored him. Jonas scanned each face, looking for the portly man with salt-and-pepper hair that he'd glimpsed briefly on the boardwalk this morning. No sign of the banker.

Conversations ebbed and flowed around him as he moved through the parlor and into another lamp-lit room in search of Mr. Castlerock. He knew he was out of place, and the disdainful looks he received from some of the partygoers only confirmed it, made him feel as awkward and unwelcome as he'd felt at eighteen in the Broadhursts' Philadelphia home.

"Can I help ya, son?"

Jonas turned at the voice and caught sight of a plump woman with an apron covering most of her ample figure. Here was someone from his class, someone who could help him. Relief flooded him.

"Yes, I'm looking for Mr. Castlerock. I'm to deliver this letter, and I need to speak with him on another matter—"

The woman took the letter from Jonas. "I'll put it aside for the boss. If he sets it down during the party, he'll never remember where he put it in the morning. Last I saw him, he was in his study, down there..." She nodded toward a door down the hall and her voice trailed off as she bustled away in the opposite direction.

"Thanks," Jonas murmured to her departing back.

He couldn't be sure which room she'd meant to indicate— there were two doorways on the left and one on the right, so he peeked into each as he passed. Finally, he had no choice but to enter the room at the end of the hall.

So intent was he on locating the banker, Jonas didn't notice her at first. But as he tried to slip through the crowd without bumping into any of the fine furnishings or well-dressed guests, he caught a glimpse of upswept copper curls, burnished to fire by the lamplight.

He'd only ever seen one person with that color hair in his entire life.

Jonas froze, dumbstruck, as a tall man in a black jacket moved away and his view became unhindered. It *was* her, with the laughing blue eyes he remembered and wearing the frilliest, fanciest peach-colored dress he'd ever seen.

The girl he'd admired from afar, back in Philadelphia. Penny Castlerock.

He'd guessed from the unusual surname that she might be a relation to the wealthy banker, but never imagined he would see her here. He'd thought she would be married to a Philadelphia businessman by now. What was she doing in Wyoming?

Penny Castlerock caught sight of the farmer the moment he stepped into her father's study, where some of the guests had congregated. His dark suit was ill-fitting, in contrast to the tailored jackets worn by her father's acquaintances, but the suit's ugliness couldn't hide the muscled shoulders most likely earned through days of backbreaking labor in a field somewhere. His crown of blond hair showed a noticeable line where his hat must have rested earlier in the day.

And there was the hat. Clutched in one hand against the farmer's leg. The man appeared to be looking for someone, if his roving brown eyes were any indication.

The moment those intelligent brown eyes spotted her, he froze, a thunderstruck look on his face.

While he seemed vaguely familiar to her, she couldn't be sure she'd met the man before. And while she prided herself on the unusual shade of her hair and had taken extra pains to powder away the smattering of freckles she could never completely eliminate, she usually didn't elicit such a strong reaction upon a first meeting. It was quite flattering, even if he was only a farmer.

She moved to intercept him, breaking off a conversation with her dear friend Merritt Harding, the local schoolmarm. After all, *a lady's duty was to ensure all guests' needs were met.*

With advice from Mrs. Trimble's finishing school ringing in her ears, she greeted him with a warm, "Good evening," and the best smile she could procure after spending a long hour with her father's guests.

He emitted a strangled sound, not words, and gripped his hat in both hands, holding it almost as if it was a shield in front of him.

"There's punch on the serving buffet just through here, if you're thirsty." Penny extended her arm to indicate the dining room.

The man still didn't move, and she struggled to keep her smile in place. Common courtesy demanded he answer her, but he remained silent. And his stare was bordering on rude.

What was he doing here? Her father usually only included

those he deemed "important" and she wasn't sure this farmer fit the bill.

"I'm sorry, have we met before? Perhaps you're one of my father's acquaintances?" she asked, when the silence between them became fraught with tension.

"Penelope, darling, there you are."

Penny half-turned at her father's booming voice, relieved for the interruption from the awkward one-sided conversation. Why didn't the farmer *say* anything?

"Father, I've just been greeting one of our guests. This is Mr…" She left off her sentence to allow the farmer to offer his name, but instead he moved past her and extended his hand toward her father.

"Sir, I need to talk to you in private, if you have a few moments."

So the farmer could speak. But she still didn't know his name.

Her father's face creased as if he couldn't quite place the man. "I don't believe we've met. What can I do for you?"

"It's a business matter, sir." The farmer glanced briefly at Penny, just a flash of his brown eyes.

Penny was used to being excluded from her father's business, but it was a matter of contention with her. She felt women were intelligent enough to be involved in business matters, but her mother had always deferred to her father, leaving Penny no choice but to do the same.

Her father chuckled, not a kind sound. "I'm sorry, son, but I don't discuss business matters during my private parties."

Penny knew that was an exaggeration. Her father often had an after-dinner cigar or drink with his associates to talk business. Why didn't he want to speak to the farmer?

"You're welcome to make an appointment at the bank."

Her father took her elbow, obviously considering the conversation finished, and began to guide Penny away from the farmer.

"Sir, I've been to the bank twice today, trying to see you."

The farmer's statement was louder this time, drawing looks from others in the study.

Penny's father didn't stop, but she saw his face redden from the corner of her eye—a sign he was becoming irritated. "I'm sorry to hear that, but I'm a very busy man, you know."

Penny stifled a snicker. Yes, and her father was also full of his own self-importance. She almost felt sorry for the farmer, and probably would've if he hadn't caused an uncomfortable scene.

"I need a loan," the farmer called out as Penny and her father moved away, his voice becoming desperate, intense. "I've a homestead with a cabin and a barn to put up for it."

Her father's face was now crimson, indicating his mood had moved from simply irritated to angry. That did not bode well for the farmer.

"Son, you'll have to come to the bank and talk to me during business hours."

With that final statement, her father swept from the room—as much as he could in the press of people now craning their necks to see what the raised voices were about—pulling her along with him.

"The nerve—" he sputtered, apparently unable to form coherent sentences. "Embarrassing me in front of guests—"

"You could've granted him a private audience," Penny admonished softly.

She knew her words were a mistake as her father's face purpled. As he opened his mouth to rebuke her, they were interrupted.

"Ah, Penelope. You look positively striking this evening."

A familiar, nasally voice silenced her father, giving Penny

a reprieve. For now. She knew her father would have much to say to her—probably in a tirade—once the guests had taken their leave. However, this interruption wasn't one she particularly desired.

She forced a smile, knowing her father was also schooling his own features. The Castlerock family was nothing if not proper when in public. Her father's position on the town council demanded no less. Nor did the man himself.

Her father's business associate, Herman Abbott, half-bowed over her wrist, and Penny couldn't help but note the clamminess of his grip, much like a limp, dead fish. She reclaimed her hand and tucked it into the folds of her gown, wishing she could wipe away the disgusting feeling but not daring to.

She couldn't help a glance over Mr. Abbott's skinny shoulders to the long case clock to gauge how much longer she had to participate in tonight's event.

"I was hoping to speak to you tonight," Mr. Abbott went on, apparently not noticing her inattention. "With your father's permission, I'd like to take you on a buggy ride tomorrow morning. I've just had the carriage resprung," he said as an aside with a proud look at Penny's father.

"I'm afraid that won't be possible," she inserted before the men could decide for her. "I'm going to help Mr. Silverton at the bank. Mrs. Shannon—the bank teller—" she explained for Mr. Abbott's benefit, "just had her baby and he has not been able to find a replacement yet."

She hadn't promised any such thing, but the bank manager would indulge her if she arrived early enough. She had no desire to spend time with her father's associate. Not only was he older, much closer to her father's age than Penny's, but there was something about him that made her uncomfortable...

"You know I don't like you working in the teller window,"

her father hissed. To Abbott he said, "Our family is certainly of a station that my daughter has no need to work. Of course, her mother and I encourage her to help those less fortunate—show compassion for the common man and all—"

Penny gritted her teeth, hoping her facial muscles approximated a smile while the two men chuckled. While she enjoyed the fine things her father's money bought, such as the taffeta gown she wore this very moment, she didn't think that same wealth gave her father reason to lord it over those around him.

The men's arrogant posturing bothered her, and she allowed her mind to wander. Why had her father dismissed the farmer so abruptly? The man seemed familiar to her, though she couldn't recall a name. Had her father been in such a hurry to partner her with Abbott that he'd been unnecessarily rude to the man?

And why couldn't her father sense that she had no interest in Mr. Abbott? Of all her father's associates, there was something about Mr. Abbott that unnerved her. It wasn't that he looked at her inappropriately, per se. But something behind his eyes…

A man in a resplendent dark jacket approached, and her father was drawn into conversation, leaving Penny and Mr. Abbott standing together.

"It seems a shame to waste the morning," he said, turning his glittering gaze on her. "Are you sure you can't get out of your commitment to the bank?"

Penny managed to keep her smile in place, but it was a near thing. "I'm certain."

"Perhaps we can arrange for a buggy ride in the evening, then," he pressed.

"Perhaps," Penny hedged. She knew an outright refusal would be considered rude, but she didn't want to encourage the man.

"I'm most interested in deepening our acquaintance—"

Why must he push so?

"Oh!" She glimpsed a flash of fuchsia skirt passing the doorway. "I've just seen a friend I absolutely *must* speak to. Will you excuse me?" She inclined her head and scooted away before he could respond.

Emerging in the hallway, Penny spied her sixteen-year-old brother Sam sneaking into the kitchen and changed her course to follow him. She slipped through the door, one hand against her midsection as she tried to catch her breath. That had been entirely too close for comfort—she had no wish to spend any more time with Mr. Herman Abbott.

Sam's head jerked up from his station behind the fancy chocolate cake that Ethel, the family's combined cook and maid, had spent all morning baking.

"Sam, you'd better not be thinking of disturbing the food for our guests. You know Papa is still angry about the nasty words you painted on the side of the schoolhouse."

At her admonishment, her brother's expression changed from guilt to something colder. "I told you that was Billy, not me."

She didn't know whether to believe him or not. He'd been in plenty of trouble all on his own, including the horse he'd tried to steal right off Main Street, and as of late she had difficulty identifying if he was lying or not.

"Just don't do anything to cause trouble tonight," she chided him.

"We just want a taste of cake, that's all."

Her eyebrows went up. "We?"

"Me 'n Louie." Sam tipped his head to the side and Penny's gaze followed to the window, where the shadow of a head and shoulders could be seen.

"Papa wouldn't let him come to the party—" And no wonder. She'd never seen Sam's friend wear anything but torn, stained clothing. He probably didn't own a Sunday suit and wouldn't have fit with her father's associates.

The comparison made her think of the farmer, who hadn't fit in at all, but there had been something about him that had drawn her...

"—and we just want a taste, anyway."

"Sam..." she warned. She had a bad feeling that this would lead to trouble for her brother.

"Aw, why don't you go back to your beau and leave me alone?"

Penny hoped he wasn't talking about Mr. Abbott. The stubborn tilt of her brother's chin told her he wasn't going to listen, so she turned to leave. She spared him one more glance as she returned to the gathering. Sam motioned his friend to come in the back door.

"I can't believe you embarrassed me like that. Herman said you just ran off and left him."

"I saw someone I needed to talk to—" Penny tried to explain, but her father spoke over her words.

"While your impulsiveness might be charming to your friends, I'm not certain it is a trait Herman is looking for in a wife."

Penny opened her mouth to tell her father that was just fine with her as she had no desire to have Mr. Abbott for a suitor, when her father continued.

"Herman has asked for my permission to pay court. It is his intention to marry soon. We've talked and decided you'd make an excellent match."

Her mother's eyes came up from the afghan bunched in her lap, but she remained still and silent on the parlor sofa.

Penny couldn't contain a gasp. "Am I to be settled like a business deal, then?" Agitated, she rose and paced to the front window. "I don't *like* Mr. Abbott. I have no wish to be courted by him *or* to consider marriage to him."

She didn't have to look in the reflection of the glass panes to know her father's face was going red. "Herman is one of my closest associates—"

"And that has nothing to do with whether he would be an acceptable husband." Penny whirled to face her father. "He is arrogant, speaks only of his own interests all the time. Why, I doubt he even knows I like to paint!"

"Those things will come as he gets to know you. You will allow him to come courting—"

"I won't—"

"You *will,* or you'll see your clothing allowance severely curtailed. I have given Herman my word."

Penny shook all over, her anger was so great.

"Darling, why don't you go up to bed?" her mother suggested, ever the peacemaker. "Perhaps we can discuss things further in the morning."

"There is nothing further to discuss—"

"Papa, can't I go to bed?" Sam interrupted from his slouched position on the other settee.

"No! I'm not through with you, boy. I can't believe you ruined a whole cake—there was no dessert to serve to my guests—"

Penny turned and stomped away, knowing she'd get no further with her father while he was in the midst of one of his tirades. Thankfully, his attention had turned to Sam, but what was she going to do?

Her mother followed her out of the parlor. "I'll come up and help you unpin your hair."

Upstairs in her room, Penny fumed as she nudged aside the romantic dime novel she'd been reading earlier and settled on the chair in front of her looking glass.

How could her father do this to her?

Her mother appeared behind her in the reflection and began removing the pins holding the intricate style in place. Her fingers in Penny's hair were a comfort—as they'd been throughout Penny's youth, whenever her father had lost his temper over something insignificant. Like a grass stain on the knees of her dress—the reason she was careful to look perfect at all times.

"I can't believe Papa would do this…"

"Your father and I want what's best for you, darling," came her mother's voice, muffled by pins pressed between her lips.

"Well, it isn't *Herman Abbott,* no matter what Father thinks."

"How can you know?" her mother asked, again with her unending patience. "You should get to know him, allow him to court."

I don't want to know him. Penny didn't voice the thought. It seemed as if her mother already agreed with her father's decision.

"But several weeks ago, I overheard him telling Papa he didn't think our church should support the needy." At the time, his words had shocked her in their callousness.

"Perhaps you misunderstood," came her mother's unruffled response.

"But—"

"Your father and I want to see you settled. You had a chance to make a match of your own when you were away at finishing school. And when you came back from Philadelphia without a husband three years ago, we didn't push…"

The reminder of Penny's failure to land a wealthy Eastern husband rankled. She'd known her father had been disappointed, but none of the men she'd met had caught her interest. She was only twenty-three, not an old maid yet.

"Give Mr. Abbott a chance."

"But—" Penny grasped onto the first thing she could think

of. "What about love?" She tapped the romance novel with her index finger.

Her mother's expression flickered in the looking glass. "Love comes later."

"Like it did for you?" Penny asked. She immediately regretted the impertinent question. Why couldn't she control her impulsive tongue better?

"I'm sorry, Mama. I didn't mean that."

Her mother was silent.

"But…what about—don't you remember what it was like between Grandfather and Grandmother?"

As a child, Penny had been allowed to spend summers with her maternal grandparents, who lived on a homestead a day's ride away. Even in the reduced circumstances they'd lived in, Penny had been awed by the love her grandparents had shared. They never seemed to argue, always put each other's needs first.

It had been a stark contrast to the relationship her parents shared, where her father made constant demands and her mother never stood up for herself.

Her mother finished removing the pins and shook out Penny's long, curly tresses. She reached for the silver-plated hairbrush on Penny's dressing table.

"Your father has not always been the easiest man to live with," she finally said.

Penny thought of the tirades, her father's unmercifully high expectations. She knew the Good Book said to *honor thy father and mother,* but didn't it also say *fathers, provoke not your children?*

"But neither was your grandfather."

Her mother's surprising statement brought Penny's eyes back up to meet hers in the looking glass. She couldn't imagine her gentle, quiet grandfather in a temper.

"Never having enough money for new dresses, or boots…" Her voice trailed off, obviously she was lost in the past.

Penny gazed at the skirt of the beautiful peach gown her father had allowed her to have for tonight's event. She fingered the soft lace at her wrist. It was an exquisite gown. And she had several more, just as fine…

"You must give Mr. Abbott a chance," said her mother at last, putting the brush back on the table.

Penny didn't argue with her, but her mind was made up. She would never accept Herman Abbott as a suitor. She just needed to discover a way to escape his attentions.

Chapter Two

Penny joined her mother at the dining table the next morning after a sleepless night. She considered herself an intelligent woman, but she still couldn't figure a way to evade Mr. Abbott's attentions.

"You don't look very rested, my dear," her mother commented before taking a sip of tea from a delicate china cup. "I suppose you're still determined not to bow to your father's wishes?"

"Missus Castlerock, I forgot to give this to your husband." Ethel bustled into the room with a plate for Penny and plunked a letter down next to her mother. "Gentleman delivered it last night."

"Which gentleman?" Penny asked curiously, pouring her own cup of tea and thankful for the interruption. Perhaps her mother would forget her earlier question about Penny's intentions.

"Didn't catch his name, but he didn't look like one of the boss's usual acquaintances."

The farmer. It had to be. Penny had spoken to most of the other people at her father's party and he was the only one who might match Ethel's description.

"What does it say?" she asked her mother, who'd opened the missive.

"It's from your grandfather, sent with a neighbor." Her mother's eyes scanned the letter and in a moment, her face crumpled. "Your grandfather has been ill. He asked if we could send someone out to help him for a few days."

Penny considered the request. "He's never asked for help before."

Her mother sniffled and pulled a lace handkerchief from her sleeve. "You're right. It sounds as if…something might be wrong."

Penny knew her mother was within moments of going into a fit of hysterics. "May I see the letter?"

She scanned her grandfather's spidery writing. "It doesn't sound so bad. Maybe he just needs help catching up with some of the chores since he's been down with a fever and a cough."

Returning the letter to her mother, an idea began to form. "What if I traveled up to Bear Creek to help Grandfather for a little while?" If she left town for a few days or a week, perhaps her father would reconsider allowing Mr. Abbott to court.

Her mother's brow wrinkled. "But you haven't been to the homestead since you were a girl. And you don't know anything about farming."

At that moment, Sam shuffled into the room, scowling. Obviously, he was still upset about whatever punishment their father had meted out last night.

"Sam could come, too!" Penny nearly bounced in her chair in excitement. It was the perfect solution to get her away from Calvin for a bit and away from Mr. Abbott. "Sam can help with the physical chores. And it would give Papa some time to forget his anger about the ruined cake."

"But how will you get there? Your father won't agree to take you—"

Penny already had an answer for that as well. "If the farmer—Grandfather's neighbor—is still in town, perhaps he could be persuaded to allow Sam and me to ride back to Bear Creek." It had to work.

"What's going on?" Sam asked, joining them at the table.

Her mother shook her head. "Your sister—"

"Has come up with the perfect idea to help Grandfather." And get some distance from Mr. Abbott, Penny added silently.

"But what about this farmer—"

"Surely if Grandfather entrusted a personal letter to him, he can be trusted to give us a ride out to the homestead," Penny argued. "And Sam could act as chaperone, so it couldn't be considered inappropriate."

Penny suddenly wilted into her chair. "I'd forgotten. I'm supposed to help out at the bank for a bit this morning." If her father didn't see her behind the teller window, he'd be even angrier about her fib to Mr. Abbott. "Do you think Ethel might go down to the hotel or boardinghouse to find the farmer and convince him to come by?"

Her mother's eyes scrutinized Penny more closely than she would've liked. Could she see behind her words to the real reason Penny wanted to visit Grandfather so badly? "I suppose it wouldn't hurt."

Spirits restored, Penny bounced up out of her seat. "I'll go ask Ethel for help."

She heard Sam's question as she left the room. "Will someone please tell *me* what is happening?"

Jonas stood awkwardly in the opulent bank lobby, wearing his same Sunday suit, hat in hand, waiting to talk to Mr. Castlerock, who sat at a wide desk behind a waist-high partition. Jonas prayed he hadn't ruined his chances of securing a loan with his outburst at the banker's party last night.

He'd known better than to go into that lavish home.

But he was desperate to get the loan. His daughter's doctor in Cheyenne, the only one Jonas had found who had a treatment for her epilepsy, demanded payment in full before he would procure the medicine. This bank loan was Jonas's last option.

Even with his money troubles weighing on his mind, he couldn't stop thinking about Penny Castlerock, who hadn't recognized him last night. He hadn't expected her to be friendly, as they didn't and never would move in the same social circles, but he'd thought she would at least remember him.

He'd worked for weeks on the stately home next to the girls' school she'd attended in Philadelphia. As a bricklayer's apprentice, his was dirty, outdoor work. Mostly, he'd seen her through the large windows overlooking the small yard where he'd repaired an exterior wall and part of a stairwell. He'd never gotten the courage to address her any of the few times she'd passed him as she left the girls' school for an errand or shopping excursion.

But he'd never be able to forget her face. Her features were indelibly imprinted on his mind. And he'd caught her gaze on him several times, though they'd never actually spoken...

How many times had he thought of Miss Castlerock on his and Breanna's journey west from Philadelphia? Especially in the dark part of night, when he'd fumbled his way through feeding and diapering a crying baby over five years ago.

He remembered everything about her. Those clear blue eyes, a hint of mischief always lurking in their depths. Her copper curls, held back in a fashionable style.

Her laugh. He hadn't heard it last night, but it was the thing he remembered most clearly about her. A joyful, exuberant noise that he'd heard once in Philadelphia as she'd walked down the street. More than five years ago now, but the sound had had the power to set a boulder in his gut then and Jonas imagined it still would.

Especially for someone like him—someone without much to laugh about in his lifetime.

She hadn't remembered him at all.

And now Miss Castlerock was behind the teller counter—another surprise—and kept sending curious glances at him over the heads of the patrons in line.

A gruff "ahem" brought his attention to the older man, who was gesturing Jonas past the partition. His expression was closed, and Jonas suspected the loan would be denied.

But he had to try. For his daughter, he could grovel. Breanna was everything to him.

Less than a quarter hour later, Jonas strode away from the bank, disappointment bitter in his throat, cold all over despite the warm summer sun blazing down on him.

Denied. Again.

He'd been to every bank between here and Cheyenne, and no one would make him a loan. How could he raise funds to pay for Breanna's treatment on his own?

"Papa!" A projectile launched itself at him, brown curls and faded blue dress flying behind her.

With practiced movements, he caught the little girl and swung her in a circle, her excited shrieks making him forget about the weight pressing on his shoulders. Breanna and the boys, his adopted sons, were his life. He couldn't let his daughter down. He had to find a way to get the money he needed.

"Breanna! You must be feeling better."

She nodded, throwing her arms around his neck and hugging him.

Mrs. Clark, the older widow who had been a neighbor

and helped him keep house and take care of Breanna when he needed to be out in the fields, nodded to him from where she stood just outside the hotel where she and Breanna had spent the night. Jonas had slept out under the stars in a bed-roll, unable to justify the expense of a second hotel room when he could sleep outside for free.

Breanna had had another seizure last night just after they'd arrived in town. Jonas still felt the terror that infused him every time her eyes unfocused and she stiffened like a board. At least now he'd had enough practice at recognizing the warning signs that he was able to lay her down on the floor or a bed when the seizure began.

He still remembered the first one she'd experienced, when she was three. She'd hit her head on a kitchen chair as she'd fallen to the ground. There had been blood everywhere. Oscar and Seb, the first two of his adopted brood, had both stood by in total panic, white-faced. For long moments, he'd thought he would lose her...

Jonas shook those thoughts away, focusing on the little girl in his arms, eyes sparkling with life, cheeks flushed. *His* little girl, the one God had gifted him with when he'd thought he'd never have such a wonder in his life. He didn't care one whit that she wasn't his by blood, she was his *daughter*.

"Papa, you said we'd go to breakfast when you got back from the bank. Can we go *now?*"

Jonas loved his daughter's exuberance. Eating at the café would be a special treat for her, one his family didn't get to enjoy often enough. Money was tight; it was hard enough to put food on the table for a large family like his—mismatched as they were. Eating at a restaurant was a rare thing.

"Mrs. Clark, would you like to join us? After that we'll need to pick up the wagon at the General Store and get going, Breanna."

"Thank you for the offer, young man." Mrs. Clark always

called him that, though she wasn't yet his mother's age, if his mother was even still alive. "But my train leaves in a few hours and I should rest up for the journey."

The reminder that he was losing his help strained his smile, but for Breanna's benefit he kept it in place. Mrs. Clark had recently been widowed and was going back East to live with family.

"I hope you will be happy living with your daughter back East." He reached out to clasp the woman's hand. "Thank you for all your help this past year." He didn't want to imagine what a mess he would have made of things if she hadn't been around.

Mrs. Clark accepted his hand, then a hug from Breanna.

"Tell those boys goodbye for me. All right, Breanna?" Mrs. Clark asked.

"Yes, I will." Breanna sniffled.

Mrs. Clark's words were another reminder that he'd left Oscar in charge and Jonas needed to get back to the homestead. The seventeen-year-old was older in spirit than his age suggested, but it was the first time Jonas had left the seven boys home with only his neighbor Walt Nelson nearby to watch over them. And Jonas knew how little it took for two of those boys in particular to get into mischief.

He tried to be a good father, but he felt as if waves crashed upon him from every side. Sometimes he felt he was drowning.

"Shall we go and get our breakfast?" he asked, hoping to distract his daughter from melancholy.

It seemed to work, for she accepted his hand and they set off down the boardwalk toward the café he'd passed on his way to the Calvin Bank and Trust earlier this morning.

"Papa, can we go and visit Mrs. Clark at her daughter's house?"

"Perhaps you can go and see her when you're older." As

for him, he had vowed never to go back east of the Mississippi River. Only bad memories waited there.

"Can I have biscuits and gravy for breakfast?"

Jonas squeezed Breanna's hand in his. "We'll have to see what they're serving this morning. It might be flapjacks or something else."

Thankfully, his daughter was a lot like him. Not a picky eater. In his childhood, he'd lived through several hard winters eating garbage back in Philadelphia. And his daughter had never known that kind of poverty. He resolved that she would *never* know it.

Penny darted out the bank door, nearly knocking into Mrs. Stoll, who ran the boardinghouse.

"Excuse me!"

Penny had had a line of customers when the farmer had been in the bank to see her father, and hadn't been able to get away to talk to him. When Mr. Silverton had arrived a few minutes after the farmer had gone, she'd rushed to count the money in her till, fumbling and miscounting once in her haste.

And now she hurried out onto the boardwalk, trying to guess where the farmer would've gone. Hoping he hadn't already left town.

There were plenty of people out on the boardwalk, wagons and horses lined the hard-packed streets. Where would the farmer have gone?

She guessed the grocery, and headed in that direction. She allowed herself to be distracted for only a moment by a lovely chestnut-colored mare with white socks on three of its feet, pausing only to admire its conformation before she hurried on.

As she passed the undertaker's, she caught sight of Mr. Abbott speaking to another man on the boardwalk and ducked into the space between two buildings. The two men had their backs to her, so hopefully Abbott hadn't seen her.

As she peeked out from her hiding place, Penny saw a tall man with broad shoulders in a black coat exit the café. Was it the farmer?

And what were Abbott and his friend doing? They appeared to be conversing in low tones but showed no indication of moving along down the street.

Penny glanced after the man in the dark jacket. He was entering one of the stores down the street, but she couldn't tell which one. She edged closer to the boardwalk, wondering if she should just cross to the other side of the street and hope Mr. Abbott didn't see her.

"Miss Castlecrock?" Penny heard the man with Mr. Abbott ask incredulously. Her ears perked at hearing her own name. "Isn't she a bit…hard to please? I mean, she's mighty fancy…"

Immediately up in arms at the mean-spirited assumption, Penny bit back a response and reminded herself she didn't want Mr. Abbott to see her.

"She's beautiful, all right," the man continued. "But high-spirited…"

Mr. Abbott chuckled, not a pleasant sort of sound at all. "Yes, she's much like Annie was in the beginning. My first wife was used to having her own way, as well."

His first what? Wife? Did Father know that Herman Abbott had been married before?

"But she quickly learned obedience was the best thing for her. Taming her spirit was…"

Mr. Abbott's voice lowered and Penny couldn't hear the rest of his words. A shiver of unease crawled down Penny's spine. While his words weren't an outright threat, they certainly sounded sinister. The question was, would her father believe what she'd overheard?

"Doesn't matter." Abbott's voice rose again. His confident

air rankled her. "Her father wants to solidify our business dealings and I've convinced him that marrying his daughter will further our connection. Once we're married, she'll do as I say."

"Not likely," Penny muttered under her breath. To either part.

"After all, there are ways a woman can be brought to my way of thinking, regardless of how strong-willed she is."

Penny's outrage would no longer be contained. "You'll get no such acquiescence from me," she spat, stomping onto the boardwalk.

The two men turned toward her, surprise registering on their faces.

Instead of being embarrassed, or getting angry, like her father would've, Mr. Abbott's eyes glinted with something unidentifiable. "Miss Castlerock. I thought you were helping at the bank this morning? If you're quite finished, I'll escort you home."

"That's not necessary. I am perfectly able to see myself home."

His eyes narrowed. "I insist." He took her arm in an iron grip and pushed her down the boardwalk. "I'm sure your father wouldn't appreciate you making a scene in front of his acquaintance."

She tried to yank her arm away, but he held fast. "If you're finished at the bank," his patronizing tone told her he suspected she'd made up the engagement at the bank, "I'll call around with the buggy after lunch."

"I'd prefer not. I usually go calling with my mother in the afternoons."

"I'm certain she can spare your company for an afternoon."

Angry at his continued presumption, she stopped cold. They'd almost reached Penny's street corner, and she wanted to be across the way, where she thought she'd seen the farmer go into one of the buildings.

"Do you honestly think we'd suit?" she demanded. Never mind her new reservations. At least for now.

Again, that unholy light sparked in his eyes. "Oh, I'm certain of it."

"But you don't know anything about me."

"I know enough."

His enigmatic comment did not reassure her. "Really? What is my favorite pastime? My favorite food?"

"There is plenty of time in the future to learn those things… Or perhaps your likes will come to align with mine in time. Your father and I both think you and I would make a fine match."

She wasn't convinced; the man wasn't even listening to her.

"I'll call for you after the noon meal." He patted her hand, tone condescending.

She pulled away from his touch and used both hands to shake out her gown. "If you'll excuse me, I'd forgotten Ethel needed some eggs and butter."

Quickly, Penny ducked into the General Store, the closest building, glancing over her shoulder to ensure Abbott hadn't followed her.

His high-handedness infuriated her, but it was the cold, calculating gleam beneath his stern manner that frightened her.

She was so intent on evading Abbott's attentions that she scarcely noticed the man with a little girl perusing the dry goods nearby. Until the small child gasped and tugged on Penny's skirt.

"Miss—"

Penny turned to the child just as the little girl's father exclaimed, "Breanna!" and pulled her away by the arm.

It was the farmer. Relief swept through Penny even as she glanced over her shoulder. No one entered the building behind her. No Abbott.

The man bent and spoke to his daughter in a tone too low for Penny to hear—though she tried—but she hated for the girl to get into trouble, especially when Penny was about to ask him for a favor. "It's all right," Penny interrupted, and the man turned a surprised face to her.

He straightened to his full height and shifted the hat he held between his hands. "I'm sorry—your dress—" One of his hands jerked awkwardly toward her skirt.

Penny glanced down and saw a handprint that looked suspiciously like melted licorice now marred the pale yellow silk of her skirt.

"Is it ruined?"

"I'm sure it isn't," Penny said, though she wasn't sure of any such thing. Perhaps Ethel knew of a remedy to remove the stain. Penny wasn't worried about the dress, though. She had much bigger problems today.

Mr. Hyer, the General Store owner, addressed the farmer and both men turned away, the farmer pulling a piece of folded paper from his shirt pocket. Probably his shopping list.

"Miss?"

This time the little girl's voice was tentative and she kept her hands clasped behind her.

Penny shifted her skirt and squatted to speak at the girl's level. "Hello. My name is Penny. What's yours?"

"Breanna," came the soft reply.

"I see you are helping your father with his purchases."

"Yes'm. Miss?"

"Yes?"

"I never seen a dress so pretty as yours." The girl's awed whisper was accented by her wide brown eyes.

"Why, thank you."

Breanna's eyes darted from Penny to a nearby mannequin wearing a frilly, child-size gown.

Penny couldn't help but notice the state of the girl's dress—a simple calico print, worn in some places, too short. She'd noticed the farmer's ill-fitting suit last night, but in the daylight, its worn condition was apparent as well. Penny knew her grandfather's homestead hadn't created much income in its early years. Not until he'd obtained a couple of good breeding mares and begun raising fine horses. It appeared her grandfather's neighbors did not have enough funds to obtain newer clothing.

Her heart pinched a little for the girl who wished for pretty things.

"Are you and your father in town for long?" Penny pried, a glance revealing the farmer still in conversation with Mr. Hyer.

"We stayed the night in a fancy hotel, but today we have to go home." This was said in such a matter-of-fact tone that Penny had to hide a smile.

The farmer glanced over his shoulder and started to turn as he caught sight of Penny and Breanna conversing, but Penny sent him what she meant to be a charming smile to reassure him. She hoped he was receptive to her plea—she wouldn't go on a buggy ride with Mr. Abbott, nor any other activity.

The farmer rejoined Penny and Breanna, putting a hand on his daughter's shoulder. "I hope she wasn't being bothersome."

"No, no," Penny said quickly, straightening up from her crouch. "Actually, I was hoping to find you."

His raised eyebrows communicated his disbelief. "Why?"

Well, it wasn't the most positive of responses, but Penny thought of Mr. Abbott's advances and soldiered on. "My mother wanted to thank you for delivering Grandfather's letter to us. And…I'm afraid I'm going to press upon your goodwill."

His expression closed. Breanna watched both adults with rapt attention.

"In his letter, my grandfather indicated he has been a bit under the weather, and my mother wishes to send me and my brother out to visit him. Unfortunately, our father is too busy to arrange to take us. I was—we were hoping we could convince you to allow us to ride along with you to Grandfather's place. If you have room in your wagon."

He was silent, mouth slightly open as if he couldn't understand her request.

"I know it is an imposition," she rushed on, praying he wouldn't say no. "We'd be willing to pay you a sum for your services, of course."

Still he didn't respond, only clutched his daughter's shoulder and stared at Penny. He was going to deny her request. Panic seized Penny's chest and she knew it must be showing on her face. She *needed* this man's cooperation.

"Please, I—" Her throat closed over the rest of her words. What else could she say? She *had to* obtain his agreement.

Finally, after what seemed an eternity, he cleared his throat. "All right."

Chapter Three

"Are you certain you want to do this? You haven't spent more than an afternoon with your grandfather since you were younger…won't you be bored on the homestead?"

I don't have a choice. I won't be pushed into courting a man I can't abide.

Penny reassured her mother with a smile, clutching the small satchel she'd quickly stuffed with a couple of her older dresses and her tooth powder. She was acutely aware of the hall clock ticking away, every moment bringing Mr. Abbott's pending visit closer. "Grandfather needs someone to help, and I'm sure Sam and I can manage for a bit."

The sound of hooves and the creaking of a wagon in front of the house were a welcome sound. Penny flipped aside the curtain to ensure it was the farmer—she'd been so concerned with getting his agreement earlier that she had completely forgotten the proprieties and hadn't properly introduced herself to the man—then moved into the foyer.

"Sam!" she called up the stairs. "It's time to go!"

Her mother trailed her onto the front veranda and across the lawn as the farmer set the brake on his wagon and hopped down. He tipped his hat. "Ma'am."

The little girl's head popped up from inside the wagon

and she leaned out over the side, arms hanging down as she smiled at Penny.

Mother looked to Penny for introductions and Penny felt her face heat. What good was an education at one of the finest ladies' finishing schools in Philadelphia if she forgot her manners at inopportune moments?

"I'm terribly sorry for my rudeness earlier, but we weren't properly introduced. I'm Penny Castlerock and this is my mother, Mary."

An expression Penny couldn't classify crossed the man's face before he removed his hat and clutched it between his hands—a nervous trait? She'd seen him do it at least twice. "Jonas White."

He seemed to be waiting for a reaction to his name, but Penny didn't know what he expected. When she'd seen him at her father's party, she'd experienced a moment of recognition, but couldn't place where she'd seen him before.

"I'm sorry—" she stammered. "Have we…met before?"

A flush rose in his cheeks. "Not formally. But several years ago, I worked as a bricklayer's apprentice in Philadelphia."

And suddenly, she knew why he seemed familiar.

"You repaired the home next door to the finishing school." And had been fired for compromising one of the other girls in Mrs. Trimble's Academy.

A glance at the brown-haired girl hanging from the wagon made Penny's heart beat uncomfortably. Was this the child born from that union? It had to be.

Penny's mother looked between Jonas White and Penny, obviously sensing the sudden tension. If Penny told her mother the truth, she would never agree to let Penny ride along to her grandfather's homestead, Sam's presence notwithstanding.

But perhaps accepting a ride from a man with such loose moral standards wasn't the best idea, either.

She'd brought this conundrum on herself—her impulsiveness in pushing for a ride. If she'd waited for her father to figure out a way for her to visit her grandfather's homestead, this never would have happened.

But she still needed to escape Calvin—and Mr. Abbott—for a while.

The front door slammed, and Sam tromped down the steps, a satchel slung over his shoulder, scowl etched on his face.

Time to decide. Stay in Calvin and attempt to ward off Mr. Abbott's advances, or go with this man and hope for the best.

This was a bad idea.

Jonas had known it the moment he'd agreed to give Miss Penny Castlerock a ride out to Walt's place. And he thought it again as recognition flared across her expressive face.

Now she remembered him. And although she carefully schooled her expression, he saw the flash of derision cross her features. He knew what she thought: the same thing that all those folks who'd believed the scandal back in Philadelphia thought. That he had fathered Breanna out of wedlock.

He knew the truth, but what if she mentioned his past, or at least what she knew of it, in Philadelphia in front of Breanna?

He should never have agreed to allow her to ride along, but he'd been concerned for his friend and mentor, Walt, who had seemed a bit under the weather lately. And Walt's place *had* been getting more run down; Miss Castlerock's brother could help him get things back in order. Although the boy, who was obviously related to Miss Castlerock with that shock of auburn hair and the same bright blue eyes, didn't look as if he knew the first thing about working on a homestead.

Jonas's last hope that Miss Castlerock would change her mind dissipated as she reached out and embraced her mother. "I'll write a note when I can to let you know how Grandfather is doing."

Jonas turned away to check the horses' harness. "Seat's not too wide. One of you will need to ride in the back." He and the general store proprietor had arranged the goods to leave enough room for someone to sit back there.

It was too much to hope that Miss Castlerock would sit in back. Instead, the boy grumbled as he climbed into the wagon. His attitude reminded Jonas of his son Edgar when Jonas had found him on the streets of Cheyenne and taken him in. Unwilling to help, sullen...but Edgar had responded to Jonas's steady presence and the hard work that had been assigned to him.

It had taken a bit longer for Edgar to settle and realize he had a permanent home with Jonas, Breanna and the other adopted boys. Over a year to erase that sense of worry about where the next meal was coming from, where he'd sleep tonight, having a place of his own...

Jonas blinked away the memories. Perhaps working on Walt's homestead was just what Penny's brother needed to settle him as well, but Jonas hoped the older man was equipped to handle a sulky teen.

Jonas glanced up and realized Miss Castlerock was waiting for him to help her up onto the wagon's bench, an inscrutable look on her features. Her gaze reminded him of being eighteen again and having a flock of tittering girls in colorful dresses watching him lay bricks. The same mortification— embarrassment that he was so far below their station, unease because he thought them beautiful—filled him now, but he stuffed it away. He was a grown man, a man with a family to take care of. If not respected by the people in his community, he at least made his own way. And that was something to be proud of.

As he boosted her up onto the seat, he wasn't prepared for the heat of her hand in his, even through her soft, white glove.

"Thank you," she murmured.

He cleared his throat, but didn't respond as he crossed in front of the horses and used the wagon wheel to lever himself into the seat.

She swished her skirts and smoothed them, and part of the fabric brushed his calf and almost sent him jumping out of the seat. Had the seat always been so small? He felt awkward and too large next to her.

Behind him, Breanna was questioning Sam Castlerock, who responded in nearly unintelligible grunts. With seven brothers, his daughter was used to teen boys and wasn't letting this one's sullenness deter her, if her chatter was any indication.

Jonas released the brake and snapped the reins, and the horses began to move. Miss Castlerock's shoulder bumped his as the wagon crawled into motion.

"You'll have to excuse my brother," she said softly. "He's been…difficult as of late."

She paused, then went on. "I think perhaps my mother hopes some time with our grandfather will straighten him out."

Jonas agreed. "Hard work never hurt a body. Walt's got plenty to do around his place." He'd learned about hard work growing up on the streets, then found there was plenty of it to be done in the West just the same as there had been in Philadelphia.

The reminder of the past between them, and what she must think of him, was sharp in his chest. With a glance over his shoulder to make sure Breanna was still engaged, Jonas spoke quickly in a low voice.

"I'd appreciate it if you wouldn't speak of Breanna's mother or the…circumstances under which I left Philadelphia." He planned to tell Breanna before she was grown, but right now she was just a little girl.

This close, he could see the curiosity and something else pass through Miss Castlerock's clear blue eyes. "As you wish," came her soft reply after a long moment when he didn't dare breathe.

And just in time, because Breanna popped her head up between Jonas and Penny. "Miss Penny, your brother is funny."

Miss Castlerock turned to address his daughter and her knee bumped Jonas's. Jonas opened his mouth to prevent her saying anything rude to his daughter, who had a tendency to be a bit precocious, but the young woman spoke before he could.

"Why, you've made a little nest for yourself."

She must've spotted the little gap Breanna had created amongst the boxes and bundles. Miss Castlerock went on, "Hmm, I suppose Sam can be funny sometimes, although I don't always appreciate his humor. Just the other night he was trying to play a prank and ruined an entire chocolate sheet cake that I really wanted to taste."

Breanna's eyes grew big in her face. "He sounds like Ricky! My brother pulls my pigtails all the time in church and sometimes I wish he wasn't my brother, but Pa says we have to be patient with all the brothers."

Staring over the horses' ears, Jonas caught the curious slide of Penny's eyes toward him. What must she think of him? Of Breanna talking about her brothers? Penny couldn't know he wasn't married, and yet Breanna referenced *more* children?

Before Penny could ask him any questions, Breanna rambled on.

"Have you ever been on a train, Miss Penny? Yesterday Pa took me to see the train come to Calvin and it was so noisy and loud."

Jonas started to caution his daughter that maybe her new friend didn't want to talk so much, but before he could speak, Miss Castlerock was talking again.

"Why, yes. My parents sent me to finishing school back East. In Philadelphia."

"Philadelphia? Pa, Miss Penny's been to Philadelphia." Breanna patted his shoulder, her excitement evident.

Jonas had to clear his throat. "I heard." He shifted on the seat, uncomfortable. His daughter had steered the conversation right where he'd asked Penny not to. What would she say?

"Pa and I rode the train from Philadelphia to Denver, and then a wagon and then we came to our homestead and lived in a little cabin, but I don't remember any of that because I was just a baby."

Breanna sucked in a breath, offering a short reprieve from her chatter. It didn't last long.

"What's a finishing school? Did you learn sums and reading and such?"

Penny could sense Jonas White's tension in the stiff set of his shoulders. What did he think she was going to do, tell Breanna that he'd gotten her mother with child outside of wedlock? It wasn't her place.

Turning to face Breanna, Penny accidentally knocked her knee against Jonas's leg again. Drat the small seat on this wagon.

She resettled her skirt to ensure her ankles weren't showing and couldn't help but take in the condition of the conveyance. It seemed to be the same wagon Breanna had just mentioned that had brought her companions west years ago, with wheels that had obviously been repaired and were bleached white from the sun.

The horses seemed to be of good quality. Penny almost wondered if they were some of her grandfather's stock.

Penny forced herself to pay attention to the conversation instead of thinking of the Whites' monetary situation. She told the young girl, "A finishing school is a special school for young ladies to learn skills to help them maintain a household. To make them more eligible for marriage." Not that it had helped her catch a mate. Even with Mrs. Trimble's training, Penny was too outspoken, too Western, for the men she'd met in Philadelphia.

It was a stark reminder of how she'd disappointed her father. So much that now he'd decided to match her with Mr. Abbott. Penny pushed away the unwelcome thoughts.

"What's that mean? To *maintain a household?*" Breanna's nose crinkled adorably with the question. "Is it like sweepin' floors and makin' supper?"

The man beside her coughed, his frame shaking.

"No. Not like that. More of dressing the table and how to make polite conversation with dinner guests…arranging flowers…" As she said the words, Penny realized how trivial they sounded. Would she even know what to do to help her grandfather? She hoped so.

But the little girl hadn't seemed to pick up on that. "Pa, I don't have to go away to school, do I?"

Jonas glanced at his daughter's concerned, upturned face. "No, miss. Not unless you grow up and decide you want to catch a rich husband." He winked, and Breanna giggled.

He still didn't look directly at Penny. Had he meant the words as a slight? She couldn't tell.

"Do *you* have a rich husband, Miss Penny?"

A wince she couldn't hide. "No."

An hour later, the little girl was noticeably drooping, her questions slowing. Sam had long since dropped off to sleep and was snoring in the back of the wagon, chin tilted to his chest.

"Why don't you curl up and take a nap?" Jonas asked his daughter. "You've got room there. Do you want my hat to shade your face?"

"Mmm...thanks, Pa."

Jonas handed the little girl his hat, and she lay down. Quiet, at last.

Penny observed Jonas as he leaned back to tuck Breanna's skirt around her legs and tilted the hat to make sure she could breathe easily. It was obvious he loved his daughter deeply. She wondered how he'd fared with an infant after leaving Philadelphia. Had he found someone to help care for Breanna? Or had he managed to care for the infant girl by himself? It seemed impossible...

"She's a lovely little girl," Penny commented when the silence between them stretched. Unable to contain her curiosity, she asked, "Was there—did you...marry after you left Philadelphia?"

"No," came his short answer. "I'm not married."

But hadn't Breanna just mentioned having brothers? Was it possible he'd fathered *more* children out of wedlock? Suddenly uncomfortable, Penny glanced over her shoulder to see if Sam still slept. Should she wake him?

Turning back to face front, her eyes met Jonas's and his gaze narrowed.

Penny rushed to fill the awkward silence. "Sam and I are very grateful for the ride to my grandfather's place. It's very kind of you."

He grunted, now refusing to look at her, squinting in the sun without his hat. His hair was matted to his head where the hat had been, a ring of darker blond showing where the hat had rested on his head. Penny was surprised to note he was quite handsome. She had been too absorbed with her own need to escape Calvin that she'd hardly paid attention to her companion, but she was unable to ignore the sculpted chin and finely arched brow.

The realization was discomfiting. Especially in light of Jonas White's moral deficiencies. The man had fathered one—or more—children outside of wedlock. And he appeared to struggle for money, lived on a homestead. In short, he wasn't a man she would consider a suitable match. In addition, she wanted to fall desperately, powerfully in love the way her grandparents had.

To distract herself from uncomfortable thoughts, Penny continued making conversation. "How did you come to be in Calvin? Isn't Bear Creek closer for purchasing supplies?"

He thought about his answer for a considerable amount of time. "It is. I had business with your father's bank, and with other banks as well."

"That's right. Was your business concluded in a satisfactory manner?" Jonas hadn't been in her father's office for very long, she'd noticed, even though she'd been waiting on customers.

"No. Your father didn't grant me the loan."

His blunt, quiet answer seemed to end that vein of conversation.

"I'm sorry," she murmured, staring down at her gloved hands. She didn't know all the circumstances, but the man's disappointment was palpable. She remembered her father's anger when Jonas had interrupted his party and wondered if that had anything to do with his denying the loan. Surely not. "Then I'm doubly grateful you agreed to convey my brother and me to Grandfather's homestead."

A long silence settled between them. Penny stood it for as

long as she was able, but finally felt compelled to make further conversation.

"How did you come to be in Wyoming?"

He frowned and glanced back at his daughter, who still slept. "I was…encouraged to leave Philadelphia."

Ah. Because of the scandal with Millie, though he did not say it in so many words.

"But how did you choose Wyoming? And…is it…do you raise cattle?"

"Some." He paused for a long time and again she wondered if he would answer. "I once heard someone read a story about Wyoming in a dime novel. With nowhere else to go, one place seemed as good as another."

"Hmm."

She hoped her interest would encourage him to go on, but he stubbornly went silent again. Well. If he wasn't inclined to make conversation, she would simply endure the quiet.

But what a coincidence that they'd ended up in the same state, near in geographic area. As he'd said, with nowhere else to go, it didn't much matter where he landed, but how had he come to be Grandfather's neighbor?

An hour passed without a word spoken between them. Breanna woke up. She seemed quieter, more reserved, and this seemed to worry Jonas, if the crease on his brow was any indication. He insisted they stop awhile under a clump of trees. Sam roused, too, though he remained taciturn and kept to himself. They ate a small picnic in the limited shade from the wagon before continuing on their way.

Breanna did not chatter this time. Penny idly wondered if the trip was a mistake—she already missed conversing with her friends from town. The summer sun made her drowsy, and she was half-dreaming about her father forcing her down the aisle to meet Mr. Abbott when a startled exclamation from Jonas roused her.

"Breanna? Do you feel ill?"

Breanna did not answer, but Penny turned in time to see the little girl collapse into the wagon.

Suddenly, the placid, quiet man next to Penny leapt into action.

"Whoa!" He pulled back on the reins and set the brake as the wagon rolled to a stop. Instantly, he scooped Breanna into his arms from her prone position in the wagon and maneuvered himself off the bench seat. Breanna appeared to be shaking. She hadn't seemed sick at all this morning...

Alarmed by the girl's pallor, Penny blurted, "What can I do to help?"

Sam jumped from the back of the wagon, shaking his head as if he'd been drowsing, too. "What's wrong?"

"Jonas?" Penny questioned again, forgoing propriety.

Jonas ignored Sam as he settled the girl in the small patch of shade cast by the wagon itself. He spoke to Penny instead. "Can you get the canteen? It's under the bench there. And find a piece of fabric to wet her face?"

She reached for the canteen tucked under the bench seat and hiked up her skirts before stepping down on top of the wagon wheel to dismount. As she pulled her other leg from the wagon, her boot slipped on the smooth wheel and she tumbled to the ground, knocking her chin on the way down. She ended up sprawled inelegantly on her backside, the canteen rolling away.

And face-to-face—albeit across the wagon—with Jonas. He was gentleman enough not to laugh at her. He only grunted, "You all right?"

She chose not to reply, instead reaching underneath her gown and ripping off a piece of her petticoat. She stood and rushed around the wagon to join Jonas kneeling near Breanna in the soft spring grasses. The girl lay on her side, her entire body convulsing.

"Will she be all right?" Penny asked, voice breathless from her fall and the suddenness of Breanna's episode.

"Yes, in a bit." Jonas did not look away from Breanna's face. He'd loosened the neck of her dress and Penny caught sight of the girl's undergarment, so worn it appeared gray.

When Penny pressed the now-damp piece of cotton from her petticoat into his hand, he used it to swab Breanna's brow. "It's all right," he murmured. "Your pa is right here, and so is Miss Penny. Just rest easy, sweetheart."

After what seemed an eternity, in which Jonas continued speaking soft words to his daughter and soothing her with a gentle touch at her forehead, the girl's body began to calm.

Sam squatted nearby, silent but watchful. Penny reached out and touched the back of his hand, hoping to offer some comfort, but he snatched his arm away and stared out at the horizon.

"Mmm, Pa?"

The whisper of Breanna's voice was the sweetest sound Penny had heard.

"Yes, sweetheart? I'm right here."

The girl's eyelashes fluttered and she opened her eyes, which were slow to focus on her father bent over her.

"Did...Miss Penny see?"

Chapter Four

Jonas knew immediately what was behind the timid question from his daughter: she was afraid her new friend would draw away because of the seizure. It had happened before, when someone didn't understand that Breanna had a medical condition she couldn't control.

It was another reason Breanna deserved the corrective treatment. His bright, beautiful daughter shouldn't have to worry about people rejecting her.

Jonas sent a warning glance over his shoulder, but Miss Castlerock's face was turned to the side, hiding her expression. She shuffled closer, dress bunching around her knees. He averted his eyes from her shapely calves and stopped her with a hand on her forearm.

"Breanna's always a little disoriented after a seizure," he warned, keeping his voice low.

Miss Castlerock looked up at him, blue eyes guileless. "All right." She started to turn back toward his daughter, but Jonas wasn't reassured that the banker's daughter would treat Breanna with enough care.

"She's just a little girl," he reminded her, tugging her arm once again.

"I understand."

Regardless, he stayed at Miss Castlerock's elbow, putting himself between her and his daughter.

"Miss Breanna."

His daughter's brown eyes opened and he experienced a desperate urge to shield her from what Miss Castlerock would say.

"You scared me a little, honey," the woman beside him said, taking his daughter's small hand between both of hers.

"Oh." Breanna gulped, and a tear slipped down her cheek. Miss Castlerock wiped it away and gently brushed back one of the damp brown curls at Breanna's temple.

"But your papa knew just what to do, didn't he? He hopped right out of that wagon and got you settled here in the shade. Are you thirsty? I've got the canteen here—let me help you hold your head up…"

And to Jonas's astonishment, she cradled Breanna's head in the crook of her elbow and helped the girl sip from the canteen. Breanna responded to the woman's gentle ramblings, her eyes brightening even though she remained lethargic and would be for several hours.

No one but Peg Nelson, Walt's late wife, had ever shown such compassion toward Breanna during one of her episodes. Even Mrs. Clark had been uncomfortable when Breanna had seizures. When his daughter had had a seizure during the Sunday children's lesson, the teacher had firmly requested of him not to bring her back.

And now the one person he might've expected to treat Breanna callously was holding his daughter close and offering her comfort.

As Miss Castlerock resettled Breanna in the long prairie grass, Jonas glimpsed a flash of scarlet beneath the woman's chin. "Did you hurt yourself?"

"Hmm?"

He mimed touching his own chin and she rubbed a hand beneath hers, smearing blood over her fingers.

"Oh. I must've scraped it when I knocked against the wagon wheel. Is it bad?" She tipped her head back, exposing the creamy span of her throat.

Jonas swallowed roughly as he became aware of the very delicate, feminine part of her body. He averted his eyes. "I— it looks—I can't tell."

She scooted closer and hiked her chin higher. "And now?"

Jonas's face flamed but the woman obviously didn't feel that she was acting inappropriately, so he glanced at the wound again.

"Looks like it's scraped." He shuffled backward and lurched to his feet, intending to get away from Miss Castlerock. "I may have some antiseptic in the wagon," he said to excuse himself.

Unfortunately, she followed him. He knew it without looking. That's how aware he was of her very presence. "Thank you. I appreciate your help getting cleaned up. Sam, why don't you sit with Breanna for a few moments?"

Jonas glanced at the young man, who looked a bit uncomfortable as he knelt by Breanna's side. Miss Castlerock leaned against the wagon, too close for Jonas's comfort. He could feel her eyes burning into him, but he kept his face averted.

He rifled through the small tack box he'd built and attached under the wagon seat and came up with the bottle of antiseptic, wrapped in cloth so it wouldn't break with the wagon's jostling. It came in handy a little too often with his seven rambunctious sons around.

Maybe that was the way. If he didn't want to make a fool of himself over a woman who outclassed him, he could treat her just like he would treat one of his boys.

But when he faced Miss Castlerock and her vivid blue

eyes, his insides clutched up. She was nothing like a teen boy and he knew it. Couldn't ignore it.

"Lift—" He choked on the word and had to clear his throat. "Lift your chin up again."

She complied silently, bracing her hands against the wagon behind her. Her eyes slid closed as she tipped her face toward the overhead sun.

Looking down on her pert nose and lightly freckled cheeks, he was unable to squander the chance to see her features up close. Jonas soaked in the image and hoped it branded to his brain, so he could remember it later. Then he gulped. The way she waited, it almost seemed…like she was waiting to be kissed.

He blinked the thought away and used his thumb to steady her chin. With the same damp cloth she'd wetted for Breanna—he resolutely kept his mind off where the cloth had come from—he cleaned the blood away.

She felt so delicate beneath his fingers, her skin as silken as a kitten's fur.

"Miss Castlerock, this might sting a little," he warned her.

With her lips in his direct line of sight, he couldn't help but notice the way they parted on a soft intake of air when he dabbed the antiseptic over her abraded skin.

As he pursed his mouth to blow air across the scrape, the same way he would for one of his kids, again the irrational desire to kiss her took him and he jerked away, moving to plug the cork back into the bottle of antiseptic and put it back in the tack box.

His hands trembled. Badly.

Had she sensed his attraction to her? Mortification swirled through him.

"I think, after all of this…we can call each other Penny and Jonas." Her soft statement turned his head; she still leaned against the wagon, her blue eyes considering him.

"And, we are to be neighbors, at least for a little while."

She wanted him to call her by her first name? He shook himself, trying to come out of the stupor her closeness had created in him. Most likely, after he dropped her and Sam at Walt's homestead, he wouldn't see her again. This was a busy time of year with haying coming up soon. What would it hurt to agree?

"As you wish." He quickly steered away from the subject. "Breanna will need to catch her breath for a while longer. Between her episode and the late start we got this morning, it will be past dark before we get to your granddad's place."

"It's all right. You couldn't help what happened, and neither could Breanna."

How he wished he *could* help his daughter. If only he'd gotten a loan, he could get Breanna the treatment she needed. The frequency of the seizures was random—he never knew when they were coming and sometimes she could go months without having one. But he wanted her *better*.

Penny must've seen the despair on his face. She reached out and laid her hand on his arm. It burned, even through his sleeve and he wrenched away, pretending to concentrate on checking the horses' harness again.

He needed distance from Penny and her overwhelming, vibrant presence, but he wasn't likely to get it until he dropped her at her grandfather's place. Why had he agreed to bring her along?

Thankfully, Penny returned to Breanna's side and plopped down, spreading her skirts around her and speaking softly to the girl.

Sam Castlerock came to him. "I could rearrange some of the crates in the back, make it more comfortable for Miss Breanna to lie down."

It was a kind offer and he doubted the boy could destroy any of the items. "Fine."

"Breanna, sweetheart? I'm going to take a short walk, make sure we're okay to stay here for a bit. You all right with Miss Penny?" He desperately needed to clear his head.

"Mm-hmm. I'm just tired…"

"I know you are. We'll get back in the wagon in a little while."

Penny huddled in the large slicker her near-silent companion had offered her after it had gotten dark and the night air cooled. She hadn't thought to bring a shawl or coat with her, had forgotten how breezy it could be out on the plains.

Jonas had barely grunted two words to her after he'd cleaned the scrape on her chin, although he'd been gentle and conversational with Breanna as he helped her settle into the newly arranged wagon bed. The girl now slept deeply, oblivious to the wagon's creaking and bumping.

Penny had been surprised when Sam had offered to help and followed through. The action was out of character for her spoiled brother, who was usually content to allow others to do work when he could get out of it. Maybe he'd been as shaken by Breanna's episode as Penny had been at first. Perhaps this trip to visit his grandfather would be good for Sam. Help him turn over a new leaf. She prayed it was so.

She was even more surprised by the man sitting beside her. The gentle way he'd treated the scrape underneath her chin had echoed his tenderness when dealing with Breanna after her seizure, and Penny didn't know what to make of it. She was used to consideration, even kindness, from the men in her acquaintance, but she couldn't imagine her father taking the time and care to treat a scrape like Jonas had.

Was that very gentleness how he had wooed Millie Broadhurst in the first place? Penny tried to imagine the ingenue that she'd shared a room with in Mrs. Trimble's Academy for Young Ladies, along with two other girls, even glancing at the bricklayer's apprentice and couldn't fathom it. Certainly Jonas's face had been pleasing, although usually smudged with brick dust or plaster, but he'd been thin and gangly... nothing at all like the way he now filled out the shoulders of the dark jacket he'd worn the night of her father's party.

Penny wished that errant thought away. There was no need to ponder the physical attributes of the man beside her.

Millie had only seemed interested in catching a rich husband. More so than Penny had been. Millie had had a practiced way of circulating the room at the different parties they'd attended, and often had afternoon callers at the finishing school.

And Penny and Millie hadn't been particularly close. The other girl *was* a consummate flirt, so perhaps she'd made the first overture and approached Jonas during a break in his work. The house he'd been repairing had shared a small courtyard with Mrs. Trimble's Academy, and they could've trysted there easily enough.

It was well known that the kitchen door was easily accessible if one of the young ladies had any desire to sneak out of the house at night. Penny had never taken advantage of it, though she'd heard some of the other girls whispering about it.

More speculations flitted through Penny's mind as she watched the nearly full moon come up over the horizon. It was better than dwelling on her own problems with her father and Mr. Abbott. Nor would she ever ask Jonas about it, as the subject was considered improper. Too improper to be broached, even by someone as curious-natured as she was.

Penny shifted to relieve the ache in her back. She wasn't used to remaining in one place for so long, and it seemed hours since they'd stopped to rest the horses and eat a small supper of stale biscuits and jerky.

Surely they were almost to her grandfather's homestead?

Unable to make out any familiar landmarks in the darkness, Penny could only guess at their location.

"We'll be there soon." The rumble of Jonas's voice startled her. "I know you're probably ready to get down by now."

"Oh." How considerate. "Thank you, but I'll be all right. I'm sure you must be anxious to get home as well."

The yellow moonlight illuminated the outline of his hat as he bobbed his head in agreement. To her surprise, he went on.

"It's a good thing you and your brother have come to see Walt."

His statement stirred the unease she'd felt since her mother had read her grandfather's letter. "His letter was a bit vague on his recent illness. Was he terribly sick?"

"I didn't even realize he'd been doing poorly until I realized we hadn't seen him in a few days. Far as I know, it was mostly just a fever and cough." Jonas rolled his shoulders, as if he, too, was tired of sitting still. "He's getting older. It's harder for him to get around, do the heavier chores. The boys and I try to get over to his place and help some, but he's stubborn...doesn't always let us help."

"Hmm. That *does* sounds like Grandfather." She'd often wondered why her mother hadn't inherited any of her grandfather's tenacity. A little would have done her good when dealing with an overbearing husband, but Penny's mother remained a yielding, docile wife.

"I can't imagine him fading away." She didn't want to, anyway. Every summer she'd visited, up to her fourteenth year, her grandfather had seemed indomitable. Always working the horses he raised, training them, loving on them. And on her grandmother, whom he'd doted on.

Her grandmother had passed away while Penny had been in finishing school. She'd been unable to attend the funeral—too far to travel—and her father hadn't wanted her to visit often since she'd been back in Wyoming. She'd never really considered why. Grandfather was a devout Christian and would never let her get into a situation that was improper. Perhaps it was just the lack of adequate companionship. After all, her grandfather's place was somewhat isolated.

"Thank you for helping Grandfather. I'm sure Sam and I can take care of what needs to be done while we're here." But what about after they returned home? Did her grandfather really need permanent help?

Jonas cleared his throat, as if he had more to say. Penny waited a few moments before he spoke. Was the man shy or did his hesitation stem from something else? "Thank you for...tending to Breanna during her episode. And after. It was kind of you."

She had the strangest urge to take his hand. She stared down at the fisted appendage on his thigh, washed white in the moonlight. He held the reins loosely, confident in his control of the horses. Why did she feel the need to comfort him? Was it simply the false intimacy crafted by the darkness surrounding them? Or that Sam and Breanna both slept, so the soft night noises created the feeling of a romantic interlude? Had he charmed Millie Broadhurst with his shy manner, in just this same way?

Uncomfortable, Penny rushed to fill the silence. "It must be a horrible thing for a parent, to have to watch Breanna go through those times. I can't imagine. Did you ever have seizures when you were a child? I can't remember if Millie ever had one."

He tensed at the mention of Breanna's mother's name. Did he still have strong feelings for her, then? Was that why Penny made him uncomfortable, why he hesitated when speaking to her? Because she was a reminder of his past?

"No. I never had one."

"Is there anything that can be done?"

"There is a medicine called bromide that has been found to be helpful to some people, but in Breanna's case, it makes her overly tired and she is still susceptible to the seizures. But…"

He paused, as if considering whether he should go on. "There's a doctor over in Cheyenne who has developed a treatment of his own that could help her."

"That's wonderful. Is it—it is safe, though?"

"I don't know much about it. This doctor doesn't want others to find out his methods. The unfortunate thing is that the treatment is expensive, and I haven't yet obtained the funds to pay for it."

"He won't consider allowing you to pay in increments over time?"

"No."

She could almost hear the frown in his voice. "That's why you came to my father's bank, isn't it? To get a loan?"

He was slow to answer. "Your father's bank and every other one between Cheyenne and Bear Creek. My homestead makes enough to feed the family, but not enough to convince them to give me a loan."

He sounded so distressed, so worn down, that Penny again had the urge to reach out to him, but she kept her fingers clenched in her lap. Didn't he have anyone to share his burdens with?

"Have you tried asking your church for the funds? Or maybe the folks in Bear Creek could take a special collection."

She thought she heard him sigh, but when she tried to look at his face, the moonlight only illuminated the shadow of his profile.

"When I asked the preacher, he said there was barely enough money in the congregation to keep him fed. And folks around here were hit hard last winter. Lost a lot of livestock and some lost everything. I can't ask them to give up what they need to survive."

"But there must be some way…" Penny knew she sounded desperate, but she wanted Breanna to get the treatment she needed. Even though she'd only known the girl one day, it was clear she was a sweet and special child. "Could you send a letter to Breanna's grandparents? Surely the Broadhursts would want to help their granddaughter—"

"No."

Jonas's sharp retort startled her into silence. "But—"

"When Breanna and I left Philadelphia, they made it clear we weren't to have any contact with Millie or the family."

That must've hurt him, to be denied contact with the mother of his child. Especially if Jonas still had feelings for Millie.

"I'll find a way to pay for the treatment. I have to."

Penny was struck by the determination in her companion's voice, could imagine the immovable set of his broad shoulders as he said the words. Was that determination what Millie had come to admire in him? And if she'd liked him enough to compromise her morals, why had Millie let her parents send him away?

Penny's whirling thoughts were interrupted when Jonas let out a soft whistle. It carried in the darkness, startling her into bumping against Jonas's shoulder.

"Wha—" Sam bolted upright from where he'd dozed off, jostling the wagon with his movement.

Breanna stirred and Jonas reached back to lay a hand on her shoulder. "We're almost home, sweetheart."

Penny couldn't see her grandfather's house, but she felt the jarring bump as Jonas guided the wagon out of the ruts made from many wagons and into the thicker grass. Had they reached her grandfather's homestead? Finally? They rounded a copse of trees, and the wooden structure, the cabin smaller than she remembered, came into view in the moonlight.

And a thin, reedy voice answered, "Who's there? I got a rifle and I'm prepared to use it."

"Walt?" Jonas's voice carried into the darkness. "It's Jonas White. I've got a special delivery for you."

Chapter Five

Penny woke to a dull thump on the door frame. Hadn't she just gone to bed?

"C'mon, Penny-girl. Time to greet the sun."

A glance out the tiny window in her grandfather's small second bedroom revealed it wasn't even light outside yet.

Ugh. How could her grandfather be so cheerful this early in the morning? Especially after their late arrival and the time they'd spent around the kitchen table catching up. While Penny hadn't shared her real reason for getting out of Calvin, her grandfather hadn't seemed to question why *both* his grandchildren had decided on a visit, and for that she was grateful.

Jonas had been right. Her grandfather was a shadow of the man he'd once been. He seemed much older than the last time she'd seen him a few months ago. Frail, almost.

Not that she'd know it this morning, if the cheer in his voice was any indication.

"You want me to come in and tickle you awake like I used to?"

"No," she warbled, voice clogged from sleep. In her hurry to escape Calvin, she had forgotten to pack a nightrail, so she'd slept in her chemise. She didn't want *anyone* coming in to see that. She pushed back the simple quilt covering her and cleared her throat to try again. "I'm awake. I'm coming."

Her grandfather's reply was a whistle; she heard the sound fade and surmised he must've stepped outside.

Still half asleep, she sat up in the small straw tick bed, wishing for her delightful feather tick at home, and attempted to stretch the back muscles that had tightened up after a day spent riding on an uncomfortable wagon seat.

Without any light coming through the curtainless window, she could barely make out the small table next to the bed and the chest of drawers across the room, but she still remembered the shock she'd suffered last night as she'd carried a lone, wavering candle into the bedroom.

What she'd remembered from her childhood as a warm, welcoming place now seemed shabby and much tinier than before. A layer of dust had covered everything and she'd had to wonder if her grandfather had even cleaned in here since her grandmother's death.

It was a far cry from what she was used to.

"But I'd rather be here than at home subjected to Mr. Abbott's advances," she said aloud, hoping the words would rouse her a bit more. She wasn't sure it was quite the truth, but she got out of bed anyway and struggled into the second dress, a blue one, she'd packed in her satchel. It was silk, from two seasons ago, though she hadn't worn it much. It wasn't one of her favorites. Putting up her hair was the work of a few moments. There was no one to see her here except family, so she settled for a simple chignon that required few pins.

In the kitchen, she splashed her face with cold water from the basin near the door, shivering at the icy blast against her skin. At home, Ethel would have warmed a pitcher for her. By the time she patted herself dry, Sam had stumbled into the kitchen and slumped into a chair at the table. "Is it really morning?" he asked, the words muffled by his arms as he buried his face in them.

"Grandfather seems to think so."

"He snores." Poor fellow. He'd been relegated to sleeping in the bigger bedroom with his grandfather, since Penny had taken the only other bedroom.

"Worse than Papa?"

Sam tilted his head up just enough to raise one incredulous eyebrow, and Penny responded with a tired smile. It was a longstanding joke between them that their father's snores rattled through the upstairs walls of their home.

The shared moment of camaraderie sent a feeling of hope through Penny.

"Good morning, children," their grandfather said as he pushed through the back door, letting in a burst of cool air.

Penny wondered for a moment if she'd been wrong about her grandfather last night. He seemed almost spry this morning. His face pink from the cold, he looked to be in good health.

"Brought in some eggs." The older man carefully settled a dish towel he'd folded around several eggs on the table close to where Penny stood. "Thought you might fry us up some breakfast, my dear. Potatoes're in the cupboard, there." He pointed to a low cabinet along one wall.

"But—" Penny started to protest, but a yawn caught her unaware.

"Come along, young man. Time's a-wasting." He thumped Sam on the back.

The boy scowled.

"The sun's almost up, m'boy. We've got chores to do. I woke up with some ideas for special projects I'd like to get done while you two whippersnappers are here."

Was one of those projects cleaning the interior of the house? In the rapidly brightening room, Penny could see just how shabby the furnishings were and the layer of dust. She was afraid to know how long it had been since her grandfather had swept the floor.

Sam reluctantly pushed himself out of the chair and followed his grandfather toward the door.

"Penny-girl, we'll be back in a bit for our morning grub."

"But—" The door closed behind them before she could form a full protest.

Her eyes fell on the eggs waiting on the table. She didn't know the first thing about frying them.

An hour later, Penny crouched next to her grandfather's water well, trying to stop coughing. Tears streamed down her face and dripped onto her now soot-covered dress.

"Whoohee!" her grandfather exclaimed as he came out the kitchen door and down the steps, waving a towel. Smoke billowed out behind him.

"Where's Sam?" Penny coughed again as she pushed the words out of her smoke-parched throat.

"Opening the front door and windows." Her grandfather stopped halfway to the well and bent over with hands on his knees.

Worried about him, Penny began to stand up, but subsided when another fit of coughing took her.

Pounding hoofbeats announced an arrival and Penny peered over her shoulder to see two teen boys race their horse up to the barn. Both boys, one redheaded and the other with a mess of black curls mashed under a soiled brown hat, hopped off the horse and ran toward the house.

"Poppy Walt, we saw the smoke!"

"Pa sent us to check on things."

Pa? The boys were certainly too old to belong to Jonas, but he was the closest neighbor, wasn't he? Could they belong to one of Jonas's cowhands? Surely they were too young to be hands themselves. The redhead appeared to be thirteen at most, still in the gangly stage of youth. The other boy appeared a bit older, maybe sixteen.

"Are you hurt, Poppy Walt?"

"Should we git some water buckets?"

Their words tumbled over each other. To Penny's surprise, Walt placed a hand on each of the boys' shoulders.

"Now, Maxwell, Davy, everything's all right." He motioned toward Penny and both boys' heads swiveled. "My granddaughter—"

The boy—Maxwell?—with curly, dark hair whipped his hat off and pressed it to his chest. The other one's face turned as red as his hair—a trait Penny could sympathize with as her face had warmed as well. How humiliating to have witnesses to the disaster she'd caused.

"M-m-morning, m-miss," the redheaded youth stammered.

"—had a little mishap while making breakfast," Walt finished.

Penny's cheeks heated further at his blatant understatement. She'd managed to set the pan of eggs and badly chopped potatoes on fire and then knocked it off the stove while trying to put it out—and caught a curtain and part of the wall on fire. Thank goodness her grandfather had come in looking for his *grub,* because she'd been failing as she tried to smother the growing fire with a tablecloth she'd found on a shelf.

Sam rounded the corner from the front of the house but stopped short when he saw the two boys standing with his grandfather, who waved him over.

"Boys, I'd like you to meet my grandson, Sam Castlerock, and my granddaughter, Penny."

Both boys moved to shake Sam's hand. Penny's brother complied but didn't say anything in greeting, only sized up the two newcomers with a frown and crossed his arms over his chest.

When the two teens turned to Penny they didn't seem to know what to do. Still silent, the curly, dark-haired one stood with a flush climbing his tanned cheeks while the redhead stammered, "N-nice to m-meet ya."

"This is Maxwell and Davy White."

White? What was going on here? These *couldn't* be Jonas's sons. In addition to being too old to be his offspring, neither boy looked anything like Jonas!

"Y'all gonna be okay then?" Maxwell finally found his voice, speaking to Walt.

"Always are." But Walt looked a little wistful as he pushed his hands into the pockets of his denims and stared at the house and the wisps of smoke still rising from the windows and doors.

"Reckon Pa would skin us alive if we didn't bring ya back home for breakfast. You want me to saddle up a couple ponies for ya?"

Walt brightened immediately. "That's a fine idea. A mighty fine idea."

The two boys seemed to be familiar with Walt's barn and corral; they hurried over and the horses came right up to them.

Sam grumbled, "I'd rather go back to bed."

Penny turned a concerned glance on him. "Aren't you hungry?"

He shrugged, still frowning.

"Gotta eat if we're gonna work today," his grandfather said, clapping Sam on the shoulder.

Apparently *his* cheer was restored. That made one of them.

Jonas's eyes kept straying to the north, to Walt's place. Just like his thoughts, ever since Davy had seen the smoke coming from that direction this morning.

All right, if he was being honest with himself, he hadn't been able to stop thinking about Penny Castlerock since last night.

She was different than he'd expected. She'd treated Breanna with care and her worry for Walt had been sincere. She was more genuine than he'd thought from seeing her at a distance back in Philadelphia.

But he wondered how she would fare at Walt's place. He'd been there to check on his friend before starting on the trip to take Mrs. Clark to Calvin and meet with the bankers. Walt's place wasn't exactly falling down, but it might as well have been a soddy compared to the Castlerocks' fine home back in Calvin. Penny had said she'd spent summers there, but Jonas just didn't see how she would adjust. Her brother, either.

He tore his eyes from the grassy plains visible through the window and swung around from the stove to set the pan of scrambled eggs on the already groaning long table that took up much of the next room. Along with the eggs, there was a huge pile of biscuits, jams and jellies, most of a ham and the last of some dried apples he'd unearthed in the pantry.

It took a lot to feed his family. But he wouldn't have it any other way.

Wiping his hands on his shirt, already marked with grease and a swipe of flour, he moved to the kitchen door and stuck his head outside to issue an ear-splitting whistle, the equivalent of ringing a dinner triangle for his crew.

"Pa, we brought some guests for breakfast!" came a shout from the north.

Jonas stepped out onto the covered porch to see Max and Davy riding double toward the barn, just the way they'd left. Behind them came two more horses, Walt in the lead and Sam and Penny on the second animal.

Eight-year-old Seb appeared from the henhouse, clutching eggs in each hand. Seventeen-year-old Oscar and fourteen-year-old Edgar approached on horseback from the near field, where they'd been checking on some cows before the meal. And Matty and Ricky, both ten years of age, popped out of the barn at a flat-out run toward the house and their breakfast.

His boys. His sons.

"Miss Penny!" Breanna shrieked and ran out the door behind him, toward the approaching riders.

Penny said something to her brother, who halted the horse and let her slide down from its back. She knelt in time to sweep Breanna into a hug.

"Who's that?" asked Ricky, joining Jonas on the porch, followed quickly by Matty and Seb.

"Yeah, she's pretty," Matty commented. Jonas agreed, though he kept silent.

"Look at her dress—fancy!" That from Seb.

Seb's words brought Jonas's gaze down to his grease-splattered shirt. Part of the collar had been ripped away, and the cuffs were worn and frayed. A glance around the excited boys on the porch revealed their clothes weren't in much better shape—pants with holes in the knees, shirts worn thin. Would the proper Miss Castlerock comment on the state of their clothing? He hoped not.

Jonas straightened his shoulders; if she said anything derogatory, he'd defend his boys. It was his job to protect them.

But as Breanna towed Penny closer, Jonas caught sight of the gray soot marring her fancy dress and forgot about his worries. Her dress was marked up worse than any of their clothes, and her hair was coming loose from its pins, some of the auburn strands framing her lovely features. Soot-stained features.

"What happened to you?" Seb blurted.

Jonas's face flamed. He clapped a hand on his son's shoulder. "That's not a kind thing to ask, Seb."

Penny looked down at herself and cringed. "Oh, dear."

"It's not so bad," Breanna offered. "Didja try to help put the fire out? I burnt some cookies once and smoked up the whole kitchen—Ricky and Matty were so mad cause it was the last of the sugar, and—"

Now that Breanna had had a night's rest to recover from her latest seizure, her good nature was restored, and she rambled on to their guest. Breanna seemed enthralled with the banker's daughter, and a gaze around the stunned faces of his younger sons—except for Edgar, the most naturally suspicious of the bunch—confirmed that they felt the same just from looking at her pretty face.

"Well, I'm afraid I caught our breakfast and the kitchen wall on fire." Penny's clipped statement had his sons staring at her with wide eyes.

"Now, Penny-girl, it isn't all that bad," said Walter, coming up beside her with Sam and Jonas's other sons in tow. A glance behind showed they'd corralled the horses. Jonas also noticed his older sons couldn't tear their eyes from Penny. He began to brace himself for the onslaught of questions they would inevitably ask as soon as Walt and the Castlerocks left. What was Walt's granddaughter doing here? Was she attached to anyone?

"Your grandmamma, God rest her soul, burned up a pair of curtains once when we were first married…"

Walt lapsed into silence, obviously remembering his late wife. His statement didn't change Penny's expression. She looked dejected, disappointed. But then, as he watched her expressive face, she visibly brightened and looked around at the faces surrounding her.

"I don't suppose anyone would care to introduce me to this bunch of…um…cowhands?"

The boys all spoke at once, giving their names and greeting her in a cacophony of sound. Jonas whistled again and the boys quieted. "One at a time," he suggested, pointing to the closest boy.

"Ricky."

"Matty."

"I'm Seb, miss. Nice ta meetcha." His youngest son, just three years older than Breanna, actually stepped forward to shake Penny's hand.

"D-D-Davy."

"Hullo. Name's Oscar, ma'am."

"Maxwell."

"Edgar." Jonas glanced over and noted the tense set of his usually easygoing son's mouth.

Both Penny and Sam scanned the faces surrounding them—Walt was long used to Jonas's makeshift family—and Jonas wondered for a moment what they would think.

He put a hand on the two closest boys' shoulders to show his pride in them. "My sons."

Chapter Six

Penny heard the words but with all the chaos from the morning and the teens surrounding her, they didn't register until she'd been ushered inside and smooshed into the center of one of the two long benches on either side of the food-laden table.

His *sons?*

She had no opportunity to ask about it as the boisterous group began dishing out delicious-smelling food. She'd never seen anything like the confusion of reaching arms, and boys half standing out of their seats to get to the food. Sam stared at her with wide eyes, sitting back in his seat across the table. This chaos was completely different from their meals taken with their parents where Ethel served each course. Mrs. Trimble's training had never discussed what to do in a situation like this!

She looked up to find Jonas's eyes on her, narrowed as if waiting for her reaction. She kept a placid smile on her face as a biscuit, then eggs and a slice of ham appeared on her plate from both sides. Their manners might be lacking, but at least they'd served their guests.

Penny kept waiting for a woman to appear to take credit for the meal, but none did. Who kept all the children in line?

Finally, when every plate was filled, the table fell silent.

From his corner of the overcrowded table, Jonas said, "Let's pray."

Penny bowed her head, her eyes flickering over the mismatched plates and cups. They were all completely different, and several of them were chipped.

As Jonas offered a sincere blessing for the meal and thanks for safe travels home, Penny fingered the worn, plain cloth that covered the table. It was far different from the fine embroidered tablecloths she was accustomed to at home.

During the prayer, none of the boys fidgeted, not even the youngest. But after the last "amen" echoed around the table, the noise level rose right back to what it had been before. Penny sat for a moment, just absorbing it. Once again, Jonas caught her eye, his face inscrutable. Was he upset she and her family had barged in on their meal?

"Do ya want some jelly, Miss Penny?" Breanna asked from close to Penny's side, breaking the connection between Penny and Jonas.

"Oh. All right." She accepted the somewhat sticky jar from the little girl's hands and spooned some of what appeared to be blackberry jelly across the fluffy biscuit on her plate.

"Butter?" The boy—she thought it was Ricky—asked from her other side, offering a small bowl for Penny's consideration.

"Umm, no. Thank you."

She didn't have much of an appetite, not after the trouble she'd caused her grandfather. Was the kitchen even usable? What would her grandfather do if he couldn't cook his own meals?

And she and Sam couldn't eat at the Whites' table the whole time they were visiting, could they?

Not wanting to be rude, Penny nibbled on the jelly-covered biscuit. It was still warm. "This is delicious! Who made all of this?"

"Why, Pa, of course," Breanna answered matter-of-factly.

"Really?" The word escaped on a gasp and the closest conversations ceased.

Jonas's face reddened.

"Don'cha think boys can cook?" Breanna asked, still shoveling food in her mouth, not noticing that Penny had committed a conversational misstep. "Pa cooks real good, and Poppy Walt can do some easy things."

"Mmm…like fry cutfish!" Sitting kitty-corner to Penny, Seb—she *thought* it was Seb, the youngest one—spoke with his mouth full, the words distorted. She supposed he meant *fried catfish*.

Penny smiled politely and took another small bite of fluffy biscuit. She couldn't believe Jonas had baked them. Was there really no woman on the premises? It would explain the lack of manners displayed by the children.

"…can't wait for the Round Up," one of the boys said to his neighbor.

Penny saw Sam's head come up from where he'd been staring at his plate, keeping separate from the conversations surrounding him.

"It's a cowboy exhibition over in Bear Creek. In six weeks." Maxwell seemed to have noticed Sam's interest as well. He'd been too shy to speak to Penny earlier, but now tried to include Sam in the conversation. "Oscar and I are thinking of entering one or two of the events."

"My friends Billy and Louie went to a Round Up over by Cheyenne last year." Sam addressed his plate, not really looking at any of the other boys, but Penny was encouraged that he attempted to make conversation. "I didn't get to go." His mouth turned down in a bitter frown.

"If you're still stayin' with Poppy Walt, you should come with us. The Bear Creek Round Up is an awful lot of fun."

Sam stared at his plate again and didn't respond, and

Penny opened her mouth to thank Maxwell for the invitation when someone laughed, spraying crumbs across the table. Some even landed on Penny's plate.

She swallowed hard. The impropriety would have been unacceptable at her parents' table. Her father's temper would have no doubt exploded by now.

And yet…there was a sense of joy here she'd never experienced at home. Brothers, biological or not, she wasn't sure, nudged each other, wrestled for the last biscuit. They were obviously close, as evidenced by the camaraderie they shared.

The question was, how had this family come to be?

Penny insisted on staying to help wash the breakfast dishes, while her grandfather and Sam headed home to try and salvage the kitchen.

She worked with Edgar to clear the table, dumping the used dishes into a sudsy tub of water. Most of the boys' plates were remarkably clean of food.

After passing the teen several times in silence, she attempted to draw him into conversation.

"Do you get stuck washing dishes often?" She offered a cheerful smile as she stacked the last of the dirty dishes next to the water tub.

His blue eyes shifted quickly to her and away. He slapped a washrag into her hand. "You wash."

"All right." She plunged her hands in the hot water, wincing, and plucked a white plate with blue trim from the bottom to scrub.

Edgar didn't answer her question, but when she handed him the clean plate to dry, he asked almost belligerently, "How come you ain't come to visit Poppy Walt before?"

She supposed it was a valid query judging by how frail her grandfather had appeared last night, but the delivery had her bristling. Still, her schooling kept her voice even and polite as she answered. "Sam and I live in Calvin with our parents. I suppose sometimes it is hard to get away for a visit."

"It ain't that far. You look old enough to drive a wagon up yourself."

She stared at the dusty blond head not far from her shoulder, but Edgar didn't look up from drying the brown and white speckled cup she'd handed him a moment ago. Was the boy purposely being uncouth, or was he unaware that he was being rude?

She couldn't tell him that her father had made his wishes clear and visiting her grandfather hadn't been what her father wanted.

"I suppose you're right," she said, patience ebbing. "It's not a good excuse, but I didn't know Grandfather had been ill."

He handed her back a chipped, crimson-rimmed plate, dripping water across her sleeve. "You missed a spot of grease, there."

Penny accepted the dish, smile becoming brittle. She scrubbed at the spot he indicated, though she didn't see any grease on the plate.

"Shouldn't matter if Poppy Walt was sick or not. He's your kin, ain't he?"

His words both irritated her and convicted her. She *had* missed time with her grandfather that she couldn't get back. Surely if she would've pushed harder, her father would've let her visit…

"Missed another spot on this one."

This time, he dropped a mug into the sudsy water, causing it to splash up onto her dress. Penny suppressed an irritated gasp, knowing from living with Sam that it would only serve to encourage this boy in his awful behavior, and strove to change the subject.

"So you're…what, thirteen? My brother Sam just turned fifteen."

He bristled. "I'm *fourteen*."

She couldn't help smiling at the offended tone he took, and apparently her smile made it worse.

"Pa says I ain't hit my growin' spurt yet," he said defensively.

"Hmm." Her noncommittal hum seemed to fuel his ire. She enjoyed it probably more than she should. "And your brothers?"

He was quiet for a moment, as if deciding whether he should answer her or not, but finally he said, "Oscar's oldest. He's seventeen. Then Maxwell, sixteen, then me, then Davy. Ricky 'n Matty are both ten. And Seb's the youngest. Well, the youngest boy. Breanna's the youngest of all."

Penny knew Jonas couldn't be much older than herself. And considering the vast range of ages of his "sons"—two of whom weren't much younger than Jonas himself—there was no way Jonas had fathered these children. So how had he ended up with all of them in his care?

"I'll bet my grandmother loved having your family close," she said softly. "I know she talked about wanting a bigger family when she was younger, but said the Lord didn't bless her and Grandfather that way."

He didn't respond immediately, and Penny noticed that his hands had slowed so he was barely drying the dish he held. After a moment, he asked, almost reluctantly, "You knew Grammy Peg?"

"Yes. I used to spend summers out here with her." Surprised by the softness in the boy's voice, Penny blinked at the sudden tears in her eyes. She sniffled, wiping a fallen tear with her shoulder as she scrubbed a spot of baked-on food from the large cast-iron frying pan.

"Are you cryin'?" The boy sounded disgusted and something splooshed back into the water tub, sending more water onto Penny's skirt.

His horrified reaction to her tears made Penny laugh. "Only a little, don't worry."

Using one arm to wipe at her face, warm water rolled down Penny's arm and dampened her sleeve. Apparently, she wasn't any better at washing dishes than she'd been at cooking; she'd gotten all wet. Though some of it was Edgar's fault.

"What's going on in here? Are you *crying?*"

Penny laughed again at Jonas's appalled tone—the very same one his son had used.

"Edgar, what did you do?"

The boy whirled toward his father, the towel he'd been using to dry dishes flicking Penny's arm. "I ain't done nuthin'!"

"Then why's she all wet? And crying?"

The boy looked at Penny with narrowed eyes. Did he expect her to rat him out for his rude questions and splashing her? Maybe she should.

Penny wiped away the last of her tears with her wrist. "I'm afraid I've been a bit clumsy is all. And Edgar didn't make me cry. We were talking about my grandmother, and my emotions got a bit carried away."

Jonas squinted a little, as if he might not believe her. A sideways glance at Edgar revealed he wore a distrustful frown. Not the reaction she'd expected when she'd covered for him with his father.

"You two about done?"

"Reckon we're close enough," Edgar answered, nudging Penny away from the bucket that was now more water than suds.

She joined Jonas on the porch, and followed his gaze to two of the older boys, who repaired something along the outside barn wall, near where it and the corral met. Breanna squatted nearby, watching their progress.

Penny took a moment to look around the homestead. From the inside, she'd observed the house was bigger than her grandfather's, but from out here, it was obvious that at least two of the rooms, probably bedrooms, had been added on after the original structure was built. Had Jonas added them as his family had grown?

The barn was newer than her grandfather's as well, and appeared to be well maintained, as was the corral where several horses grazed. The yard was clean, with a few chickens scratching.

"You've built a fine home for yourself here," Penny said softly.

Jonas startled, as if he'd forgotten she stood at his elbow. He didn't move other than a slight turn of his head in her direction, but she sensed his perusal. "It isn't a mansion, but my family is happy here."

She wanted to ask more about his family and how it had come to be, but held her tongue. Mrs. Trimble would've been proud of her restraint.

"Thank you for sharing your breakfast," she said instead.

He shrugged, moving down the porch steps. "That's what neighbors do out here. Walt and Peg helped me out plenty when I first came out here."

"Really?"

"Yep." He motioned her to join him on the ground. "I'll walk you part way back. Ease Walt's mind."

"Will Breanna be all right with the boys?" she asked, glancing over her shoulder to where the girl seemed awfully close to the swinging tools the teen boys used.

"They'll watch out for her. And I won't be gone long."

Penny slipped her hands into the pockets of her gown as she fell into step with Jonas; her right hand touched the dollar bills she'd tucked there this morning. In the disorder of arriving at her grandfather's place last night, she'd forgotten to give Jonas the money they'd agreed on for the wagon ride.

"Before I forget, here's what I promised you yesterday." She extended the bills to him.

He hesitated, eyes lingering a little too long on the cash before looking ahead. "I brought you as a favor to Walt."

His hesitation made her think he probably needed the money, but was his pride standing in his way?

She pushed the money into his palm, then tucked her hand back in the folds of her dress. "I insist."

Penny hadn't noticed earlier when riding double with Sam, but Jonas's property must be in a slight valley, because they seemed to be ascending a hill. Jonas touched her elbow when she stumbled over a dip she hadn't seen.

"Thank you," she panted. Certainly the walks she took in town when visiting her friends hadn't prepared her for this much exertion. She was perspiring in a very unladylike manner.

"I'm sorry if Edgar was unpleasant to you," Jonas said suddenly. "Especially if it was his fault you got all wet. I hope your dress isn't ruined."

A glance down at her damp, soot-stained gown was less than reassuring. Likely it *was* ruined, but it had been so before the breakfast dishes had even been started. She chose not to comment, only asked, "How did you know?"

"He tends to…he doesn't always take well to new people."

"Hmm." The boy's actions and almost belligerent attitude seemed to support that. And also reminded her of her brother, who seemed to have a bad attitude about everything these days.

"I noticed both of you got a little nervous at my tears. What do you do when Breanna cries?"

He looked at her askance. "She doesn't. Well, hardly ever."

"Whatever did you do when she was an infant?"

He kept trudging along beside her, even though she could see the top of her grandfather's house now above the tree line.

"She rarely cried when she was a babe. Mostly just when she was hungry."

Penny's teasing attitude flowed away as she imagined the sleepless nights and feeding after feeding the man beside her had endured...

She knew Breanna was his responsibility; after he'd compromised Millie what choice did he have but to accept his duty? But he must've been so unsure, not knowing how to care for an infant.

"I'm curious," she said because she *had* to know. "How did you...that is...where did you come by the boys? I know they can't be your biological children. Their looks are too disparate for that to be true."

He was slow to answer and when she looked at him, his jaw was set.

"They are my sons. We belong together."

"Yes, but—"

"They are *mine*," he said fiercely, and the closed expression on his face told Penny the subject was finished. He pointed ahead. "Walt's place is right over that rise. I've got to get back."

Chapter Seven

Penny's day did not improve. She hauled buckets of water until her shoulders ached, scoured the soot and burn marks in her grandfather's kitchen until her hands blistered. At one point she scrubbed so hard she pushed through part of the wall that had burned away.

Even after all her work, her grandfather came in as the sun was setting and declared that the kitchen was unusable until it received some repairs.

Penny dropped the worn rag into the bucket of water at her feet and plopped onto the floor. After all, she couldn't get any dirtier than she already was. "How will we cook meals?"

"We'll take meals over at the Whites'. Jonas won't mind. I'll turn over our eggs 'n milk to him to make up for what it'll cost to feed us."

"Do we have to?" Sam asked gruffly, leaning against the door with arms crossed. His face was pink from being out in the sun. He hadn't been his usual self since they'd left Calvin with Jonas and Breanna, and it worried Penny. If he caused trouble for her grandfather, she'd be very disappointed in him.

"Unless you want to try cooking over an open fire. Might be fun."

Sam grumbled something unintelligible and slammed out of the house.

Penny started to apologize for her brother's behavior, but Walt waved off her words. "He'll come around. You ain't been out to see my horses yet, girl. Used to be your Gran and I couldn't get you out of the barn."

She hauled herself off the hard plank floor and hooked her arm through his, turning them both toward the door. "Then we'd better go see what kind of stock you've got now."

They passed Sam, sitting on the ground just around the corner of the house. Probably pouting.

Penny had always thought her grandfather's horses the finest around, and a visit to the barn revealed that even though his house might be in disrepair, his animals had been well taken care of. Two mares nearly ready to drop foals were in the last two stalls they visited.

"Saved the best for last," Walt said, pushing through the barn door and gesturing her to join him at the corral.

Penny leaned against the railing and admired a stallion that cantered around the ring, obviously wanting to be out in the open fields. "He's magnificent."

"Bought this fella last year off a drifter who didn't know what he was worth."

The animal's shiny black coat attested to a recent grooming; his muscles rippled as he moved in an easy gait. It was obvious he was a well-built, powerful animal.

"The two foals are his. Just waiting to see if they'll turn out as fine as he is."

"If the foals are anything like him, you'll make a fortune... um, hiring him out."

"Mmm. Well, money ain't everything, Penny-girl." He raised his eyes to the horizon. "Look at that sunset. You ever seen anything so beautiful?"

Penny placed one hand against her aching back. What she

really wanted to do was go inside and rest awhile, but she obediently took a moment to study the pinking sky over the mountains in the distance. The colors were lovely, reminding her of a gown she'd admired in the dressmaker's window recently. She couldn't wear that particular color of pink, not with her complexion and hair, but she admired it just the same.

"Sometimes it's the moments of beauty in yer life that are worth the most…" Walt's voice trailed off, and Penny determined he must not require a response. She stood and watched the sunset with him.

"You want to tell me what's really bothering you, Penny-girl? Other than your ornery brother, that is?"

"Hmm?" Could he have guessed that her frustration today wasn't simply about her disastrous morning?

"I might not be as perceptive as your Gran was, but I can tell you've got somethin' on your heart."

She stared at the sky, now turning a deep red. "My father wants me to marry a man I can't abide."

Walt grunted.

"If it was someone I could possibly see myself with, I would give things a chance, but this man…he is…" She couldn't explain the feeling Mr. Abbott inspired in her, but she shivered just thinking about the disturbing way he looked at her and the words she'd overheard before she'd left town.

"You know, I didn't think your pa was worth much when your mama first brought him home."

Penny had heard the story before, how her father had seen the most beautiful girl during a visit to Bear Creek and followed her home.

"It's more than that," Penny said, shaking her head. "There's something…unsettling about this man."

Walt was silent; Penny knew he was still thinking. Her

grandfather certainly wasn't a man to speak quickly. Sort of like Jonas White.

"What should I do? I know I'm supposed to honor my father, but I won't marry Mr. Abbott."

"Penny-girl, if I know one thing, it's that your father loves you and wants the best for you. Maybe this Mr. Abbott of yours has some redeeming qualities you don't know about."

Well, sure he did. He was one of her father's associates and would solidify her father's business connections. That seemed to be enough for him, but it wasn't enough for her.

"But…"

Walt turned to her and placed a gentle hand on her shoulder. "Maybe it was God's will for you to come out here and visit me. Get away for a little bit and think things through. Remember what really matters."

She pondered his words as the sky turned purple. What really mattered…yes, finding a husband was important, but what about love? Just being around her grandfather today reminded her of the deep love he'd had for her grandmother.

That's what she wanted, that kind of unending love. And she was certain she wouldn't find it with Mr. Abbott. But how to make her father understand?

Penny's muddled thoughts were interrupted by hoofbeats announcing a rider's arrival. She and Walt turned to see Oscar White rein in close to the cabin, carrying a large hamper.

"Pa sent a cold supper and asked me to see how things were going over here. If y'all need to, you're welcome to come for breakfast tomorrow."

Well, at least they wouldn't starve.

Sunset nearing, Jonas finished rubbing down the mare he'd ridden to the south pasture earlier and tucked her into her stall for the night. Her neighbor, a mule with a graying muzzle, stuck its head over the partition and lipped at Jonas's shirt.

"Hello, old friend." Jonas paused a moment to pat Bailey's nose and forehead. Five years ago, the mule had traveled with Jonas, Oscar and Breanna from Denver, after they'd disembarked from the train that had carried them from Boston and bought a buckboard to bring them the rest of the way to Wyoming. The animal had heard many a confession from Jonas's lips, including the truth about Breanna's parentage.

Jonas hadn't had anyone else to tell about the scandal with the Broadhursts, Millie's accusations, or his rage when they'd refused to care for Breanna. His determination that the innocent baby girl wouldn't know the loneliness he'd known for what seemed his whole life…

Jonas still didn't know how anyone could've held the tiny baby—even looked at her!—and not fallen in love with her.

After he'd joined Jonas and Breanna as they left Boston, Oscar had still been wary, unsure that Jonas really intended to treat him as a son. Jonas had spoken with the mule often about the mistrust… It was an emotion Jonas could understand, especially after the events that had caused him to leave Boston.

And when they'd added Seb to their unusual family in Denver thanks to the help of a kindly judge, Bailey had heard all about the trials of taming a small boy who was too curious for his own good.

Then when Jonas had fought through those first days and months of homesteading, the mule had gotten an earful about just how hard it was to make a home for them on the Wyoming prairie. At the time, Jonas had felt so inadequate for the task set before him. With a toddler, a teen boy and Breanna to care for…and not knowing much about living off the land, he'd been drowning in his own failures until Walt and Peg had got ahold of him. Not only had they taught him what he needed to know about farming, but they'd taught him about God's grace and Jonas's worth in God's eyes. They'd changed Jonas's life, and in turn, the children's lives, too.

Until today, Jonas had thought those old feelings of inadequacy were gone for good. What was it about Penny Castlerock that brought thoughts of not being good enough back?

"I couldn't face her tonight," Jonas told the donkey, speaking of Penny. "I brushed her off this morning, afraid…" *Of what she thought of my makeshift family.*

Although some of the people in nearby Bear Creek accepted his family, most were wary. He'd heard whispers of *rag-tag, misfits, orphans,* although no one had dared to say anything to his face, at the general store, outside church and other places.

The same names he'd heard throughout his childhood, directed at Jonas himself. Words that had stung each time. *Worthless. Trash.* Words that infuriated him when directed at his children.

They might not be his by blood, but the boys had chosen him, chosen each other. Chosen to be a family. That made them Jonas's by *right.* And he protected his own. Even from the pretty, highborn neighbor, and her curiosity.

She had completely discomfited him. He felt like he was eighteen again, catching glimpses of her through the windows in the fine house as he laid bricks…the feelings of insecurity when she and her friends had giggled behind their gloved hands, not knowing if they were laughing at him.

He'd secretly daydreamed of speaking to her. Not courting her. Just talking to her.

Not that he would have known what to say. He'd never conversed with a pretty young woman before. The girls that hawked papers and worked in the factories, ones he knew from the streets didn't count. And he likely would have been too tongue-tied to say anything at all.

She'd been the inspiration behind his most secret wish. One that he'd never shared with anyone before. A dream of having a true family of his own: a wife, children.

He loved the boys and Breanna more than anything. They'd become a family. He was happy.

But seeing Penny again, sitting next to her in the wagon all day yesterday had resurrected Jonas's secret dreams. And her presence had brought back his insecurities, as well. He felt awkward and unsure.

He didn't have time to worry about his neighbor's pretty granddaughter; he needed to focus on his family. With the days he'd taken to visit the banks, he'd lost time getting the cattle ready to drive down to Cheyenne. Haying was about to start, and he had yet to find a way to pay for Breanna's treatment. Selling off some of the cattle would help, and he prayed for a good price since it wasn't really the right time of year to be selling, but it wouldn't account for the entire amount.

"Need to forget about her, old boy," he told the donkey with a final pat, exiting the barn. If only it was that easy to push Penny from his mind.

"Pa!" Davy jogged toward him from the house. "Mr. Sumner's here. Wants to talk to you."

Sumner was another neighbor, a bit farther out than Walt's place. A handshake was enough of a greeting. It was late for a social call.

"I won't stay long," the man said, sitting at the table across from Jonas. "My wife's ma is in a bad way, down in Colorado. And my wife's in…ahem…the family way." The man's neck reddened under his tan. "So I cain't send her off on her own. I'm goin' along. What I need is someone to bring in my hay."

Jonas started to speak but the other man held up his hand and kept on talking. "I know you've got your own place to look after, but my wife and I won't make it through the winter without our crop. You've got enough boys to help you and I can pay you…"

He named a sum.

Enough to make Jonas sit back in his chair, reeling. The extra money could help pay for Breanna's treatment. But he was already in enough of a bind with Breanna. With her condition she needed someone to watch her at all times. If she suffered a seizure and fell, she could injure herself badly. And with Mrs. Clark's departure, he had no one to rely on.

On the other hand, how could he pass up this opportunity? The money would nearly pay for Breanna's treatment… How could he say no?

After they'd consumed the cold supper, Penny wilted in front of the fire in what used to be her grandmother's rocking chair. Her head lolled to the left and took in her brother who was lying on the floor with his head on the rag rug.

"You as exhausted as I am?"

"Mmm," he grunted, eyes closed. "Ready to go home."

It was on the tip of her tongue to chide him for his earlier behavior, but something held her back. If she made Sam angry, he might cause more trouble. And with the barn in disrepair and now the kitchen needing to be fixed thanks to her ineptitude, she needed Sam on his best behavior to help with the work to be done. All right, to *do* the work.

Walt bustled into the room, carrying a large tin tub and huffing with exertion. "Here ya go, missy." He set the tub full of water in front of the crackling fire.

"What?" Penny wasn't sure what to make of it.

Disappearing into his bedroom, he soon returned with a worn towel and a bar of rough soap. "Since the stove's out of commission, it'll have to be a cool bath. Sam and I'll sneak down to the stream and wash off there."

Penny grimaced. A *cold* bath?

"You'll want to be clean for Sunday services in the morning."

She'd forgotten tomorrow was Sunday. Or maybe she'd put it out of her mind, because the two dresses she'd brought with her had been ruined. She had nothing to wear.

"Grandfather, I've ruined both the dresses I brought with me." One with soot and the other with milk and mud.

"Don't guess folks will care if you're a little messy. We're a casual bunch in Bear Creek."

"Well, *I* care." She regretted her sharp tone instantly. Her grandfather had enough troubles without having to worry about clothing her. But she *couldn't* wear either of her gowns to church, where people would see her. It was bad enough that Jonas and his family had seen her all a mess.

"Reckon you could wear one of your grandmama's gowns. They're plainer than what you're used to…" His voice trailed off as he went back into his bedroom.

Penny grimaced. Wear something her grandmother had worn? But they would be old and out of style! How could she let her grandfather down gently?

Walt brought out a plain blue calico dress and presented it to Penny with a proud flourish. "It should be a close fit. You're as tall as your grandmamma and near enough the same shape."

Penny flushed at his frank words, and Sam chuckled. She glared at her brother, who shrugged in false innocence.

The dress was unembellished, with none of the lacy frills Penny liked. But it was unstained, and that's what her grandfather seemed to think mattered.

"She made it herself." Pride colored her grandfather's voice.

Penny wasn't surprised by his statement. She remembered learning some of the basic stitches at her grandmother's knee.

Probably at a much older age than most other girls would have learned. Penny's mother didn't believe her daughter needed to know how to sew a garment, not when she could afford to buy finery from the seamstress in Calvin or one in Cheyenne. But her gran had shared her love of sewing, and Penny had learned as much as she could during the summers she spent at the homestead.

It was the one wifely skill Penny *did* have. Though her abilities were probably rusty from disuse now.

But she couldn't wear this dress. "I can't—" She swallowed back the instant denial on her lips as her grandfather pushed the dress into her hands.

"You can, Penny-girl." His gaze seemed to intensify and she remembered how kind he'd been to listen to her worries about her father and Mr. Abbott out by the barn. "'Sides, it's what's on the inside of the dress that's beautiful. That's what matters."

She frowned, but accepted the dress. Maybe, after her bath, she could try to wash out one of her gowns. If she could get most of the stains out, perhaps it would dry by morning? Then she wouldn't have to hurt her grandfather's feelings by not wearing this dress.

"Thought you might like to borrow this while you're visiting, too." Walt placed a well-worn Bible in her lap. "It was your gran's. What made her so beautiful on the inside."

Penny looked down at the faded book. How many times had she seen her gran reading this at the kitchen table, in-between cooking or sewing or other chores?

But the Bible wasn't likely to make her grandfather forget about the dress he wanted her to wear to church tomorrow.

Chapter Eight

Penny felt numerous eyes on her as the Whites' wagon rolled into the churchyard. She was conspicuous on the wagon seat; everyone could see her in her grandmother's dress.

The results of washing one of her gowns had been disastrous. The silk had still been a damp, wrinkly mess this morning and most of the stains hadn't come out anyway. So she'd had no choice but to wear the scratchy calico that was sadly out of date. She'd almost considered pretending to be ill, but knew she couldn't disappoint her grandfather.

And the first people to see her this morning had been all of the Whites, because apparently her grandfather liked the company on his way to church services every Sunday. Thankfully, Jonas and his sons had been too polite to comment on her appearance.

"You planning to come down from there?"

She looked down into Jonas's frowning brown eyes as he reached up for her. Not waiting for an answer, his strong hands clasped her waist, spanning it easily. He hoisted her off the wagon seat without ceremony and deposited her on the ground.

"I feel like everyone's looking at me," she whispered, huddling behind him, half-aware that his hands remained at her waist. Had his shoulders been this broad when he'd helped her in and out of the wagon just days ago?

"They probably are."

She looked up at him sharply; his eyes squinted a little, scrutinizing her face, their brown depths unreadable.

"We don't have a lot of visitors, so newcomers like you and Sam are a novelty."

"'Specially someone as pretty as you, Miss Penny," Breanna inserted, face appearing between the two adults as she looked up at them. Her presence spurred Penny to step back, leaving Jonas's hands to fall away from her waist.

"Especially someone as pretty as you," Jonas echoed softly, looking surprised even as the words left his mouth. He took his daughter's hand, and they turned toward the clapboard building, following the gaggle of boys.

Penny joined her grandfather, noting the way his eyes glanced curiously from Jonas to her.

Jonas's compliment had bolstered her spirits for a brief moment, but a glance at a pair of prettily dressed young women approaching the church building on foot brought Penny's discomfort right back.

Sam shuffled his feet behind them.

Inside Penny ended up squished into a row between Breanna and Sam, next to the rest of the Whites.

Jonas's robust baritone, from his place just on the other side of Breanna, surprised her into distraction as the small congregation stood and sang the first songs, but as the group sat down for the sermon, she caught a glance from a young man across the aisle.

His eyes held a frank appraisal, but all Penny could feel was embarrassment at being caught out in her grandmother's dress. She knew she was blushing, her face most likely mottling red, but she couldn't help it.

Movement from Breanna gave Penny an excuse to look

away, and she glanced down at the girl to find her with her head turned in Penny's direction. Jonas cleared his throat softly and Breanna returned her attention to the preacher. Jonas sent Penny a reproving frown above his daughter's head.

Blushing even more furiously, she attempted to pay attention to the sermon.

But the unexpected attraction to Jonas White made it difficult. The shared moments as he'd helped her from the wagon before services had surprised her.

No longer was he the shy teen she remembered from Philadelphia, the boy who would barely meet her eyes if she encountered him on her way out of the finishing school. Although he still seemed to be somewhat quiet in disposition, he had obviously made a success of his homestead, in order to support himself and eight children.

The reminder of his circumstances brought an abrupt halt to her musings. Even if the fluttering in her stomach *was* attraction—and it could possibly be accounted for by the single biscuit and glass of milk she'd eaten this morning— she would never act on it. She wanted to fall in love with and marry someone who could support her in the style to which she was accustomed. She would simply have to be careful in her interactions with the homesteader.

Sam shifted next to her and her attention shifted as well. He'd been sullen and silent this morning as they'd readied to leave from their grandfather's home; then he'd been downright rude and ignored two of Jonas's sons when they'd tried to engage him in conversation.

If Sam caused trouble for Walt, he was likely to get them both sent home. And she didn't want to be back in Calvin, where she would be subject to Mr. Abbott's attentions.

In addition, Walt needed help. If Sam messed up, who would take care of things at his homestead?

* * *

"Hey!"

"Oomph!"

The sound of fists meeting flesh and the knowledge that her brother had slipped away had Penny scurrying around the side of the church building in time to see Sam wrestle another boy to the ground.

"Sam!" she shrieked, lifting her skirt to try and reach her brother before he could hurt the other boy.

"Hey, stop!" Another voice joined hers, and one of Jonas's older sons joined the scuffle. He made a valiant effort to contain the fistfight, but managed only to receive a punch in the face when he got in the middle.

Before Penny could determine if she should step in, Jonas and Walt pushed past her and took control of the situation. Penny saw Walt receive an inadvertent elbow to the ribs and he hunched over, wheezing as he tried to breathe. She rushed to his side. "Grandfather!"

Jonas drew both fighting boys to their feet, grasping each by their upper arm. His son, she thought it was Oscar, stood nearby, one hand holding his nose.

"What's going on here?" Jonas demanded. "Why aren't you boys over at the food tables? You're supposed to be joining the picnic."

"He insulted my sister," said the boy Penny didn't know, pointing a finger at Sam.

Sam stood silent, clothes mussed. His sullen refusal to meet any of their eyes made him look guilty.

Jonas looked to his son who said, "I wasn't close enough to hear. I only saw them go for each other at the same time and tried to stop them fighting."

"Sam, how could you?" Penny asked, still supporting her Grandfather's elbow as he continued to wheeze. "We're supposed to be helping Grandfather, not getting into trouble."

"I didn't ask to be sent out here. That was all you and Mama. I'd rather be back home."

"Sam!" Penny exclaimed, but her brother jerked away from Jonas's hold and stalked off among the wagons parked in front of the church building. Penny wondered if she should go after him, but her grandfather still wasn't breathing correctly and she knew anything she said to Sam in the heat of the moment would be brushed off.

"He reminds me a bit of Edgar when he first came to me... Needs some hard work and some discipline." Jonas uttered the terse words and then moved away, clapping a hand on his son's shoulder as he guided the boy away from the scene of the confrontation.

Walt still fought for breath. The rattle in his chest concerned Penny deeply. He hadn't seemed sick since she and Sam had arrived, but this breathing trouble could be serious. She hooked her hand under the older man's elbow as he coughed once more and then finally seemed to catch his breath.

"I think Jonas is right." Walt straightened, wiping a stray drop of spittle from his chin with the back of one hand. "Your pa's spoiled that boy. A strong hand is what he needs."

Perhaps so, but who would provide it? They were only visiting Walt for a couple of weeks, and then Sam would return to the same situation at home.

"Are you certain you're all right?" Penny asked, instead of commenting on her brother's actions. "Have you caught your breath?"

"I'll be fine, Penny-girl. Why don't you go get some grub?"

In the scuffle and resulting chaos, she'd nearly forgotten they were to join the picnicking families from the church. She didn't particularly feel like socializing, not wearing this uncomfortable dress, and not after her brother had just caused a dust-up. She could see several people on the fringes of the food tables glancing in their direction.

"Miss Penny, Miss Penny!" Breanna came running, hair flying loose behind her. Why hadn't Jonas put it in a braid?

"Come sit with us! I helped fill you a plate…"

Letting the girl's words flow over her, Penny allowed herself to be dragged by the hand to a worn, quilted blanket where Jonas sat alone. Head down, he seemed pensive and separate from those surrounding him; alone in a crowd of chattering families.

"I found Miss Penny," Breanna announced, flouncing down onto the blanket with no sense of decorum, her skirt flying up as she did so.

Penny gently lowered herself to the blanket, smoothing the calico skirt so that no one got a view of her legs. She accepted the overloaded plate Jonas handed her with a silent nod of thanks.

"What happened with your brother?" Breanna waved an ear of corn toward the direction they'd just come from.

Penny waited for Jonas to correct his daughter's impolite behavior as it wasn't fitting to gesture with one's food like that, but he had tucked into his own dinner and hadn't seemed to notice Breanna's action.

"He's caused a bit of trouble, hasn't he?" Penny knew the young girl was likely to ask more questions, so she changed the subject. "Where are your brothers? Aren't they going to join us?"

Penny spared a glance to see if her grandfather had gotten his food yet. She wanted to ensure he was all right after that coughing fit.

Breanna waved her arm around, this time thankfully without the ear of corn clutched in her fingers. "They's too busy playin' with friends to eat now. Reckon they'll get somethin' afore we leave. 'Sides all they want to talk about is bronc ridin' in the Round Up."

The young girl scrunched up her nose as if disgusted with her brothers' chosen topic. Then with a shrug, she dug into her food, with no regard for the fork lying on the blanket nearby. She used her hands to bring a piece of pie to her mouth.

Penny looked down, unable to watch. Why didn't Jonas say something to his daughter? Didn't he mind that her manners were lacking? Penny remembered the chaos surrounding the Whites' dining table just yesterday and couldn't be sure.

"I'm disappointed Grandfather and I couldn't bring anything to contribute for supper." Although it didn't stop Penny from taking a dainty bite of fried chicken. Delicious.

"'s a'ight," Breanna said around a mouthful of corn. "We brung loads of stuff."

"Breanna, it's not polite to speak with your mouth full of food." Penny couldn't help gently chiding the girl when it was obvious Jonas wasn't going to correct her.

"Miss Castlerock—" Jonas started.

Breanna looked abashed. She gulped a huge swallow, brown eyes large in her face. "Sorry, miss."

A glance at Jonas revealed his tight jaw; he probably wasn't happy with her interfering, but the girl needed to be taught. Penny comforted Breanna with a pat on her hand. "It's all right."

Penny dabbed her mouth with her handkerchief. "A lady must be polite at all times."

Breanna started to open her mouth midchew, then apparently thought better of it. She swallowed, then spoke. "Reckon I ain't much of a lady, Miss Penny."

"Breanna is just a little girl," Jonas stated, looking as if he wanted to say more.

Penny admired his desire to defend his daughter, but without a mother's influence, how could the girl learn? "Yes, but it's never too early to learn proper manners," Penny insisted.

Jonas looked as if he wanted to argue, but how could he? Breanna *did* need to learn manners.

Breanna seemed so disheartened, staring down at her plate with a wobbly bottom lip, that Penny offered, "Perhaps I could teach you some of the social graces."

Breanna's face lit up.

"Just while I'm staying with my grandfather, you understand," Penny was careful to clarify.

"Oh, Miss Penny, yes!" Breanna exclaimed, plate clattering to the blanket as she clapped her hands together. A little gravy spilled over the side of the plate, staining the blanket.

Breanna became distracted when a little girl who looked to be about her same age approached the blanket.

Jonas's expression remained closed off; he kept his gaze on his plate. Penny's offer had been sincere, but she hoped she hadn't offended him.

"I hope I've not overstepped where I shouldn't have," she said softly.

A muscle ticked in Jonas's jaw, though he kept his head bowed over his tin plate. "Perhaps my parenting skills are suspect, but Breanna doesn't know any better than to act as she does."

She *had* offended him. Why couldn't she learn to curb her tongue? "I'm certain you're doing the best you can with the children. I wouldn't have the faintest idea where to begin…"

"Well, I don't know much about…what did you say? *Social graces.*" His words were quiet and she had to lean closer to hear him, bringing their heads close.

Penny regretted her handling of the situation. Jonas had been nothing but kind to her and her family, first by providing her and Sam a ride in his wagon, and then allowing them to share meals at his table. Was there a way she could make things right?

"Perhaps... Have you thought that Breanna might need a woman's guidance? Is there anyone—someone you would consider marrying?"

A flush of red swept up Jonas's neck and into his face. "I suppose you think I can just go into town and procure a wife at the mercantile?"

She'd said the wrong thing again. Penny started to apologize but was interrupted when a young woman about her age approached their shared blanket with a welcoming smile.

Is there anyone you would consider marrying?

Jonas forced Penny's impertinent question from his mind as the schoolteacher, Miss Prince, struck up a conversation with his neighbor's granddaughter. The sour woman didn't think too much of him after the confrontation they'd had over Breanna attending school a few months back. Even now, the brown-haired tyrant was glaring at him from the corner of her eye. It made him uncomfortable.

He was used to people looking down on him, thinking he was lesser than them, but he didn't want that for Breanna. Especially not because of a condition beyond her control.

"My brother and I are staying with our grandfather, Walt Nelson, for a few weeks," Penny said to the schoolteacher.

Breanna shifted on the blanket, and Penny smiled down at her and wrapped one arm around his daughter's shoulders. "And I've been getting to know one of your students, Miss Breanna White, here."

The teacher's smile drooped, her gaze turned icy. "I'm afraid the girl is not allowed in my classroom."

Jonas wanted to protect Breanna from any disparaging remarks the teacher might make. "Honey, why don't you run and find Seb for me? I haven't heard his yell in a while, so he might be getting into trouble."

Breanna left after giving him a quick hug around his neck.

Penny looked between Jonas and the teacher, puzzlement evident in her creased brow. "Why isn't Breanna allowed to come to school?"

He should have known she would just ask outright. She was a forthright person and not afraid to speak her mind. But he didn't want her to hear what the teacher would say about Breanna, or about the other members of his family. True, Penny had seen one of Breanna's seizures up close, but she might change her opinion of his daughter when she understood the censure Breanna faced from others because of her condition.

"She had an *episode*," the schoolteacher spat the word, "and I simply can't have such goings-on in my classroom."

Penny met the other woman's gaze without faltering. "It's not Breanna's fault she has the seizures. She can't control it."

"It is disrupting and scares the other children. There's no telling when she could have another *episode* and—"

Penny didn't wait for the other woman to stop speaking, just interrupted with squared shoulders. "I've witnessed one of Breanna's seizures, and it wasn't a terrifying experience for me. I'm sure if someone explained her condition to the other children, they could be made to understand—"

"I don't want that kind of distraction in my classroom. I won't have it."

Penny's eyes flashed. Jonas was surprised she was fighting so vehemently for Breanna's right to be in the classroom. Breanna was only a neighbor, not a relation, but the way Penny was acting, Breanna could have been her own daughter.

"Miss Prince, are you sure *you* aren't the one who is frightened of Breanna's seizures?"

The other woman didn't respond, only turned and walked away.

Jonas watched Penny sit in silence, staring down at her hands. She interlaced her fingers once, then again.

When she finally looked up, her blue eyes still flashed fire. "I cannot believe that woman."

Jonas didn't know how to respond to her indignation.

"She isn't the only one who feels that way," he said quietly. No, there were several others in the community who avoided Jonas and his family, both covertly and blatantly. Just before Penny and Breanna had joined him on the picnic blanket, another family had moved away.

Penny settled one hand over Jonas's, her fingers curling under the edge of his palm. The move startled him into looking up into her bright blue eyes, compassion shining from their depths.

"I'm sorry you have to deal with their ignorance. Sorry for Breanna's sake."

Penny's strident defense of his daughter, and her compassion at this moment dissolved Jonas's earlier indignation at her interference. It sounded as if she *cared* about his daughter. What if her insistence that Breanna learn manners stemmed from concern?

But how could he be sure? He didn't know anything about fine ladies like Penny Castlerock.

Before he could fully understand her motives, she squeezed his hand and then released him, just in time for Matty and Ricky to slide onto the picnic blanket on their knees, bunching the blanket and almost toppling Penny.

"Sorry!" they chorused as one.

The moment was lost, but for a second, Jonas wondered

if he'd seen something more than compassion in Penny's eyes—something like admiration.

Penny glanced behind her to the passel of children in the wagon—all asleep. The gentle rocking motion, along with the rowdy play they'd engaged in at the church picnic had put them to sleep.

The four older boys, Sam included, rode ahead on horseback with Walt.

The group was nearing the Whites' home, and Penny's chance of talking to Jonas about her grandfather's problems was dwindling. Jonas had been pensive and quiet since they'd spoken on the picnic blanket, hardly saying anything, even to the children. She hoped she hadn't offended him again with her unkind words about the schoolteacher. It had just made her so *angry* that the woman held a prejudice against sweet little Breanna.

"Can I ask your advice about something?" She took care to keep her voice quiet. She didn't want to wake the children, but more so, she didn't want her grandfather to overhear.

"About what?"

Well, his response wasn't exactly the enthusiastic "yes" she'd wanted, but she continued regardless.

"My grandfather. He...trusts you. Counts you as a friend."

She saw Jonas's eyes flicker up to where her grandfather rode with the boys.

"I know his health has been a concern; he's seemed...not ill, exactly, since Sam and I have been with him, but...slower than I remember."

Jonas nodded. "We spoke before about his place being run-down."

"And then this afternoon, during the confrontation Sam caused, Grandfather couldn't stop coughing. I've heard him in the mornings, as well…sometimes it's almost as if he can't catch his breath."

Jonas's brow creased.

"Do you think…" Penny hesitated, trying to word her question appropriately. "Do you think he might consider coming to Calvin to live with my parents? There's plenty of room in our home."

Jonas's eyes narrowed. He considered her words for a moment, eyes fixed on the group ahead.

"Some men have the West in their blood," he finally said. "Your grandfather's one of them, I think. He loves his place, loves the land. His horses. I don't know if you'd be able to persuade him to move into town."

He was right. She knew he was right. But the helpless feeling that had come over her earlier, after Sam's fight, wouldn't lift. She threw up her hands. "Sam and I aren't prepared for the kind of work Grandfather needs around his place. You've heard what I did to the kitchen…"

She took a deep breath and forged on. "And Sam…well, I'm worried Sam is going to cause even more trouble for my grandfather. Even if he doesn't, neither of us knows how to fix the leaky roof in the barn or the chicken coop that's half blown away because of the wind out here."

He was silent, still staring ahead. What was he thinking? Was he sympathizing with her plight? Or did he think she was a grumbler, complaining when there was plenty of work to go around?

"Can't your father send some money? Or hire some workers?"

Considering the way her father felt about her grandfather, that wasn't likely. "I doubt that my father would be willing to do so. He and Grandfather don't really get along."

Jonas bit back the retort that wanted to escape. How could anyone dislike Walt Nelson? The older man had taught Jonas what it meant to be a believer, was always willing to pitch in and help when Jonas needed it. And his own son-in-law wasn't willing to send funds to help the older man?

Here was more evidence of the different worlds Jonas and Penny came from. And yet, maybe they weren't so different. Jonas's father hadn't been what a real father should be, either.

"Plus, there were…extenuating circumstances that led me to leave Calvin. I'm quite sure Father isn't happy with me at the moment. He would probably ignore any letter I sent him just now."

Jonas thought the man sounded like a tyrant, if he wouldn't listen to his daughter's request for help. He wanted to ask what had prompted her to leave town, but it wasn't his place. And she didn't offer the information. Did she think he wouldn't be able to understand her reasons for leaving town?

"I don't suppose…" Penny cleared her throat delicately, and her head tipped to one side, giving Jonas a full view of her face.

His mouth went dry, even as he tried to ignore his attraction to her.

"I know you're busy with your own homestead, but would there be any way you could find some time to help my grandfather with some of the repairs he needs? At least until I can find another solution…"

Jonas was already shaking his head by the time her voice faded away. He had enough work—an overwhelming amount of work—to do on his own spread, plus he'd agreed to take on the job of cutting Mr. Sumner's hay for the extra cash. He'd already be putting in extra hours, would be missing sleep. And still needed to find someone to care for Breanna.

But…

Walt was a good friend. He and Peg had been there for Jonas during times when he'd needed help with the kids. With Breanna when she'd been a baby. Walt had taught him everything Jonas now knew about horses. Walt had taught him about being a father, since Jonas's own example of a father had been pitifully lacking.

Jonas owed the man.

"I want to help. Walt is a good friend. I just don't see how I can manage all the work I already have to do."

"I understand." Her voice was low and laden with disappointment. Her shoulders slumped, and she gazed off into the distance. She seemed so discouraged that Jonas felt the need to explain himself.

"I've agreed to help another neighbor bring in his hay. His wife's mother is sick and he's going to pay me, but the boys and I are going to have a time of it getting all the work done before fall sets in."

She nodded, touched her cheek. Had she wiped away a tear? Her face was turned away, so he couldn't tell. He hoped not as he had no idea how to handle a teary woman. He wanted her to understand.

"With the money I'll earn, I should be able to pay for Breanna's treatment."

And after today's demonstration at the picnic, she had to understand how important that was to him.

"I just need to find someone to watch Breanna. I can't have her underfoot." Maybe that was the solution. "What if—do you think…?"

Now his tongue was getting all tangled. Penny did that to him. Discombobulated him.

"If you were able to watch Breanna for me, maybe handle some of the easier tasks around my place—not cooking," he hurried to say, "maybe doing the washing, gathering eggs— Ricky and Matty can help show you how things are done— then perhaps I could spare Maxwell for a couple of days to help out at Walt's place. Show Sam how things should be done," he explained. He had no intention of sending his son over to Walt's to do all the work, but Maxwell was a capable teacher.

Her expressive blue eyes settled on him, and the joy in their depths made his chest expand with an answering emotion. "Thank you."

Chapter Nine

Early Monday morning, after Walt and Sam had breakfasted and returned to the family homestead, Penny followed Breanna and Seb outside for her first lesson in gathering eggs. She hoped to accomplish this without getting her arms pecked. She already bore a long red scratch from her battle with her grandfather's hens.

Approaching the coop, Penny was distracted for a moment by the sight of Jonas's tall figure striding into the barn. She was grateful that he'd agreed to help her grandfather, but he'd been distant, almost preoccupied this morning. Not that any of the children had seemed to notice. They shared a rowdy breakfast as usual, although Seb and Ricky had been curious about the manners she'd tried to teach Breanna.

A loud whinny drew her attention to the corral, where Oscar and Maxwell had a rope around the neck of a sorrel filly. The horse bared its teeth and reared, obviously not co-operating with the teens.

Seb let loose a low whistle and followed Penny's distracted feet as she moved toward the corral to watch.

"They aren't trying to break that horse themselves, are they? Where's your father?" Penny asked Edgar, who sat on the corral's top rail, dirt-streaked blond hair peeking out from under his hat. "Shouldn't he be out here?"

"Don't need him, prob'ly," the rangy boy answered shortly. "Oscar broke three fillies last summer, and Pa wants him to teach Maxwell how t'do it this year. Besides, it's good practice for the bronc ridin' competition if they can get a saddle on her— Whooheee!" the boy shouted, startling Penny and causing the horse to rear up again.

"Get outta here, Ed!" Maxwell shouted.

"Don't make noise like that! You're scarin' him!" came Oscar's reprimand.

"Rope 'im in, pull 'im in," Ed crowed, ignoring his brothers. "Jest like Oscar roped that Sally Hansen in for a kiss yesterday behind the church."

Neither boy took their attention from the stomping, snorting horse, but both reacted to Edgar's statement. Maxwell flushed, deep red running up into his face beneath his tan. Oscar grinned, his teeth flashing white against his tanned face.

Indignation rising, Penny turned to Edgar, conscious of Breanna and Seb listening at her elbow. "What do you mean, he *roped* a girl in for kissing?"

Edgar laughed. "Well, from where I was spying, she didn't look none too much like she wanted the kiss. Least not at first. Until you laid a good one on her, right, Oscar?" He directed his last words to his brother, who grinned again.

Oscar wrestled the horse a few feet closer, wrapped the rope around his gloved fist. "That's right, Eddie-boy. Sometimes ya gotta steal a kiss to get the filly settled down—" He grunted as the horse pulled against him.

Penny looked between the boys, offense making her words sharp. "Girls are not fillies. They are not to be cornered or corralled and *kissed!* And it is certainly not appropriate to be stealing kisses behind the church. Or any other building!"

Oscar and Edgar laughed, while Maxwell remained silent, focused on the horse. His ears were still red.

"Does your father approve of this behavior?" she demanded.

Edgar shrugged. "He ain't said one way or t'other."

Cheek pressed against old Molly's side as he milked the placid cow, Jonas heard the ruckus outside before the barn door burst open, spilling light into the building's dim interior.

"Jonas?"

He could tell from Penny's voice that something—more like *someone,* one of his sons—had riled her up.

"Back here," he murmured, purposely keeping his voice calm so the cow wouldn't react to his sudden tension.

"Do you know what your sons are talking about, out in the corral? Oscar is proud that he cornered a girl and stole a kiss yesterday. He's bragging about it to the other boys."

Jonas didn't think that was much to holler about. But she seemed pretty riled up, if the sound of her stomping feet was any indication.

"Umm—"

She went on, apparently not requiring a response, her swinging skirt appearing in his peripheral vision. "As if that is an appropriate way to court a girl—not that your boys are of an age where they need to be worrying about kissing girls yet. Why, I couldn't believe it…"

Her voice faded as she paced toward the front of the barn, her words too low for Jonas to make out with one ear pressed against the cow's flank.

"Aren't you going to do anything?" *That* he heard, along with her outraged tone.

"What do you want me to do?" he asked, still working at keeping his voice calm.

"Talk to your sons!" Now she sounded exasperated, as if

he should have agreed with her assessment from the beginning and already known the answer. She must still be a few stalls over, because her voice was somewhat muffled. "Tell them it's not okay to steal a kiss! It isn't appropriate. Tell them when the time *is* appropriate."

"How should I know when it's *appropriate* to kiss someone?" he mumbled into Molly's hide. "I never have."

Her face suddenly appeared in front of him; she squatted close to Molly's shoulder, laying one hand on the docile cow's side. "What do you *mean,* you've never kissed a girl? What about Millie?"

Immediate, hot color boiled into his cheeks. He hadn't meant for her to hear that! "Wait—you didn't—I meant—"

But she was already shaking her head, eyes wide with realization. "You aren't Breanna's biological father," she whispered the words and plopped down in the straw, as if her legs wouldn't hold her anymore.

He eased away from Molly, taking a moment to look around and make sure none of the children were around.

"I am Breanna's father in every way that matters," he said in a low, firm voice. "I've taken care of her since the day she was born, and that makes me her pa. Not blood, not relations."

Penny opened her mouth, probably to ask more questions, but shouts from outside drew Jonas away from Molly. He raised one hand for Penny to be quiet and when he heard, "Pa!" again, he rushed from the barn to help.

Penny couldn't stop thinking about what Jonas had inadvertently revealed as she helped his children perform chores throughout the day.

As Matty showed her how to rub the clothes along the washboard for their weekly washing, she questioned everything she knew about her grandfather's neighbor.

Her memories of the events from Philadelphia had grown vague as the years had passed. There had been whispers that Millie had been with child for weeks before Mrs. Trimble had called a meeting with the four girls from Penny's dorm and shared that Millie would no longer be a part of the Academy. Penny had seen her roommate only once before Millie had been whisked away to an unknown location; the other girl had whispered that the bricklayer's apprentice was the baby's father. Penny had had no reason to disbelieve Millie, but now...

She'd only known Jonas as a laborer, someone in the peripheral sphere of her life. He often watched her with his piercing dark eyes when she came or went from the finishing school, though he'd never spoken to her. With his dust-covered hands and bricklayer's apron, she'd thought him beneath her notice, but she would not turn away an admiring glance. She'd imagined he fancied her, but all of that changed with Millie's revelation.

Then Penny had known—or thought she knew—that he was someone of loose morals. To compromise her friend's virtue...

And now it seemed she'd been completely wrong all this time. Had Millie's accusation caused Jonas to lose his livelihood? Had *he* been the one taken advantage of?

But why had he taken charge of Breanna? If he wasn't the girl's father, he couldn't be held responsible for her.

Penny shook out a light-colored shirt that must belong to one of the bigger boys, turning her head when water droplets sprayed her. She clipped it to the hanging line, as Matty showed her, and couldn't help but notice its worn condition and a tear near the bottom of the garment.

Jonas obviously worked himself to the bone to provide for these children. Children that weren't even his responsibility. What kind of a man would do that, expecting nothing in return? An honorable one.

But she still didn't understand *why*.

Jonas stayed in the fields as long as he could, avoiding Penny and the questions he knew she must have. He didn't want to dredge up his past, didn't want her to know how little his own parents had valued him and what their abandonment had caused him to do to survive.

He knew she hadn't thought much of him, not if she'd believed Millie Broadhurst about Breanna's parentage. But his pride didn't want her opinion to worsen when she found out about his past.

When his belly was roaring for some sustenance and it was almost dark, he couldn't avoid home any longer.

After bedding down his horse, he approached the house and saw that she was waiting for him on the porch, backlit by the soft glow of a lamp shining out the window. As he got closer he could see she dozed in the chair, head lolling to one side. A quick glance revealed her dress was dirtier than he'd seen it before, with water-spots all down the front.

Matty and Breanna must've worked her pretty hard today.

Warmth flooded through him as he imagined coming home to her waiting for him like this every day…and he quickly shook that dangerous thought away. She'd made it clear several times that she was only here to help Walt for a little while. Best to keep his heart uninvolved.

Only he was afraid it was too late for that, after the way she'd defended Breanna yesterday.

She sighed in her sleep, the soft sound parting her lips and drawing his eyes. He could gaze at her for hours and not tire of learning her lovely features…and there was another dangerous thought. What he needed was to stay far, far away from his neighbor's granddaughter.

"Penny," he murmured, moving closer.

She stirred but didn't wake. One copper curl slipped loose and fell across her cheek, tempting him to brush it away. Just brush his fingers against the softness of her cheek…

"Penny." He shook her shoulder more forcefully than he'd intended.

She roused with a soft, "Hmm," and an open smile that was like a fist to his chest, knocking his breath away.

He stepped off as she arched her back and stretched, trying desperately to keep the image of that joyous smile from burning into his brain. It made him want to pull her into an embrace…

"I must've fallen asleep," Penny said, standing and a little wobbly on her feet. He reached out and her hand fell onto his forearm, burning fire through his shirt. "I wanted to talk with you…" Her voice faded away on a yawn.

"We should get you home. Plenty of time to talk later." Or never, if he had his way.

"Ricky?" Jonas called quietly. The boy came to the back door. "Can you fetch a fresh horse and get him tacked up? I think Miss Penny is too tired to walk home on her own."

Ricky hopped from the porch and raced across the rapidly darkening yard to do Jonas's bidding.

"Should I have had him harness the wagon?" Jonas teased quietly as Penny wobbled again and this time settled right up against him, shoulder to shoulder. She was warm and pliant, felt a little like Breanna when she fell asleep in the wagon and he carried her inside. And nothing like Breanna, with curves only a woman could have.

He tilted his chin up and stared at the stars, denying the urge to wrap his arm around her shoulders and bring her closer. She wouldn't want that.

If she'd been up in arms about Oscar stealing a kiss, she would surely be offended by his unwanted embrace.

"No…" Another yawn. "I'll be fine. You don't even have to take me home. I can bring the horse back in the morning."

Ricky guided the horse close to the steps and Penny moved toward the animal, stumbling down the porch steps and into Jonas. He righted her with a hand on her upper arm, getting a whiff of her scent, something sweeter than flowers.

"I think I'd like to make sure you get there in one piece. And you don't wander off in the wrong direction. Thanks, son."

Jonas mounted up and Ricky helped Penny settle behind him, her small hands clutching the sides of his shirt, body supple and boneless against his back.

"All right?" He worried she'd fall asleep and slide off the horse behind him. "Do you need me to—hold you?" He bit off the strangled words.

"No, no," her soft protest was spoken into the back of his shirt, the words heating his skin. "'M fine. Just go. Night, Rick."

Half-disappointed and half-relieved, he nudged the horse into a walk. At least if they went slowly, she wouldn't be hurt much if she dropped off the animal.

True to form, she was only silent for a moment. He was almost getting used to her chatter.

"Mmm. You smell like the barn."

He tried to concentrate on her words instead of the brush of her chin against his shoulder blade. It didn't sound like a good thing. He knew what he smelled like. Sweat and horse. "I've been working in the fields all day. Barely in the barn."

"Reminds me of hugging Poppy when I was a girl."

Her words reflected the affection she felt. He'd never heard her call Walt *Poppy,* it was always Grandfather. Her speech was always proper, just like she was. Except for now.

Then she was quiet, her breathing even as it puffed against

the back of his neck. He was still afraid she would fall asleep, so he asked a question.

"How often did you visit your grandparents?"

"Mmm…" she hummed, the soft sound vibrating through his shirt and making his stomach swoop. "Haven't visited much since I left for Philadelphia. My father doesn't want me to come. Before that…every summer."

"Really?" That was surprising. He couldn't picture her following Peg into the barn to milk cows or gather eggs. "I wouldn't think you'd enjoy the homestead much. Too quiet."

"I do like conversing with my friends, but…" She sighed. "I love the horses. I helped saddle-break Patches, you know."

Another surprise. "No, I didn't know that."

They crested the final hill before Walt's place and the moonlight showed the small house, barn and corral in stark relief against the darker landscape. A light burned in the window. Probably Walt waiting on his granddaughter to arrive home.

"I didn't know a lot of things about you." Her words came slower now, almost dreamily.

Jonas kept his eyes focused ahead, wondering what Penny thought every time she saw this place. It sounded like she had good childhood memories here, but now that she was used to finery and wealth, did she see Walt's homestead differently?

"Thought you had loose morals…"

Her hands fisted in the material of Jonas's shirt, brushing against his sides and making him jump. The horse beneath him shied a bit, reacting to his abrupt movement, and Jonas patted the animal's neck, calming it. He knew it shouldn't bother him that Penny had thought the same as all the others had, that he was capable of fathering a child out of wedlock, but it rankled. He'd wanted Penny to see past the bricklayer's shy apprentice to who he was inside.

"But I found out I was wrong."

Jonas hadn't meant for her to find out about Breanna's parentage; he still didn't quite know what to say to her to convince her to keep it between the two of them.

They entered the yard between Walt's cabin and the barn, and Jonas slowed the horse.

"…Found out you're a man I can admire."

Jonas's heart pulsed at the same time he reined in the horse. His mind shouted *distance! distance!* because she didn't know about his own past and she'd most likely think differently about him when she did. But his heart caught on her admiration. He wanted her to think highly about him.

He didn't say anything as he dismounted from the horse and reached up for her waist.

"Oh!" she gasped softly, wobbling but not coming toward him. "My foot's caught—"

Jonas rounded the horse and freed her ankle from one of the saddle straps. She swung her leg over the horse's back and slid to the ground, putting them face-to-face with the horse between. Light from Walt's window painted her features golden and Jonas knew his must be in shadow—an apt metaphor for the difference in their circumstances.

"Why did you do it?" she asked, her gaze aware and frank with curiosity. She wasn't as sleepy as he'd thought. "Why did you take on Breanna's care instead of telling the truth?"

He could still remember being in the Broadhursts' stifling parlor, hat in hand, too afraid to sit for fear of getting brick dust on the fancy furniture. Remembered Millie's formidable father and the accusations he'd thrown at Jonas while Millie had sat crying on a sofa nearby. And he still remembered his own rising anger that had caused words to spew from his mouth before he'd really thought.

"They were going to just *throw her away*," he said, dropping his voice at the end of his sentence so maybe she wouldn't hear the anger still simmering all these years later.

"What? Who, Breanna?"

He looked away, pretending to adjust one of the buckles on the saddle, because he didn't want Penny to see the emotion he knew was written on his face.

"The Broadhursts paid me to take Breanna and leave Philadelphia. I think they still wanted to try and make their daughter a society match." Something he knew Penny wanted as well. Something impossible to someone like him. "If I hadn't…" He swallowed, the remembered words Mr. Broadhurst had said ringing in his ears. *Don't want the disgrace. Atrocity. Trash. Mistake.* Words he'd heard applied to himself as a child…

"If you hadn't taken Breanna…" Penny prodded, touching the back of his hand and bringing his gaze back up to meet her compassion-filled eyes.

He made himself say the words. "They would have given her up. Put her in an orphanage—" He exhaled heavily, trying to steady his voice. "Abandoned her." As his parents had done to him.

"Would that have been so bad? Aren't—don't orphanages, I mean, they help children who don't have anyone else, right?"

He could see in her face she didn't understand. She had probably never ever set foot in one of the overcrowded, noisy, lonely places. Had never been told she wasn't wanted. Something he never wanted Breanna to feel.

"But she did have someone," he stated simply, matter-of-factly. "Me." Unwilling, unable to tell her more. "You'd better go in."

Her face crinkled at his dismissal, but the emotions crowding his chest made it necessary.

He'd known she wouldn't understand what abandonment felt like, or what it meant to grow up in a place with a hundred other kids, crowded and with no privacy, no hope of finding a place, a family. Or on the streets, in the cold, moving from place to place.

Well, he'd made his own place, his own family. And he was happy out here on his homestead, with his kids.

"Penny?"

The porch flooded with light and the outline of Penny's brother filled the doorway.

"Grandfather's ready to turn in."

"All right. I'm coming." Her gaze continued to pierce Jonas as she backed toward the porch. "Thank you for telling me," she said softly.

She seemed to think he'd done something admirable, even if she didn't understand exactly what he'd saved Breanna from.

So why did he leave with such a bitter taste in his throat?

Chapter Ten

"Whatcha doin'?"

Taking a break. Exhausted from a morning spent on her knees forking potatoes out of the hard-packed soil, Penny looked up from the letter she was penning to smile at Breanna as the girl wandered into the dining room. Breanna had been playing with a crude corn-cob doll in her bedroom, and now emerged with tousled hair and bright eyes. She'd probably fallen asleep.

"I'm writing a letter, Miss Breanna."

"To who?" The girl plopped onto the end of one of the table benches, straddling it in a most unladylike fashion.

"Hmm, I think it's time for a manners lesson," Penny said, hoping to divert the girl's attention.

She stood and moved next to Breanna. "A lady never sits with legs apart. You may sit with your feet together on the floor." Penny demonstrated. "Or with your ankles crossed, like this." Penny tucked her crossed ankles beneath her, showing Breanna the proper position.

Breanna scrambled to sit up straight and copy what Penny was doing. She almost toppled from the bench because her feet didn't touch the floor, but Penny righted her and took the opportunity to put her arm around the girl's shoulders and hug her.

"Is this right, Miss Penny?" Breanna looked up with an eager expression. "Am I doing it?"

Penny nodded. She couldn't help but notice that Breanna's skirt fell well above the girl's ankles. Not to mention its state: worn and stained. The other dress she'd seen Breanna in was just as bad. The girl needed some new clothes. But Penny hesitated to broach the subject with Jonas, who already had more than enough worries about money.

And Penny couldn't help but think of her wardrobe full of silks and satins back at home. It was a shame the silks would not fare well on a farm with this many rowdy children, or she'd send for some of her older dresses and remake them into something that would fit Breanna.

"May I have a cup of tea?" Breanna asked, brown eyes shining up at Penny. "Isn't that what ladies drink?"

"Yes," Penny said with a smile. "But how about some milk instead?"

Breanna shrugged. "Okay."

They were going to throw her away. Jonas's words from the previous night reverberated in her head as Penny fetched Breanna's drink. Even with Breanna's tendency to follow her brothers around and her propensity to become dirt-smudged and the rips in her hems, she was a beautiful, vibrant girl. She was kind to animals, especially one of the chickens she'd taken to. And Breanna always saw the little things like Walt talked about, like a pretty wildflower or an unusual patterned leaf.

The beauty that shone through her reminded Penny of her grandfather's comments when they'd spoken privately near the barn. Between keeping track of Breanna and learning the farm chores, Penny had barely had time to ensure that Sam wasn't causing too much trouble and her grandfather wasn't too worn down. She hadn't had a decent conversation with him since.

And still, his words echoed through her mind at the oddest times. Like now, in a child-like moment spent with Breanna. Her grandfather *was* right. Breanna didn't need frilly, lacy dresses to make her beautiful. She was that on her own.

Of course, it wouldn't hurt to augment that beauty with a new, better-fitting dress…

But what could Penny do about it?

She brought Breanna's milk and sat back down to finish her letter. At least this was one thing she could do for the girl who'd started blooming in Penny's heart.

A letter she had no intention of telling Jonas about. After his disclosure last night, she'd thought back over every interaction she'd had with Millie and her family, trying to see them as Jonas must have seen them: a wealthy family intent on getting rid of a problem their daughter had caused. It wasn't a nice picture.

She herself couldn't call Breanna a problem, not after getting to know the girl.

But she'd remembered a vague memory, one of Millie talking about episodes or seizures she'd had during her childhood. Penny couldn't remember the young woman ever having a seizure during their acquaintance, but if she'd suffered them during her childhood, perhaps it meant they'd lessened or even disappeared as Millie had grown older.

And if that was the case, then perhaps Breanna didn't need to have the expensive treatment that Jonas was worried about. Not only could Jonas save money, but if the operation was dangerous for Breanna and they found it was unnecessary, Penny could save the girl from possible danger.

During the wagon ride from Calvin, Jonas had been adamant about not seeking help from the Broadhursts. If he knew about her letter, he could very well be furious. Although

Penny had yet to see him lose his temper, even with all the mischief the boys got into. He was a remarkably even-tempered man.

Shaking her head to clear the distraction, Penny continued writing. If Jonas found out about it and objected, she would simply tell him she was corresponding with a friend. Which she was. Millie Broadhurst.

Shouts from outside brought Penny to her feet, Breanna following. She knew Jonas was driving down cattle from the southern field today with several of the boys. Maxwell was helping at Walt's place, alongside Sam. If something was wrong, what should she do? Ride home and fetch her grandfather?

A wild whinny and more shouts drew Penny outside and down the porch steps before she even realized she'd headed toward the corral. Oscar and Ed had roped the same sorrel filly they'd been trying to break yesterday and were trying to settle her, but the mare kept rearing and whinnying.

Penny willed Oscar to release the rope as the horse's hooves came within feet of his body, but he kept reeling her closer, putting himself and Ed in danger of getting kicked.

"Drop the rope," she said under her breath. Didn't the boy know what danger he was in?

The horse whirled, jerking its head against the noose. Ed got jostled by its hindquarters and fell in the soft dirt, and the horse chose that moment to rear again. Its hooves came perilously close to Ed's head as he tried to scramble away, unable to get to his feet—

"Drop the rope!" Penny screamed.

Oscar released the rope in time for the animal to turn and gallop to the opposite side of the corral, narrowly missing Edgar, who scrambled to his feet and slipped through the cross-planks to stand outside the corral. He was shaking all over.

Oscar threw up his hands, a crude word slipping from his mouth. "The horse won't cooperate! I've never met a meaner piece of meat. She won't listen to me at all." He spat in the dirt in disgust.

"Don't curse," Penny corrected absently, watching the mare dance and try to shake off the bridle.

"What about ol' Blackie? He's plenty mean." Breanna crossed her arms on the middle corral railing and leaned her chin on top.

"Aw, why don't ya two gals go back inside where ya belong?" asked Edgar belligerently. He still hadn't warmed up to Penny since their first encounter over the breakfast dishes.

Penny paid no attention to the argumentative boy; she was focused on the animal quivering at the back of the corral.

"Blackie's a mustang stallion Pa got last year," Oscar put in, still breathing hard. "He's wild, and even Pa couldn't break him." This was said as if it was unimaginable.

"Don't worry. Blackie gets his own pasture. Pa has him in a special fence so's he don't stomp on any of us kids or visit with the mares or anythin'," Breanna said.

"Hmm," Penny hummed, still considering the idea that had come to her. "I'll be right back."

She went into the house and quartered the early apple she'd set aside as a snack for later. She slipped three of the pieces into her apron pocket and held onto the other. Jonas had lent her the apron and she still had a hard time visualizing him wearing it. When she returned to the corral, Oscar had joined Ed and Breanna outside the corral, arms crossed. The horse still dragged the lead rope from her neck.

Penny hiked up her skirt and maneuvered her way through the rails into the corral. The horse immediately reacted, neighing a warning for Penny to stay away.

"Miss Penny, what're you doing?" Breanna gasped.

Penny ignored her. "Don't speak too loudly, you three," she ordered. "I'm going to try a trick my grandfather showed me."

"*You're* going to tame that filly?" Oscar scoffed.

"Why doncha get outta there before ya get hurt?" Edgar chimed in, crossing his arms across the top railing and putting one boot on the bottom.

The boys' remarks rankled, but Penny didn't show her reaction outwardly. She needed to be calm so the horse would trust her. Pretending to ignore the horse, Penny leaned on the fence about halfway between the children and the animal, one arm outstretched against the top railing, the apple piece dangling loosely from her fingertips.

"There's more than one way to break a filly," was Penny's response to Oscar. "You can try to manhandle her into submission… Perhaps to steal a kiss…?" She still couldn't believe he'd done such a thing with a young woman last Sunday. Maybe she could use the horse-breaking to teach two lessons at once and encourage him on the proper way to treat a woman.

Breanna and Ed watched; the young girl with rapt attention, Edgar wearing a skeptical look.

Oscar's eyebrows arched, his jaw lifting defiantly. She'd seen that look on Sam's face many a time. "Or…?"

Penny held her breath as the horse snorted. She watched from the corner of her eye as the animal bobbed its head, trying to determine who Penny was and just what she was doing in the corral. Penny could wait.

"Or you can woo your filly."

"Woo her? Yer joking."

Edgar snorted as if to agree with his brother.

"I'm not." Penny remained perfectly still as the horse took one step in Penny's direction. "Yes, woo her. Just like when you're trying to catch the attention of a girl you might fancy."

Now Oscar's eyebrows met his hat. He crossed his arms over his chest.

"When you want to get a girl's attention, you don't demand it." Penny held her breath as the horse took two more hesitant steps forward. Still several to go before the rope would be within reach.

"You speak softly to her." Penny kept her voice low and soothing. "Tell her things she wants to hear. That she's pretty, if you like her dress, that kind of thing." Another step. And another. "But don't simply ask about surface things. You want to find out what is close to her heart. Her family, her dreams…"

One more step brought the horse close enough to stretch its neck and sniff the apple in Penny's palm, tickling her with its warm breath.

"That's right," Penny encouraged the animal under her breath. "Take it…"

The horse lipped up the apple piece, crunching it between its teeth.

"And giving a girl—a filly—gifts can't hurt your chances, either," Penny finished, pride coloring her voice. It had worked!

Penny caught sight of a sharp motion from the corner of her eye. Suddenly, the horse shied and reared. She jumped away, banging her side hard into the corral post. The horse's hooves narrowly missed her. She heard the air whoosh by as the filly galloped away to the other side of the corral.

"Miss Penny!"

"What's going on here?"

Heart pounding so loudly that she only dimly heard Breanna's shout and the second voice—Jonas's—Penny clung to the corral post. The horse didn't settle, instead heading around the corral and back toward Penny, who couldn't seem to make her legs work. She knew she needed to duck between the rails and get out of the corral, but her feet felt like lead. She couldn't move!

A pair of hands clasped her waist and she was bodily lifted over the top corral rail just before the horse thundered past, dirt flying up behind its dangerous hooves.

"What do you think you're doing?" Jonas demanded.

Penny gripped his shoulders with both hands, trembling uncontrollably. "I just lost my footing. I'm all right." She said the words to convince herself.

Over Jonas's shoulder, Penny saw Oscar's mouth twist snidely. "She thought to teach me how to tame that filly."

"What?"

Pressed up close against Jonas like she was, with her nose nearly in his neck, Penny felt as much as heard his curt question as it vibrated through his chest. His heart thudded against her cheek, as if he'd run across the yard to get to her. Looking past Oscar to the horse saddled near the barn, where Davy and Ricky looked on from their own horses, she supposed he might've done just that.

She felt safe in his embrace. The sheer breadth of his shoulders made it seem as if he could protect her from any harm. He smelled of sweat and horse, but somehow the scent was more potent than the colognes some of her acquaintances wore. Jonas was purely male.

As suddenly as she'd become aware of Jonas's physicality, she realized the children watched them curiously, and pushed away. Her legs were still wobbly, but they held her weight.

"Breanna and I came outside to watch the boys for a moment, and I saw Oscar having trouble… I told you that I helped Grandfather train Patches," she finished quickly as a disbelieving look crossed his face.

He shook his head as if he didn't know what to say to her. "You could have been hurt," he chided.

"My method was working, until something startled the

horse." She lifted her chin. "I'm sure you and the boys are hungry. Breanna and I already started laying out lunch."

Breanna joined them and began rattling off items, "We've got a cold ham, and some biscuits and the leftover potatoes from last night, and the pickled okra!"

As the group made their way indoors, Penny hung back, still a little uncomfortable with the realization that she *was* attracted to Jonas.

"Miss Penny, I saw ya makin' friends with the horse," said Davy, joining Penny as she crossed the yard a little behind the others. "I saw my brother wave his handkerchief and scare the horse just when you was about to win her over."

Penny followed Davy's pointed finger to a dark blue bandana tucked in Edgar's back pocket. She thought she'd seen something moving just before the horse had shied, but she couldn't be sure.

"Do you want me to tell Pa?"

Edgar glanced over his shoulder, eyes narrowed at Penny. It bothered her that the boy didn't like her, but surely he wouldn't do something to endanger her—would he?

"No, Davy," she said, putting a hand to the boy's shoulder. "Maybe it was an accident."

The boy shrugged. He turned away and spoke to his brother as Ricky joined them, leaving Penny to ponder Edgar's behavior. And her attraction to Jonas.

She followed the family into the kitchen, scooting past when the boys and Jonas all stopped at the water pitcher near the door to wash up. She still needed to set out the plates and utensils for the meal, but that didn't stop her from noticing the way Jonas's shirt stretched over the muscles in his back as he leaned over to splash his face. Or the way his throat worked when he swallowed several sips of water from the dipper.

She forced herself to turn away, focusing on the jostling boys now at the table.

Where had this awareness come from? What was wrong with her? She'd been around handsome men before—many handsome men!—and none of them had had this effect on her, this level of attraction.

Even if she *was* attracted to Jonas, nothing could come of it. She wasn't staying with her grandfather forever, only until she was able to get the repairs settled at his homestead. And Jonas wasn't the type of husband she wanted. Oh, he was kind and good-tempered, unlike her father, but he had eight children and lived on a small homestead.

She wanted to live in town and have fine things, pretty things. There wasn't anything wrong with that, was there?

Later that evening, Penny had made her escape back to her grandfather's place a little earlier than usual. She needed the space to try and figure out her feelings for Jonas.

"You've been awful quiet since you've been helping out at the Whites'."

Penny glanced over to her grandfather, who joined her at the corral to watch his stallion.

"I guess I'm just more tired than usual."

He seemed to accept that answer, asking, "Those boys behaving?"

"Mmm, for the most part." Except for Edgar, who still distrusted her. What did he expect from her, that she'd earned his suspicion?

"Your gran sure did admire Jonas and what he was doin' with those kids."

In light of Penny's earlier discovery that she was mightily attracted to Jonas, Walt's comment brought up her defenses. She'd just opened her mouth to refute what she knew he was going to say next, when Sam joined them at the railing.

"She doesn't want to marry a poor farmer, Grandfather. Not when Papa's got suitors swarming around back in Calvin."

"Jonas is more than just a farmer," Penny said without thinking.

Her grandfather's eyes took on a shine. She realized that he could think her words meant she was developing feelings for the homesteader, and quickly went on, "He *is* admirable for taking in the ch—the boys," she stopped herself before she slipped. If Walt didn't know about Breanna's true parentage, she didn't want to reveal Jonas's secret.

"But…I'm not…I don't think we could be anything more than friends."

Walt didn't seem disappointed by this, only kept smiling as he watched the horse round the corral, muscles rippling in the fading sunlight.

Sam grunted and swung around. "I'm still hungry. That cold chicken you brought over for supper wasn't enough. Maybe there's something else in the cabinets."

Penny shook her head and sighed as her brother stomped toward the house. The supper she'd brought over from the Whites' place had been plenty and she knew it. She guessed Sam just wanted an excuse to be by himself.

"I'd hoped…"

"Mmm?" Walt urged her.

"Well, I'd hoped that being out here would settle Sam a little. I couldn't say whether Father has truly spoiled him or not, but I know being with you and Gran are some of the best memories of my life."

As she said it, she realized it was true. She'd been happy at her gran's knee, doing simple things like sewing curtains or mending her grandfather's shirts, and helping him with the horses.

But she was happy back in Calvin, too. She loved attending ladies' socials with her mother and visiting with friends and having the opportunity to wear her fine dresses. There was nothing quite like getting dolled up for an event to make a girl feel beautiful.

Thankfully, her grandfather didn't press her, just stood at her elbow in silence. Uncomfortable with the turmoil of her thoughts, Penny changed the subject. "I noticed the barn roof looks much better."

"Yep. That Max is awful handy. Shouldn't leak a bit now."

"Is Sam behaving himself?" she parroted her grandfather's earlier question, curious to know if her brother was causing trouble.

"Sure is. Jonas couldn't have picked a better one of his boys to send. Maxwell is quiet, won't push Sam if he don't want to talk. But Max is also steady and a good example. Jonas has done well with him."

Penny wondered what her grandfather's cryptic words meant. Jonas had done what for Maxwell? Given him a home? Or more? She huffed as she realized her thoughts had tracked right back to the homesteader. She wouldn't think of him anymore tonight.

As Penny watched the horse round the corral once more, her hands twitched on the railing. What she'd really like to do was take an evening ride—feel the wind against her cheeks and keep remembering earlier times here with her gran.

"You want to give him a try? Reckon he wouldn't mind if you took him out for a ride."

How had he guessed her thoughts? "I shouldn't. It's getting dark."

"Sure you should. You'd both enjoy a little fresh air. Sam and I will be here when you get back. I'll help ya saddle up."

And that was that.

Riding through her grandfather's pastures as the sun set red over the mountains, Penny was careful to keep within sight of the house. She would never live it down if she managed to get lost in the dark.

Out here, there was a certain freedom that she didn't have back in Calvin…and she almost thought she could feel her gran smiling down on her from above.

But her problems back in Calvin hadn't been resolved, only delayed.

Chapter Eleven

Penny was conscious of two things during Sunday morning services at the little Bear Creek church. One was the finished letter she'd tucked into the pocket of her grandmother's simple calico dress. The other was the man beside her.

From his broad shoulders filling out the dark jacket of his Sunday suit, to the slightly off-key baritone, after three days of trying, she still couldn't ignore Jonas. Especially not when she'd ended up wedged next to him in the pew, Breanna on her other side.

This morning she'd felt much more comfortable coming to services. She hadn't noticed any stares from other people and several folks had greeted her warmly as she entered the sanctuary with her grandfather and Sam, making her feel welcome and not so out of place, even though she still wore one of her grandmother's nicer but simple dresses. Today it didn't bother her.

And she couldn't help noticing how beautiful the congregational singing was, even though not all of the voices carried perfect pitch. Ever since the midweek ride she'd taken on her grandfather's stallion, she'd been noticing little things more. Like the exuberant joy with which the boys consumed their meals. What she'd taken for chaos those first couple of days was actually them enjoying the good fare. Breanna's constant cheerful state was another thing to admire.

And it seemed she couldn't turn around without noticing Jonas and her continued awareness of him.

She ducked past Jonas as soon as the last "amen" was said, angling to meet up with the mercantile owner's wife in the milling crowd. She'd met the woman last week at the picnic and learned she was also the postmistress for Bear Creek.

"Good morning, Mrs. Peterson."

"Hello, dear. It's nice to see you again. Has anyone told you about the barn raising planned for two weeks from now at the Smiths' place? They're newlyweds," Mrs. Peterson confided, voice lowered. "Moved out here from back East not too long ago and haven't got one put up yet. Men'll be building and us womenfolk are providin' the noon meal."

"Oh," Penny hedged. "I'm not much of a cook."

"That's all right. Just bring yourself. And that lot of boys, if you can get them to come. Most times they're too busy to come to community events."

That didn't surprise Penny. Jonas was committed to making his homestead profitable, taking care of the children. But maybe he needed an event like this to remind him he wasn't alone out here. Maybe she could talk to some folks about raising money for Breanna—without Jonas knowing, of course. Jonas was a proud man, and she didn't want to offend him if he didn't want folks to know he needed money.

"Mrs. Peterson, I was wondering if you could post this letter for me. I don't think I'll be able to make it back to town tomorrow, and it'd be a great favor to me."

"Oh, certainly, dear." She glanced down at the envelope. "Miss Millie Broadhurst, in Philadelphia. Is that a friend of yours, dear?"

Penny glanced over her shoulder. Had Jonas heard? Thankfully he was deep in conversation with another man across the sanctuary.

"Miss Penny!"

Breanna ran up to the two women, interrupting anything else that Penny might've told Mrs. Peterson about the letter.

"Pa says we can't stay long because there's a storm comin' in," the girl reported and then was off again, chasing and calling after one of her brothers.

Mrs. Peterson's gaze followed the brown braid Penny had put in just this morning. "She's a sweet girl. My Katie, my youngest, is that age." She shook her head. "Gets into everything. Follows her older sister into trouble."

Penny agreed. "Yes, Breanna can be a handful, but all of her brothers dote on her. But she needs…" New dresses. And while doing the wash, Penny had noticed how worn some of the boys' shirts were as well.

"I don't suppose…" Penny leaned close to the older woman and asked for another favor. This time a big one.

"I'm coming!"

Jonas worked to keep the annoyance off his face as he turned toward the sound of boots hurrying along Bear Creek's wooden boardwalk along Main Street.

Penny approached, face lit up from within, clutching a paper-wrapped package to her chest. Wrapping he recognized from the mercantile. She'd been *shopping* while he waited, while the storm clouds grew darker?

He didn't vent his irritation, didn't say anything as he boosted her up onto the bench seat. Gritted his teeth as he walked around behind the wagon and vaulted onto the seat on his side without even using the wheel for leverage.

"Where is everyone?" she asked, glancing around and finally realizing that they were alone, save Oscar, who held his prancing mount in place a few paces away.

"They all doubled up to hurry home. Oscar waited," he nodded to his son as he snapped the reins, putting the horses in motion. "The others didn't want to get wet."

Penny tilted her chin up to the cloud-filled sky, giving him an open view of her delicate features in his peripheral vision. "Oh, dear," she half sighed. "I *did* hurry. I'm sorry."

He stared at a point just over the horses' ears. Was two weeks too long for her to go without having a new gown or some other frippery? Had she asked the Petersons to open their store for her just so she could have her fine things?

It shouldn't bother him. He *knew* she liked fine things, pretty things. Knew she would never settle for someone poor. Someone like him.

For a moment when he'd held her in his arms after he'd scooped her out of the corral, he'd thought they'd connected. There had been something on her face, some emotion he couldn't name had flashed across her expressive features and his heart had pounded even harder than when he'd seen her almost get trampled on by Oscar's filly.

And then in the last three days, she'd seemed to pull away. Not *quite* avoiding him but not addressing him with the open warmth he'd come to expect. He didn't know what to make of it. Maybe he'd done something to offend her, but for the life of him, he couldn't figure out what.

"I'll be even sorrier if we get soaked," she muttered.

Jonas didn't reply as they left the town behind and moved directly toward the building storm. He'd secured most of the animals before hitching up the wagon this morning, but the cattle he planned to take to Cheyenne tomorrow were still penned out in the open. He prayed there wouldn't be much lightning or thunder with this storm, and the animals would ride it out without kicking up a fuss.

"Miss Penny, you steered me wrong."

Jonas's head came up at Oscar's frustrated statement.

His son had brought his horse right next to the wagon on Penny's side.

"What do you mean?" Penny smoothed her skirt and addressed the boy.

"You told me to woo Sally, and I tried but she didn't take to it."

"You told him to *what?*" The words were out before Jonas could temper his frustration.

"What did you do?" Penny asked, ignoring Jonas's question with her face still turned to Oscar.

"I told her she looked real pretty, just like you said."

"I did say he should compliment her. Women like compliments," Penny said to Jonas with a quick glance. "What else?" she asked the teen.

"Well, I asked her about her family, like you said. She has an older sister, Sarah, who's away training to become a teacher and I asked how she was doing and was she well and did she like the schooling and all of a sudden Sally jest turned real red in the face and walked away. I tried to ask her what was wrong but she jest ignored me." His son shrugged, the gesture seeming to convey his confusion.

Jonas couldn't help his son—he had no idea what had gone wrong for the boy, either.

"Oh," Penny said, lips clamped together as if she was holding back laughter. "Oh, my."

"What? Why didn't she take to my wooing?"

Penny cleared her throat once. And again. Then when she could apparently speak without her mirth showing she said, "By asking all those questions about her sister, Miss Sally might've thought you…um…fancied her sister."

"Fancied? Sarah Hansen?" The incredulity in Oscar's voice made it evident that thought hadn't crossed his mind whatsoever. "Sarah's no fun at all. Before she left home all she did was nag the other kids. 'Don't horse around.' 'You're yelling too loud.' She's *awful*—"

"Oscar," Jonas warned. He'd taught his son better than to talk badly about a lady, no matter if he did think all those things about her.

Penny shrugged, her arm brushing against Jonas's. "I'm just letting you know what I suspect happened. If you asked all those questions about her sister, Miss Sally might've thought you were more interested in her sister than you were interested in her. What do you usually talk to Sally about?"

A flush rose up Oscar's neck. "We don't rightly talk much. I wanted her to know I liked her…um…fancied her," Oscar looked uncomfortable using Penny's proper word, "so last week I jest, well, kissed her so she'd know how I felt. But you said I shouldn't have done that."

A slight *tsk*ing sound emerged from the woman next to Jonas. Her lips were pinched together again.

"So she really has no idea what your intentions are then?"

The boy shrugged.

She sighed and went on, "The correct way to catch a lady's attention is first with a gentle compliment. Let's practice a bit. Here, Jonas, you can help us. For instance, if you wanted to show your admiration for me, you might remark on my appearance."

Instant heat radiated up Jonas's neck and bled into his face. He hoped the shadow from his hatbrim was enough to keep her from noticing. He swallowed, but all the moisture in his whole body seemed to have evaporated, leaving him dry mouthed. She wanted him to compliment her, but he hadn't any idea how to go about it.

"Go ahead," Penny urged.

Oscar looked at him with raised brows, expecting…what? A smooth-tongued example?

Jonas cleared his throat, but it didn't help much. His voice sounded hoarse when he dutifully said, "Miss Castlerock, you look…" *more beautiful than a summer sunrise over the mountains.* He couldn't say the words. "…very nice in your Sunday dress this morning."

Her eyebrows knit together and then smoothed. "Thank you." She offered him such a genuine smile that he felt it all the way to the toes of his boots.

"And then you would continue to make conversation. Perhaps ask about my family…"

Hadn't he just seen Walt for himself, before and during Sunday service? Should he ask about her parents, then? Afraid he would say something he shouldn't, Jonas beseeched her for more guidance with a half-panicked glance.

"Honestly," she huffed under her breath. "It's as if you've never spoken to a woman of courting age."

"I told you before, I can't just walk into the mercantile and pick a bride," he muttered, tugging on the collar of his shirt that was suddenly choking him.

"Well, I don't see why you have to make it so difficult," she sniped right back at him. "It's not as if I'm an ogre."

Her silly comment struck him, and he couldn't help the half smile that dragged a corner of his mouth upward. She responded with a warm smile of her own, one he hadn't seen in a couple of days.

"If you prefer to ask about my interests, I enjoy—"

"Pretty dresses and frilly hats," he finished quickly.

She looked at him sideways. "I was going to say *painting.* I left my oils at home in Calvin, but I've been sketching a bit in the evenings. When I have time," she amended.

"I remember you used to set up an easel in the courtyard back in Philadelphia." The memory came upon him quickly, and he'd said the words before he really thought about them—he hadn't wanted her to know how closely he'd watched back then.

"You remember that?" she asked, tilting her head to one side and appraising him with those blue, blue eyes.

"I—guess so," he choked. Was that an appropriate response?

The moment seemed to stretch and Jonas's breath caught in his chest until Oscar interrupted them, still looking perplexed. "But how do I fix things with Sally? I really like… um, fancy her, you know."

The teen looked to Jonas, but Jonas didn't know what to tell him. "You know just as much about women as I do."

"Miss Penny, can you tell me what to do?"

She hesitated, glancing at Jonas, but he gestured for her to carry on. As if he could stop the flow of advice from his pretty neighbor. "Just be honest with her. Tell her that you want to get to know her better and that's why you were asking questions about her sister."

"But what if she don't believe me? Should I corner her and kiss her again?"

"No!" Exasperation rang in her voice. "You can't just go around stealing kisses, Oscar. If the girl likes you—really likes you—you'll know it just by her actions. Maybe she'll invite you to Sunday dinner with her folks, or maybe she'll allow you to hold her hand. But kisses aren't to be taken lightly, and they aren't ever to be stolen."

"All right." Forehead wrinkled in thought, Jonas's son urged his mount a little ahead. Aware that they were now alone, Jonas shifted on the seat.

Suddenly, as if they'd crossed an invisible line, a wave of cooler air washed over them, and Penny shivered.

Jonas turned to grab the slicker he'd tucked behind the bench seat this morning and pushed it into Penny's hands. "Rain won't be far behind."

She tried to hand it back to him. "What about you? What will you do?"

He shrugged. "One of us is getting wet. Might as well be me."

"Are you certain?" Her question irritated him. He might not know much about women, but did she think him so uncouth that he wouldn't offer her a simple courtesy?

He didn't know the answer, but was gratified when she shrugged into the coat. The shoulders were too big for her, and it hung about her like an oversize blanket, but perhaps she would stay somewhat dry.

They weren't far from the homestead. He could see the stand of trees that marked the edge of his property, but they weren't close enough to outrun the rain. The first drops plopped against his hat and shoulders.

Penny cried out as the sprinkles turned to torrents, and Jonas snapped the reins to make the horses move faster, though they already strained in their traces. He hunched his shoulders and kept his hat tipped down to try and keep the worst of the rain from his head.

They were nearing the house when a shout brought Jonas's head up. Matty galloped toward them, waving his arms and yelling, though Jonas couldn't make out his words. Jonas reined in the horses.

"Pa!" the boy gasped as he got close and brought his heaving mount next to the wagon. "The cattle broke out of the corral! They're stampedin' toward the McCoys' place. Th' other boys already went after them—"

Jonas reacted, jumping from the wagon and reaching to unhitch the nearest horse from its harness. Time was of the essence. He didn't want any of the cattle getting injured in a stampede, and he didn't have extra time in the next days to round up lost cattle, either. He knew Oscar and Maxwell were capable riders, but if the beasts were good and scared, one of the younger boys could get hurt. He needed to join his sons and take charge of the situation.

"Thunder must've scared them," Matty shouted over the pounding rain.

Jonas didn't waste time arguing that the thunder was too far away, he just kept working on getting the nearest horse undone so he could join his sons. If he had to ride bareback, so be it. The horses he'd hitched up this morning were some of his more placid animals and this one wouldn't balk at it.

"Where's Breanna?" Penny called out, and Jonas looked up to see that she was out of the wagon and attempting to unbuckle the straps on the opposite horse.

"What're you doing?" he demanded at the same time Matty replied, "She's with Poppy Walt. Oscar sent them back to the house."

"Good," Penny said, and stunned him with her next words. "I'm coming, too."

Freezing, he looked up, straight into her vivid blue eyes.

"No, you're not. Walt would—"

"He would want me to help," she interrupted, still struggling with the heavy harness.

"I don't have time to argue. Matty can take you home and catch up with the rest of the boys."

"I'm not going home," the exasperating woman said through gritted teeth, pulling on the leather strap with both hands. "If I can get this to cooperate."

"Penny. There's no reason for you to do this."

"I can ride—"

"Bareback?" he demanded, remembering her experience with the rearing horse last week. The last thing he needed was a fool woman getting in trouble or getting hurt.

"I'll be fine. I'm helping." She gave him a steady look over the horses' backs, sodden hair drooping into her face.

He didn't have time to hide his displeasure or to help her get the harness undone. He needed to get to his sons before the cattle got any more out of control. They needed those cattle for sale.

"Fine," he spat, finally getting the horse on his side un-hitched. Jonas wasted no time in swinging up on its back. "I'm going to head straight for the McCoys' from here—hope I can cut off some of the cattle and turn them. You and Penny follow the old cattle trail between here and the ravine," he pointed toward the place he was talking about, knowing his son would know where it was, "and try to catch any strag-glers."

"Watch out for her," he told his son, who nodded seriously.

Penny sent him a speaking glance, but he didn't have time to worry about her hurt feelings.

He raced off into the pouring rain after the cattle and his sons, praying the whole way. He had a feeling his gang was going to need it.

Chapter Twelve

Penny threw one side of the heavy corral gate closed and tried in vain to wipe some of the moisture from her face. Jonas closed the other side of the gate, trapping the milling, bawling mob of cows inside.

He leaned back against the gate, face raised to the sky. Penny followed his example and rested on the fence, her shaky legs protesting just how long she'd asked them to cling to a horse bareback.

The boys wheeled their horses not far away, whooping their excitement. Somehow both Penny and Jonas had been the closest to the corral when the last of the cattle had been ushered in, and she'd followed his example and jumped from her mount to shove the gate closed without even a thought.

"We did it," she gasped, panting from exertion. A sense of pride she hadn't felt in a while rose up in her chest and she laughed aloud, turning to Jonas as she repeated, "We did it."

His answering smile warmed her from the inside out, no matter that she was soaked to the skin, her dress clinging to her uncomfortably. She didn't even notice.

She hadn't ridden so hard or fast since her childhood—or maybe ever. And she'd certainly never chased down a bunch of rangy cattle. If her mother could only see her cowgirl daughter now… She laughed again.

Jonas shook his head, a chuckle escaping. "Walt was telling me the other day how you wanted to ride in a cowboy exhibition back when you were around Edgar's age. I didn't believe him, but after the way you rode today…"

A hot flush crept up Penny's neck and into her face. She'd forgotten about that summer. She'd been, what…twelve? It was the first time her grandfather had really let her help with breaking the horses, and she'd been the happiest she could remember.

"I've never even been to a round up," she admitted, attempting to wipe some of the rain and mud from her face. "My mother thinks the crowds are too rough for a *young lady of my deportment.*" She finished the sentence with a bit of mockery in her voice. Now that she was finding her feet between Jonas's homestead and her grandfather's place, her mother's concerns of propriety seemed a bit too much.

Jonas's eyes rested on her face for a long moment.

"Well, today you were amazing," Jonas's baritone rumbled. He lifted his head back to the sky, face open to the now softly falling rain.

"Really? Why, thank you, kind sir." Penny pushed away from the fence to drop an exaggerated curtsy.

Her wobbly legs threatened to fold at the movement and his arm came around her shoulders, steadying her, pulling her close to his broad chest, covered only by the shirt that clung to him like a second skin.

"We make a good team," Penny said, face upturned to his, their accomplishments still making her giddy.

He stared down at her, silent and serious again, eyes tracing her face and lingering on her…mouth?

Then he nodded, and the movement of his hat sent rivulets of cold water splashing onto her heated cheeks and ruined the moment. She stepped away, gripping the railing to steady herself, staring blindly at the animals before her.

Had he been about to kiss her?

Would she have resisted if he had?

She didn't know anymore. She was finding it hard not to like the quiet rancher who'd built a life for himself. Poor or not.

"We should get back to the house." Jonas rubbed the back of his neck with one hand so his arm blocked her view of his face. "I'm sure Walt's worried about you."

"Mmm," she agreed faintly. "And we should check on Breanna. I hope the excitement hasn't upset her."

She fell into step with him, one of the boys—Davy—waved at them from atop his horse and motioned to the two unsaddled horses he held by the reins.

"You want to ride back to the cabin?" Jonas asked.

She shuddered at the thought of getting back on that horse bareback. "It's not far, is it?"

Jonas waved off his son. "No, not far. Just watch your step," Jonas cautioned. "Might be slick."

His concern reminded her of the way he'd told Matty to *watch out for her* just before he'd ridden away. He was a man who took care of his own. And his concern made her feel as if he cared for her.

Would she welcome it if he did?

Her earlier joy faded, leaving her out of sorts as she contemplated the possibility of a relationship between herself and Jonas. It couldn't work. Could it?

She didn't want to live on an isolated homestead. Not even one with her grandfather as a close neighbor. She liked visiting her friends in town, being able to walk down to the café and have a cup of coffee with Merritt, the schoolmarm back in Calvin.

And her fine gowns, including the peach taffeta she

adored, had no place here. Her first days working with her grandfather had taught her that. Both dresses she'd brought from home had been utterly ruined.

If Jonas *did* feel something for her, wasn't it better to draw away now, before his feelings could be engaged any more than they already were? And before her own heart became involved?

Foot slipping on a muddy patch, Penny nearly toppled, but Jonas steadied her with a hand on her forearm, then offered her his arm. She took it, even though they were getting close to the house. Better to be safe and not have a bruised posterior to go with her tired legs.

Penny snuck a glance at the man who'd trudged silently next to her while she ruminated and who now stared ahead at the snug cabin. Except for offering her his arm, he didn't even seem to register her presence.

Perhaps he wasn't even attracted to her. He'd freely admitted he didn't know how to woo a woman, so wouldn't she be able to tell if he fancied her?

Maybe he *didn't* think about her as a potential wife. Maybe his concern only meant he was being polite.

If that was the case, why was she strangely disappointed?

Jonas couldn't get away from Penny fast enough. He needed the distraction his sons provided—to keep him from thinking on the way her face had looked turned up to his and shining with joy.

And that hint of awareness that had entered her eyes. Had she expected his kiss? Wanted it?

Or was he being foolish and imagining what he wanted to see in her eyes? He didn't know much about women, and didn't have a ma to ask.

Regardless, the camaraderie and shared success he'd felt with Penny after rounding up the cattle had been powerful.

He couldn't believe how well she'd ridden. Her childhood skills must have come back to her in a moment of need. He was proud that she'd accomplished it, glad the cattle were back where they belonged.

Jonas released Penny's arm and stomped up the porch steps, grateful that he could turn her over to Walt and send her home. He needed distance.

He opened the door to a cacophony of noise. Sounded like the boys were regaling Walt and Breanna with how they'd rounded up the cattle, and all talking at the same time. As usual.

The scent of fried chicken and warm bread registered at the same time the blast of heat did. He didn't realize how cool it had been outside.

"Oooh," Penny murmured from behind his shoulder, at the same time he heard her stomach gurgle. "I'm starved."

"You worked hard," he told her, and no one even seemed to notice they'd come inside. "You did good."

She flushed at the compliment and he looked away before she could see how much her pink cheeks affected him. "C'mon, let's get some grub," he said gruffly.

She looked down at herself, her dress soaked and muddy under the too-big slicker. "I'm a mess—need to get dry—"

"Miss Penny, you can borrow some of my things. They'll probably fit." Davy appeared with an armful of clothing: some of his trousers and a button-up shirt, wool socks.

Jonas waited for Penny to refuse the items, thinking she wouldn't wear boys' clothing, but she just thanked his son and slipped into Breanna's room. Minutes later, after he'd donned a dry set of trousers and homespun shirt himself, she stepped out into the living area.

He stared, mouth dry. The boys and Breanna had already sat down at the laden dining table, ready to dig in to the delayed noon meal and didn't seem to notice anything unusual about Penny's appearance.

Apparently, Jonas was the only one fascinated by the sight of her in his son's clothing. The shirt didn't reveal any more curves than other shirtwaists he'd seen women wearing before. It was the trousers that showed her long legs. When he was able to tear his eyes away, he was gripped by the auburn curls that turned dark when wet, falling around her shoulders and halfway down her back. He itched to run his hands through those locks. But he had no right, Jonas reminded himself sternly.

Penny self-consciously ducked her chin as she neared where he stood, halfway between the table and the bedrooms. "I must look a sight."

She did. An attractive, beautiful, breathtaking sight.

He cleared his throat, tried to get his voice to work. "You look…just fine. It's only family anyway."

Thankfully, she didn't call him on the understatement, but just moved toward the table. He followed dumbly, now immune to the smells of the food, attuned only to Penny. She'd enchanted him.

Penny took the second-to-last seat left at the long table, leaving him to scoot in on the end next to her. Would he even be able to eat with this sizzling awareness of her at his elbow?

"Miss Penny, you were amazing!" Ricky called from the far end of the table, after Walt had prayed for the food. "I saw you race down that ornery ol' red dogie and bring her back in."

She shifted on the seat next to him, shrugged off the compliment as she dished some corn pone onto her plate.

Oscar chimed in, "I saw her collect two steers at once—"

And so did Seb, who'd mostly stayed out of the way by Jonas's plan. "You ride real good for a girl!"

Perhaps most telling of all was Maxwell, who was usually too shy to speak at all around young women. "I couldn't believe she was riding bareback in the rain. I almost slipped off old Silver's saddle twice myself!"

Jonas had had his own moment of nearly being unseated, so he knew Maxwell's compliment was genuine.

"Maybe Miss Penny should think about riding in the Bear Creek round up."

Jonas had been distracted by Penny's beaming smile and wasn't sure which boy had thrown out the teasing comment, but he winked at Penny anyway, remembering their exchange near the corral. Her joy at the boys' plain-spoken admiration made Jonas's gut feel funny inside.

"I'm just glad I was useful," she said between bites, still as proper as she could be. "Not like burning the food—and the kitchen." She paused, her next words were spoken softly, almost to herself. "I actually felt like a part of the family."

Problem was, he was starting to imagine her as a part of the family, too. His wife.

He cleared his throat, trying to keep his thoughts from traveling down that road. "I noticed Sam did a good job, too."

The usually reserved teen's head came up and his eyes glanced off Jonas's steady gaze.

Maxwell clapped him on the shoulder. "It's true. Saw you cross in front of two steers and drive them back into the herd."

Sam endured some good-natured ribbing from the boys and actually smiled. Penny gifted Jonas with another beaming smile and he felt as if he'd accomplished something, simply by encouraging her brother.

Jonas wiped his hands on the damp towel and set it aside, finished with the dishes. He leaned one hand on the wall above the washing tub, looking out the window without really seeing. Too much rain still falling to see much, anyway.

When he'd built the cabin, he'd arranged the kitchen so there would be a window his future wife could look out of and enjoy the view of the mountains in the far distance. At that time, with only Breanna, Oscar and Seb to look after, he'd had dreams of finding a wife. He'd had dreams of having someone to love him since his childhood. It wasn't until his bricklaying apprenticeship in Philadelphia that those dreams had coalesced into a vision of a wife, a partner, a friend closer than any other.

Oh, he knew the kids loved him, but it wasn't the same as having someone who didn't depend on your for their well-being—someone who *chose* you.

What had happened to those desires? Had Jonas become too busy with the daily hubbub of life and those dreams had faded into the background? If he wanted a wife, he could find a wife!

With eight children to watch after, he didn't have a lot of time to think about courting. In fact, he had none during the busy months of summer. But if it was important enough, he could make time for it.

Or was it a deeper issue than time? Was he scared that if he got close to someone, they would find him lacking, just like his own parents had? What if he fell in love, completely and deeply in love, and the woman left him like his parents had?

And why had Penny's presence resurrected his dreams of finding a true partner? Could it simply be because she'd been there during his tumultuous eighteenth year, when he'd first dreamed of having a wife?

Or was there something special within her that attracted him? Like the fact that she treated Breanna as if she was completely normal?

He didn't know. This confusion and insecurity didn't

sit well with him. He liked things ordered. Liked his quiet, homesteader's life.

And yet, he couldn't be disappointed that Penny had come into his life, even if the disruption was temporary.

Dishes done, he looked over his shoulder. It had grown awfully quiet in the other room, where Penny had been playing parlor games with the children to keep them busy while they were stuck inside. Last he'd checked, Walt had fallen asleep in the rocker near the fire, amidst all the noise.

Jonas felt a little isolated in the kitchen away from the laughter and shouts, but he was the one who had insisted on it after lunch. He'd needed the space to catch his breath and try to figure things out. Not that it had done him much good. He was still as confused as he'd been before.

A peek through the doorway revealed Breanna curled up next to Penny on the sofa, head on the woman's lap, fast asleep. Maxwell was the only boy left in the room and sat against the wall facing Penny.

Jonas suspected Davy and Ricky had snuck out to the barn to check on a new foal and the others had probably retired to their rooms for a rainy-day nap, a luxury they rarely got.

"She's a real sweet gal. Helps her folks with their store, and keeps her little sisters."

Jonas realized Maxwell was talking about a girl. His son had never expressed an interest in the fairer sex, at least not to Jonas, but this certainly sounded like admiration.

"She sounds sweet. Do you know her, Jonas?" Penny asked, bringing him into the conversation though he wasn't aware she'd even noticed him standing in the doorway.

Maxwell looked up from his spot on the floor. Jonas stepped into the room, hoping his son wouldn't shut down because of his presence. Maxwell still kept some things private, even from his adoptive father.

Maxwell cleared his throat, face reddening. "We're talking about Emily Sands."

"I didn't know you were sweet on her." Jonas sat on the end of one of the benches, close enough to be part of their conversation without having to speak loudly and possibly wake Breanna.

"I ain't really said anything to anyone, because..." Maxwell looked down and fiddled with his pants leg. "Well... she's really somethin' special and I'm..."

Jonas held his breath. Would Maxwell share about his past? He was remarkably closed-mouthed about it, even to Jonas, who only knew bits and pieces.

Penny reached out, stretched a little, and ruffled Maxwell's curly black mop of hair. "You're something special, too."

His son looked up, his face open, hopeful. Yearning for Penny's approval to be real.

Jonas knew exactly what Maxwell was feeling. His stomach had tightened into a knot as he waited to see what she would say to his son. He wanted her approval for Maxwell.

He tried not to think about what it would feel like to have Penny's approving gaze rest on him.

Penny moved her hand to rest on Max's shoulder. Jonas saw the boy tense before he relaxed at the simple touch.

"You work hard to help your father on this homestead. I've seen you with Oscar and the horses. You're a smart fellow."

Maxwell's face was still pink under his tan. He looked down again. "I cain't read," he said, his voice barely audible. "And I'm too old to go to school anymore."

Jonas's breath caught again. He'd known the boy couldn't read, but not that it bothered him this much. Jonas himself couldn't read, could only work a few sums, enough to make sure he didn't get taken at the general store, but he'd grown used to it. Oscar and Davy could read well, and the other boys continued their schooling in the winter months. With only his kids on the homestead, reading wasn't a skill Jonas needed often.

But if it bothered his son, he would find a way to help Maxwell.

"Just because you can't go to school, doesn't mean you can't learn," Penny said, her hand still on Maxwell's shoulder. "If your father agrees, we could borrow a primer from one of your brothers and practice your reading in the evenings, when you're done with chores for the day."

Maxwell looked up. "You'd teach me to read?"

"Of course."

His eyes started to shine, but then his brows creased. "But what if…could you…I know you gave Oscar some advice about wooing Sally. I ain't…I cain't talk to girls. Maybe you could…you could…help me?"

Jonas couldn't imagine what it had cost the boy to admit both to the fact that he couldn't read, and also his painful shyness.

"We can do some lessons on that subject, as well. If your father agrees."

Maxwell looked to Jonas, dark eyes shining, face full of hope. How could Jonas say no?

"It's fine with me, if Miss Penny doesn't think she'll be too tired after supper. And if Walt doesn't need you," he qualified.

"Thank you." When Penny looked at him, her eyes were shining, too.

He was a little surprised she'd agreed, but less so than when he'd first begun getting to know her. Penny had a compassionate heart and she was sensitive to the needs of his children. No doubt she had heard some of the things Maxwell hadn't said and had responded to his needs.

"Is it all right if I go out and check on Ricky and Davy? Make sure they aren't getting into trouble?"

"That's probably a good idea." Those two had a knack for getting into scrapes.

Jonas watched him troop through the kitchen and disappear out the back door. For a moment while he had the portal open, the sound of rain intensified, then faded again to just the sound of drops hitting the plank roof.

When Jonas turned to face Penny again, she was staring at where Maxwell had disappeared. He became conscious that they were alone for the first time since the corral. Well, alone except for the sleeping Breanna and Walt.

"Your sons are…interesting."

Jonas bristled. No one insulted his family—

"Oh," Penny said, her eyes on him now. "No, I didn't mean anything bad. Just that each one has his own character. They are all so different."

Jonas's tension flowed away.

She clucked, a funny sound, and shook her head. "And none of them have a clue about women. Girls."

"You're probably right. Maybe Ricky. His ma raised him in a bordello before she died."

Penny's open mouth conveyed her surprise. "That's—" She looked as if she couldn't find a word strong enough.

Jonas shrugged. "She did the best she could by him. Some parents would've just abandoned him." Like Jonas's had.

"I've been wondering where all the boys came from. That seems like such a crude way to say it. Where did you find them?"

"Met Oscar on the train out of Boston. I guess to be correct I should say he was being thrown off the train. He'd snuck on board without a ticket."

Her wide blue eyes showed what she thought of that. He was sure she'd never contemplated doing something so improper.

"Why was he alone?"

Jonas looked away, looked down so she wouldn't see anything in his face if he revealed too much. "His parents died. Uncle took him in for a while but it wasn't a good situation." To say the least. "His uncle was pretty mean."

Penny seemed to understand what Jonas wasn't saying; her eyes darkened with compassion.

"And the rest?"

Her gentle reaction made it easier for him to tell the boys' stories.

"I paid for a ticket so Oscar could come West with me and Breanna. By the time we'd reached Ohio, I'd talked him into staying with us. He's the one who found Seb when we disembarked the train in Denver. The little tyke was grubby, sitting on the street, wailing. No one around knew him or who his parents were. No one seemed to want him, thought maybe he was sick because of his crying.

"When anyone would have been able to see he was just hungry, if they'd just looked. I picked him up and he clung to my neck and I couldn't leave him…" Jonas still remembered the tearing feeling in his gut when he'd picked up the small boy who obviously hadn't had a meal in days and had clung to him like a vine. "Finally, we discovered his parents had died days before. A judge put him in my custody."

"You settled a homestead with a teen, a toddler and an infant?"

Jonas didn't know what to think at the amazement in her voice. He ran his hand along the length of the finely sanded table. "I did what I had to. Couldn't leave them behind. Your grandmama was a big help. Peg taught me to cook, helped when Breanna got a fever and I didn't know what to do."

"She was a great cook." Penny's smile held a touch of nostalgia. He imagined she missed Peg, a wonderful lady with a heart of gold. "But how did you do it?"

He shrugged. "There were a lot of days where I did chores with Breanna bundled in a sling across my back, with Seb following along behind me and chattering to her. Oscar was easy. He wanted to earn his way and I could understand that. He was more help than anything else."

She shook her head gently, one hand resting on Breanna's brown curls. He continued his story because she'd asked.

"Edgar came to us next. He'd been on an orphan train and was the only boy not taken. Someone had told the train lady I might take him.

"Looking at his sad blue eyes, I knew what he was thinking." That no one wanted him. "He stayed.

"Stumbled on Davy and Ricky camping next to the creek a ways up." He remembered the smell of a too-smoky fire and the two hungry boys who'd looked so guilty and so afraid when he'd come upon them. "They'd run away. Wouldn't tell me where they were from, only that they weren't going back.

"Then Matty… His family lived a few miles from here. They'd settled a homestead but his parents got sick and passed away. The preacher brought him to me."

She must've been counting, because when he paused and tried to decide the best way to tell Maxwell's story, she asked softly, "And Max?"

Jonas exhaled hard. "I don't think he ever knew his dad. His ma was…unkind to him. She'd passed on by the time I met him. I'd taken Breanna down to Cheyenne to see the doctor there. Maxwell was in the street, scrapping with some bigger, older boys. It was clear he'd been on his own for a while—and he was losing the fight. I stepped in, but instead of thanking me, he turned on me."

Jonas shook his head at the remembrance of the gangly boy with too much anger inside. "I told him I'd take him home with me if he wanted, and where Breanna and I were staying, but I didn't hold out much hope that he'd come. But he did. Showed up the next morning next to our wagon, bruised and with a black eye and came with us. By the next town, Breanna had won him over.

"Took me longer."

"Of course. You had to earn his trust. It's clear that he thinks of you like a father now. All of them do."

Jonas allowed himself a moment of pride for his sons. He'd taken each of them in with a lot of prayer, and so far they'd been blessings to his life.

Oh, he expected them to be boys. They could rustle up mischief in a matter of seconds. But he loved them all, and thought they probably loved him back.

He'd made his own family, and it was something special.

And then Penny asked the question he most assuredly didn't want to hear. "And what about your background, Jonas? You've told me all about the boys, but I'd like to know your story, too."

Penny watched Jonas's face, so open and full of affection while he'd spoken about his boys, shutter and close off. The only clue she had that she'd asked something she shouldn't have was the muscle fluttering in his now-clenched jaw.

"Of course you don't have to tell me, if you don't want to," she offered. "I think I've guessed part of it, anyway."

He stared into the fire. Was he going to ignore her query, or was he gathering his thoughts?

"You grew up without your parents, didn't you?" she prodded gently.

His expression darkened. "What do you mean?"

"Just…some of the things you've said…makes me think they weren't around." Things like how he could relate to how the different boys felt…

He grimaced. "I guess you could say that. In a manner of speaking." He paused and she thought that would be all he was going to say. She resolved not to push him anymore. She didn't want to ruin their friendship by prying where she wasn't wanted.

"My ma left when I was real little. I barely remember her at all. And my pa walked away when I was five. Left me on a street corner without so much as a goodbye."

He spoke the words dispassionately, as if it didn't hurt to say them, but Penny knew it must. "Oh, Jonas," she breathed.

She wanted to touch him, to reach out to him in comfort, but with Breanna asleep across her lap, she didn't dare move.

He shrugged again, an offhand movement, but his face hadn't cleared. Was there more to his story than just parents who had abandoned him?

"I grew up mostly on the streets. Did a stint in an orphanage around my tenth birthday, but I hated it. The other boys were cruel, and there were too many of us."

She remembered his comment about Breanna and how he didn't want an orphanage for her. Of course he would feel that way after living in one himself, especially an overcrowded one.

"But how did you survive?" she asked, curiosity erasing her determination not to ask more. "After only two winters in Philadelphia, I can't imagine how you kept warm."

He shrugged. "Sometimes you could find a bed in one of the homes. Sometimes it was just curling up in some newsprint over a heat register outside a house or business. There were a lot of us on the streets. We made do."

She didn't even have to close her eyes to remember the dirty street urchins she and her friends from Mrs. Trimble's Academy would pass sometimes on their way to the stores to shop. She'd turned her face away from the poignant stares, unable to bear even looking at them. Remembering her coldness shamed her.

"But how did you eat? And get new clothes?"

"I hawked papers for a bit. Did my best business as a boot-black."

He must've seen her puzzled look, though he wouldn't meet her gaze. He explained, "I shined shoes."

Oh. Absently, she wondered how much money one could make doing that. It couldn't be much. And yet he had managed to survive.

"One of my customers was Pete, who happened to be a bricklayer. He was a regular, and after a while he saw me keep doing a good job. He decided to take me on as his apprentice."

"So that's how you came to work at the home next door to Mrs. Trimble's."

"Mm-hmm, eventually. I worked with him for a year and a half. He gave me a room in the back of his shop. Really it was a little closet. He taught me a lot. Was one of the first people to show me respect."

"And then you started working next door…"

His face tightened, and she knew there was more he wasn't telling her. "What?" she asked.

He shook his head. "I don't want—Breanna might wake."

Something he didn't want his daughter to hear. And sure enough, even as he spoke, Breanna rustled and a soft "hmm" slipped from her lips. After a moment, she popped up on the couch, one side of her hair sticking every which way out of its braid.

"When's dinner?"

Breanna's question preceded a stampede of boys coming from their bedrooms. Walt roused, as well, and after gathering his bearings, nodded out the window to the moisture that had turned to a fine mist.

"We'd better be getting home, girl."

And Penny found, for the first time, she didn't want to leave.

Chapter Thirteen

Jonas shifted in the saddle, keeping one eye on the boys curled in their bedrolls around the campfire and the other on the small herd of bovines rustling quietly in a bunch nearby. He and his sons had driven the cattle hard the last two days and should reach Cheyenne tomorrow mid-morning. With Oscar left at home to take care of the basic chores, and Breanna and Seb staying with Walt and Penny, Jonas didn't feel he had to rush the trip, not like he usually did.

He'd reluctantly agreed to Maxwell's request that Sam come along on their short cattle drive, and so far he'd been pleasantly surprised by the boy. Sam and Maxwell seemed to have developed a rapport while working together to fix Walt's barn and some fence line, but Jonas still didn't completely trust Penny's brother.

Thinking of Sam made him remember Penny, and one thought kept running through his mind over and over again, especially in the quiet of night, like right now.

Will she ever look at me the same again?

After two days on the trail, he'd hoped to gain some perspective; he'd felt raw, as if his insides had been scraped clean, from the confessions he'd made to Penny in the aftermath of the rainstorm.

She had been so attentive when he'd told the boys' stories. Was that what had pushed him to tell her his own? He'd shared it with only a few people. And none, not even Walt, knew what he'd nearly confessed before remembering Breanna was in the room and could wake at any moment.

His deepest secret.

That he'd bitterly disappointed Pete, the man who'd taken him in off the streets and taught him about bricklaying. Up until Breanna's conception, he'd thought of Pete as a surrogate father.

He'd gone to Pete when he realized the mess with Breanna's mother wasn't going away. Pete hadn't believed him when Jonas had said he hadn't touched Millie Broadhurst. His mentor didn't understand Jonas's need to take care of the helpless baby that would be born.

Pete had kicked Jonas out of the little room in his shop and refused to listen. Jonas had spent two nights on the street until the Broadhursts had sent him and Millie to an aunt's home in Boston to wait for Breanna's birth.

Pete's unbelief had hurt almost as much as Jonas's parents' desertions because he'd thought Pete had had a better opinion of him, would believe him. Apparently, Pete hadn't been able to overlook Jonas's past and upbringing on the streets.

Now that she knew, Jonas worried that Penny wouldn't see him the same way, either.

And unfortunately, she seemed to be the only thing his sons wanted to talk about. They were still singing her praises for her skilled bareback riding when she'd helped bring in the cattle. She'd surprised them all, including him, with her finesse and determination to see the job through.

Thinking about the loose cattle gave Jonas a little relief from thinking about his lovely temporary neighbor, but brought another puzzle before him. When he'd gone back to the corral, he'd found the fence post that had supposedly been knocked down by the cattle when they'd panicked from the storm.

Only it had appeared to have been tampered with. It looked like someone had partially dug it up and then used a heavy leather strap of some sort to pull it out of the ground. But who would do something like that? And why?

Jonas knew not everyone in town agreed with his actions, taking in the boys like he did, but he didn't think anyone would let his cattle out on purpose. It was a dangerous thing to do and could've lost him the money he hoped to gain by selling the animals.

Maybe he'd been wrong about the post. He'd have to look at it again when he and the boys returned from Cheyenne.

Movement from the bedrolls near the fire alerted Jonas that it was almost time to let Maxwell and Sam take their turn watching the herd. The two boys spoke softly and moved to saddle their horses, picketed near the fire but not close enough they'd trample the group as they slept.

Jonas walked his horse over and dismounted, preparing to rub down the animal and settle it for the night. He nodded silently to Sam as the boy worked at saddling a sleepy mare.

Then, remembering the joyful expression on Penny's face when he'd encouraged her brother once before, he paused and turned to the teen.

"Thank you for your help on this trip. You've proved yourself a good hand."

Sam's surprised glance and the bashful hint of pride before he turned his face to his task told Jonas enough. He wasn't used to compliments. Probably not used to having to work for himself, either, but Jonas had spoken true: Sam had done a good job so far.

"And I know your granddad is happy to have your help around his place."

Sam kept his eyes on his saddle fastenings this time. Jonas

wanted to encourage him in the same way he would've encouraged Maxwell or any of his other boys. What could he say that would connect with Sam?

"A man feels a certain sense of pride when he does a good job. Even if no one else notices."

Jonas clapped one hand on the boy's shoulder and then turned to find his bedroll.

Breanna and Seb settled for the night, Penny joined her grandfather in the kitchen, hoping to steal a few moments to work on the dress she was sewing for Breanna. Walt sat across from her at the scarred kitchen table.

With the light from the flickering fire and a tapered candle, Penny carefully reviewed the lines of the fabric she'd already pieced together before she tucked in with her needle.

Mrs. Peterson from the mercantile had given her such a deal on the fabric that she'd bought enough to make a shirt for each of the boys and one for Jonas, too, but with two children underfoot in the evenings, she'd been hard-pressed to find time to make the new garments. She wanted them to be a surprise. She could just imagine the looks on the children's faces when they saw their gifts.

"You know, Penny-girl…" Her grandfather started to speak, then hesitated. "I was dozin' on Sunday afternoon while you and Jonas were talkin', but I came awake before the end of it. I know you're used to your high society fellas—"

Penny interrupted him, holding up a needle pinched between her fingers, to halt his words. "I don't look down on Jonas because of his upbringing, if that's what you're getting after."

Her grandfather looked surprised. He shifted in his seat. "Well, good."

"In fact, what he's had to overcome makes me admire him more."

It was true. She'd thought he had a soft heart when she'd guessed what he'd done for the boys and after she'd learned the truth about Breanna, but finding out that Jonas had been abandoned and yet had managed to make a successful life for himself and his family made her admire him even more.

And those vulnerable moments where he'd shown her the boy inside still searching for love…well, they touched her heart.

She didn't know what to do with her growing feelings. She hadn't planned to feel anything more than friendship for her grandfather's neighbor, but her emotions hadn't waited for permission to become engaged.

"Jonas is a good man. He'll make a good husband."

A flush climbed into her cheeks. "Grandfather—"

This time it was her grandfather who interrupted her. "I'm not saying you're looking—I'm not saying you're not, mind—but he's got as many good qualities as those highfalutin fellas you're used to. He's got the strength to survive this land. He cares for those young'uns like his own kin. Your gran loved him."

Penny looked down at the pink-sprigged material spread over the table, traced one of the lines with her index finger. "I'm learning that Jonas is all those thing. But, Grandfather… I'm not sure I could be a homesteader's wife."

She looked up to find him considering her patiently. It gave her the courage to go on. "I remember Gran being so good at things…she was the best cook around. Could sew anything, managed the household…" She waved her hand to indicate the charred wall behind the stove. "I can't even fry an egg!"

He chuckled, his bristly white mustache quivering. "Your gran didn't start out that way. Oh, her ma taught her some things, some basic cooking skills. But when she married me at seventeen, she didn't know anything about living on a homestead. She burnt our biscuits a few times 'fore she got the hang of things."

Her grandfather's voice trailed off, a sad smile lingering on his face. Penny knew he still thought about her gran often. They'd loved each other so much. That was what Penny wanted in a husband, that kind of devotion.

"She loved this land," he went on. "And she loved me. That's what made our marriage work, even through the hard times."

Her grandfather stood up and moved toward her, clasped her hand in one of his wrinkled paws. "That's what kind of love Jonas deserves. And you do, too." He patted her hand. "G'night, sweetheart."

"Goodnight."

Penny contemplated her grandfather's words as she tied off her thread and nipped off the extra. She remembered Breanna's wide eyes when she'd admired the store-bought dress back in Calvin's General Store, and Penny wanted this gift to be perfect for the girl she was coming to love.

She agreed with her grandfather that Jonas deserved someone special for his wife. Problem was, even with her burgeoning feelings, she wasn't sure that person was her.

The sun had set, but Penny remained at the Whites', trying to concentrate on mending a tear in Ricky's shirt and listen to Maxwell practice his words at the same time. While ignoring the noise emanating from Davy and Seb wrestling on the floor and Edgar picking at a banged-up banjo.

"You're doing well," she said when Maxwell paused, giving the boy a gentle smile.

And he was. Although his schooling had apparently been spotty, he could make out most of the letters and knew their sounds. And he was intelligent. Penny thought he'd be reading just fine with a few months of additional practice.

It was Jonas's curious, furtive glances from across the room that intrigued her and made her think perhaps Maxwell wasn't the only one with an unfinished education.

But the last thing she wanted to do was embarrass him in front of his children. She would wait to ask him about it later.

Instead, she asked, "Jonas, Mrs. Peterson asked me to remind you about the barn-raising next week. Grandfather said he wanted to go. Are you taking the children?"

Her query was met with a tense look, but before Jonas could answer, Breanna exclaimed, "Oh, yes, Pa, let's go! Can we?"

"May we," Penny corrected gently.

"May we, may we?" the girl chanted, bouncing on the balls of her feet. The wrestling boys quieted and looked expectantly to their father for his answer.

Oscar, next to Penny, lowered his head over his clasped hands with a slight shake.

"I don't know," came Jonas's quiet reply.

"Aw, Pa, we *never* git to go!"

Maxwell shushed Seb, while Breanna cried, "But I want to see my friends!"

Penny wondered what she'd started. Her question had been asked in innocence, just relaying Mrs. Peterson's query, but the children's reactions surprised her.

"We still have some things to get done around here before we start haying; Maxwell's trying to get his filly trained, and there are other tasks as well. We may not have time to attend the barn-raising. We'll have to see."

A couple of the boys' shoulders slumped, and Breanna wilted. Maxwell and Oscar showed no reaction. Jaw tight, Jonas rose and went to the door, grabbing his hat off a peg on the wall.

"I'm sure you're tuckered, Miss Penny." He spoke without

looking back to see the children's disappointed miens. "I'll get the roan saddled up and take you home."

"I can walk," she said, because her grandfather had mentioned there was a full moon tonight. It would give her enough light to see by.

"That's all right." His words rang with finality, and he shut the door behind him without looking back.

The children were unnaturally quiet as she tucked the mending into a basket and gathered up the shawl she'd borrowed from amongst her grandmother's things. Even in summer, the Wyoming evenings cooled off.

"Is Pa ashamed of us?"

Her head came up at the question and its asker. It hadn't come from Seb or Breanna, like she might expect, but from Ricky, who always seemed confident, but now wouldn't quite meet her eye.

"He ain't," Oscar said, voice lacking conviction.

"I agree." Penny infused confidence in her voice. "Your father is very proud of each of you."

"Then why won't he take us to the barn-raising? Or Patty Neel's weddin' last month?" This came from Davy, still sprawled on the floor.

"Does your father always tell you the truth?" Penny's query earned frowns all around as they tried to dissect her question.

"Yep," Seb answered matter-of-factly. Some of the other boys nodded.

"Then, if your father says there's work to be done, is there really work to be done?"

"Yes," a couple of voices chorused, sounding more sure of themselves.

Maxwell's head remained down, though, as if focused on his work, but as Penny watched, the finger he'd been using earlier to trace the words didn't move. He just stared down at the primer. She wanted to reassure him, so she placed a hand on his shoulder. He jumped, finally looking up, surprise on his face.

"Your pa loves you."

She squeezed his shoulder and he nodded, but he still seemed too serious. Unfortunately, with Jonas waiting, she didn't have time to reassure him further.

"Goodnight, everyone."

Jonas waited for Penny at the bottom of the porch steps, one of the horses saddled nearby. He could see her saying her goodbyes through the lighted window, but he remained in the shadows.

It was an appropriate metaphor for how he felt tonight, the first night his family had been back together since he and the boys had driven the cattle down to Cheyenne. It seemed as if Penny had bonded with each of them, although Edgar still looked on her somewhat suspiciously, and they surrounded her like a flock of chattering sparrows.

Leaving Jonas an outsider, the way he'd felt for most of his life.

He was glad for his children. He knew the boys and especially Breanna needed a woman's touch in their lives, but part of him also wanted to be part of their grouping.

And that was the real problem. His few days away from home hadn't resolved his feelings in the least. When he'd ridden into the yard this afternoon and seen Penny, his heart had leaped in his chest.

He was troubled. He might be falling in love with her. And if he was, that would be a disaster, because she was going to go back home to Calvin and find a well-to-do husband.

The door opened, spilling light onto the porch. Penny murmured a final goodbye over her shoulder and the door closed, leaving them alone.

The moon gilded her hair to gold when she joined him. He turned away, afraid of what he might do—reach out for her?—if he looked too long. Instead, he quickly mounted up and boosted her up behind him.

They rode in silence, until he couldn't bear it anymore and asked, "Were the children upset?" His voice emerged rougher than he intended it to be.

"They were trying to understand why they don't get to attend many community events." Her soft-spoken words warmed his ear; her chin pressed against his shoulder.

"It's just that…"

She squeezed his sides when his voice trailed off.

He wasn't sure she would understand, but knew she wasn't likely to drop it. Nosy woman. "I don't want them to be ashamed to be part of this family."

"What do you mean?"

"It's—we can't afford new clothes every season and I don't want folks looking down on my children."

It was more than that. He didn't want the children to hear the snide remarks some people made. Couldn't she understand he was trying to protect his family?

"So if you had some new clothes, you'd go to the barn-raising?"

He exhaled hard, hearing something masked in her voice but not able to tell what. "It's not just that. Not everyone in the community likes us. Some of the folks think the boys are troublemakers, just because of where they've come from. Worried they might steal things or get into fights or…I don't even know."

"Not everyone feels that way."

He assumed she meant Walt. "I know. Walt has been a good friend."

"It's not just him." Penny shook her head, her chin brushing against his shoulder. "There are others who admire you and what you've done."

Was she talking about herself? Was it possible she admired him? He was scared to know.

"If you asked, some of them might be willing to speak on the boys' behalf."

He opened his mouth to say something, and she must've felt his tension because she rushed on, "Not publicly, but if some of the people in town spread the word that the boys can be trusted, maybe some of those bad feelings would dissipate."

It was a kind thought, especially for someone like him, who'd never had anyone to stand up for him, but—

"It's nice that you want to make things better for them."

"And for you," she put in.

"But what happens when you go back to Calvin and your life there? When they have to face the Bear Creek residents without your support?"

She was silent for a long moment. "Then I would hope that what I've given them—whether reading lessons or confidence to speak to others in town or…anything else—" he wondered at the catch in her voice "—would stay with them."

Again, it was a tender sentiment, but as someone who'd been left behind before, the memories that remained when someone left you weren't always the nice ones like Penny mentioned.

"I…um…" He'd never heard her so unsure as she sounded now. "I noticed…well, I thought—would you want to join in on Maxwell's reading lessons?"

He ground his back teeth. How had she guessed he couldn't read?

"I know you didn't have an easy childhood. Were you able to go to school at all?"

"For a few months," he said tightly. The months he'd been in the orphanage, before he'd run back to the streets.

"You could certainly sit in on Maxwell's lessons. If you wanted," she added quickly. "Or we could spend a half an hour with a primer during lunchtime if you didn't want the children to know."

She finally stopped talking, maybe realizing he hadn't responded. He didn't mean for his lack of education to be a sore point, but he wanted her to think well of him.

"Thank you for the offer, but I'm already stretched thin trying to get everything taken care of on our place and the Sumners. And you're staying late with Maxwell already. I don't want to make more work for you." And he didn't think his heart could take any more time spent closely with her. Not if he wanted to remain unattached.

Chapter Fourteen

"Careful," Jonas warned Oscar from his perch on the skeleton frame of the Smiths' new barn roof. The teen nodded, lips pressed around a handful of nails.

Jonas had reluctantly agreed to the barn-raising for the young couple from church because some of the boys kept asking about it—and because Maxwell did *not* ask. Penny had told him of Maxwell's subdued reactions, and Jonas hadn't wanted any of the boys to think he was ashamed of them. Penny and Sam had ridden along, but Walt had elected to stay home for the event.

He hadn't taken up Penny on her offer to teach him to read. Jonas knew she'd made the offer out of kindness, but he didn't want her to feel sorry for him. Not in any way.

And he'd been anxious about getting closer to her. His emotions were already out of control. He didn't want to fall further in love with her, not when things could never work between them.

Now, mid-morning, he was part of the roofing crew, and he couldn't help but be aware of Penny on the ground as she weaved among the visiting women, Breanna sometimes by her side and sometimes off playing with the other children. Breanna with her new dress…

Nor could he ignore an awareness of his sons, each wearing a bright, clean, *new* shirt. Usually, the boys wore hand-me-downs, with Oscar and Maxwell receiving the new items because they were biggest. The joy they'd expressed last night when Penny had gifted them with the shirts and again this morning as they'd donned the brand-new clothing pinched his heart. He wished he could do more for them.

He hadn't yet worn the pale blue shirt she'd given him along with a sweet, sincere smile. He'd sat on the edge of his bed for a long time last night, moonlight streaming through his window, fingering the garment Penny had made for *him*.

It had been a very long time since anyone had given him a gift, other than the little trinkets he received from the children at Christmas.

And no one had ever given him something so fine. He kept thinking of all the time she must have spent making it.

Almost like a wife or mother, making clothing for the ones she loved. How many nights had she sat up late, working on the garments for his family? Why had she done it? Not out of pity or surely he would have seen it on her face. But he couldn't figure it out.

Those thoughts had crowded his mind, making sleep impossible until the moon had passed much farther across his window than he'd intended.

He hadn't dared to wear the shirt this morning. Too afraid to soil it or rip it while he worked with the other men, he'd worn one of his older work shirts. And Penny hadn't seemed to mind, if her cheerfulness this morning was any indication.

Nor did it seem to bother her now, as he glanced down to find her shading her eyes and looking up at him.

She waved. "You thirsty? I'll bring some water."

He found himself nodding even as she scurried away and returned with a water bucket. For a moment he thought she was going to ascend the ladder herself, but Ricky's head popped up over the edge of the half-finished structure.

"Stay there," he told his son. "We'll come to you."

Oscar was much more light of foot than Jonas on the roof. Jonas kept thinking about how far they were from the ground. Oscar met Ricky at the ladder first, quickly slurping from the community dipper. Jonas arrived as Oscar finished and accepted the dipper from his son. "Thank ya, Ricky."

"You all right up there? Not afraid of heights or anything?"

Penny's teasing tone drew his gaze downward. She was holding the ladder for Ricky, looking up at him with her face open and radiating happiness. Something inside him tightened like a fist, and then loosened and took flight.

"Jonas?"

He swallowed hard, fighting against the emotions swamping him. "Yep, we're all right. You and Breanna okay?"

"Mmm. Making friends. I'm going to try to secure a place under the tree for our lunch blanket."

He couldn't help the way his heart jumped when she said *our blanket,* as if they were all one family. He kept his face impassive, afraid she could still see his feelings in his eyes.

"All right." Was that his voice, that husky, grating sound? "Be careful."

Careful. How could he tell his heart to be careful when it seemed determined to reach out for her?

Wanting Penny in his life, in the children's, was impossible. But it hadn't seemed so impossible this morning as they'd rode up to the gathering, with her sitting close next to him on the wagon bench.

And it didn't seem so impossible when she said things like *be careful,* as if concerned about his safety.

He found it hard to concentrate for the rest of the morning, slipping once but catching his balance. Then he whacked the side of his thumb with his hammer and had to hold back a shout. *Concentrate!* he told himself, but still found his attention following the vibrant auburn head from his high vantage point.

He'd never been so relieved to hear the dinner bell before.

Instead of going straight to Penny like a lovestruck boy, he forced himself to follow the other men to the water trough and rinse some of the dust and sweat off his face and hands before joining his family at the blanket that Penny had located in the shade from a large oak on the hill.

Penny handed out tin plates to the jostling boys, who then made their way toward the groaning makeshift tables laden with food.

"Pa, can I eat with Sissy Peterson? Her ma said it was okay and—"

Jonas gave in with a nod and Breanna ran off to join her friend. Leaving Jonas and Penny alone.

Penny fell into step beside him, their shoulders brushing. She handed him his plate and gasped when she caught sight of his purpling finger. "Jonas—"

She grasped his wrist and pulled him to a halt, still far enough away from the crowds that their conversation wouldn't be overheard. "What did you do? Are you all right?"

"Just banged it a little. It doesn't hurt." Much.

Her head bent close to his chest as she examined his thumb, and his heart beat painfully against the inside of his ribs. He hoped she couldn't hear it.

"Are you sure? It looks painful." Then her blue eyes rested on his face, questioning, worry emanating from their depths.

He wasn't sure anyone had ever looked at him that way before. It erased the distance he'd spent the past week and a half trying to put between them. Made him want to be what he couldn't: someone who had enough to give Penny everything she wanted. Someone she wouldn't want to leave.

Her concerned gaze also made him want to kiss her.

His eyes flicked down to her slightly parted lips and he wanted—

"You two had better get to the food 'fore it's all gone," someone called out to them, breaking the connection and bringing Jonas to his senses. Heat filled his face and he ducked his head, hoping his hat would hide his embarrassment from anyone who might be looking—and from Penny—and moved away. How long had he stood there, stunned by her? The crowd around the food tables was much thinner now. Most folks were already back at their blankets or sitting in the grass, eating.

But Penny slid her hand into the crook of his elbow, not allowing him to outdistance her, keeping him by her side.

His heart thundered like a stampeding herd, crashing loud in his ears. Did she really want to be with him? He couldn't wrap his mind around it.

Penny clung to his elbow right up until she had to start filling her plate. She greeted the women still helping serve and when they responded, their welcome included him. Something else he'd never experienced before, not from most of these women; he'd never spoken to many of them.

A young woman served pie near the end of the tables, and Penny stopped to speak to her in a low voice, leaving Jonas standing awkwardly alone. *This* he was used to. Should he wait for Penny? Retreat to the quilt under the tree?

Then Penny returned to his side, this time with the girl's arm tucked in hers and wearing a beaming smile. "I've been getting to know Emily all morning and she's agreed to join me for the meal so we can speak some more."

It took Jonas a moment to recognize the girl as the same one Maxwell had spoken to Penny about, then he realized that Penny must have something in mind. He knew Maxwell was eating on the blanket with the other boys. And now Penny was bringing the object of his son's affections right to him.

He couldn't do anything but follow along, an unwitting accomplice.

Penny hadn't planned to invite Emily to eat with the family until she'd seen her serving pie. With most of the folks already finished filling their plates, the girl would be free to sit down and eat herself...

And it *was* true that Penny had been conversing with her all morning, whenever they would pass each other. She could see why Maxwell was smitten. Emily had a sweet disposition and a gentle, ready smile.

Now if only Maxwell could overcome his extreme shyness and manage to speak to her himself.

The boys were eating and talking when she, Jonas and Emily approached. So far she still hadn't been able to force manners on most of them. She didn't want the girl to be scared off without even speaking to Maxwell.

Penny cleared her throat and the boys looked up. Ricky and Davy with mouths hanging open. Maxwell choked, coughing. Penny pretended not to notice and Seb thumped his older brother on the back. Sam glanced curiously from Emily to Maxwell.

"Boys, I've been making friends with Miss Emily and she's going to sit with me for lunch. I know you can all be polite since there are ladies present." She *hoped.* "Here, why don't you scoot over?"

Maxwell finally got his breath, his cheeks pink. When Penny nudged him with her foot, he turned cherry red, but he obediently shifted to one side, allowing room for Emily to settle beside him with Penny on her other side.

With the extra body on their blanket, Penny was forced close to Jonas, her knee pressing into his leg. He, too, looked a little pink, and Penny patted his hand, hoping he didn't think her actions were too forward. Maxwell *had* asked for her help.

The usually boisterous boys had gone unnaturally silent, some of them staring at the new young lady in their midst. The only sounds were the clinking of their forks and the soft rustle of the breeze in the leaves above them. Emily politely kept her gaze on her food.

"I'm sure some of you know Miss Emily from school. Is that right?" Penny asked, trying to get the conversation started. She tried to catch Maxwell's eye to encourage him to say "hello", but he kept his face turned down. Both his hands were clenched on his plate, so hard his knuckles were white.

"Mm-hmm," someone replied, and Penny found herself grateful that Matty hadn't spoken with his mouth full.

"And we get supplies at her pa's store," Seb supplied helpfully. He seemed to be the only one unaware of the tension surrounding those on the blanket. Hopefully Emily wasn't aware of it, either.

Maxwell continued to stare down, jaw locked. A soft snicker from one of his brothers made a muscle jump in his cheek.

"That's right." Emily brightened, smiling at the faces around her. "I happen to know that Seb likes caramels the best. Ricky, Davy and…is it Oscar? You all like the black licorice." The girl's nose scrunched up, making it obvious that it was not a liking she shared. "Matty and Edgar prefer the taffy, and Breanna and Mr. White like to share a bag of Turkish delights."

Emily paused, and everyone on the blanket seemed to hold their breath, aware that she hadn't mentioned Maxwell. The teen sat so still Penny couldn't tell if he was breathing. Emily turned to address him directly, "But Maxwell asks for something different every time. What *is* your favorite candy?"

"I dunno," he said, almost too quietly to hear. "I like them all, I guess."

"Oh, but surely you've got a favorite," Emily prodded. "Everyone has something they like better than all the others."

"Maxwell always gets sumpin to share." Seb's helpful remark made Penny reach out and pat the boy's foot.

Ricky, Matty and Edgar lost interest in the conversation and began their own, thankfully in lowered voices.

Maxwell dared to glance up from his plate, although he quickly looked back down when he saw Emily watching him, waiting for an answer. Penny saw his chest rise and fall before he spoke, again in that soft tone. "Ain't had much candy before Pa took me in. Guess I wanted to try the different kinds to see what they were like."

His words pinched Penny's heart. She knew from what Jonas had told her that Maxwell had had a hard life, but this confirmation stung. She rushed to fill the awkward silence that threatened, not wanting to give Emily a chance to say something that might hurt the boy.

"Miss Emily's been telling me she has plans to visit her aunt in Texas next summer."

"That's right. Marjorie—my sister—" Emily directed this to Penny, "will be old enough to tend the counter next year. At least that's what Pa says. Ma isn't so sure, but they've agreed to let me spend some time with my aunt in Austin and I'm so excited!"

The thrill in her voice must've drawn Maxwell's gaze up, because his eyes fixed on her face. Behind him, Ricky and Matty were now mimicking her excited hand gestures.

Emily didn't seem to notice. "I love to read and my aunt has a well-stocked library. We've been corresponding about it."

"You like to read?" asked Seb.

"Mm-hmm."

"Oh, Miss Emily! Miss Penny's been teaching Maxwell to read cause he didn't get to go to school when he was younger." Seb proclaimed the news proudly, happy to help his brother.

Maxwell turned desperate, pained eyes to Penny as Ricky and Matty dissolved into laughter, while Davy pretended a high-pitched rendition of a girl's voice, "Oh, Maxwell, won't you read to me?" before collapsing off the blanket in laughter himself.

"Boys," Jonas barked and the three troublemakers scattered, running off and leaving behind their empty plates and utensils, callous laughter ringing behind them.

"I'll deal with them later," Jonas murmured, but Emily was already rising.

"I'm supposed to help with cleanin' up," the girl said.

"Oh, but—" Penny's protest came too late. Emily was already scurrying toward the food tables.

Maxwell's shoulders hunched, head lowering nearly to his chest, face scarlet. Oscar sat beside him, stoic, then reached one hand up to rest on his brother's shoulder, showing his support. Sam sat silent and wide-eyed, watchful.

Seb looked to Penny, eyes wide. "Did I say somethin' wrong? Miss Penny?"

She started to shake her head, trying to form words to explain that Maxwell hadn't wanted Emily to know he couldn't read.

What a mess!

"Miss Penny, I spilled on my new dress!" Breanna's wail interrupted anything Penny might've said, either to comfort Maxwell or explain things to Seb. The young girl threw herself on the blanket at Penny's knee, sobbing.

She met Jonas's eyes as he rose. She desperately wanted

to ask how he dealt with all these children on his own—because she wasn't doing a good job at all! Look at the trouble she'd caused.

Working alongside Maxwell and Sam during the afternoon, Jonas wanted to say something to comfort his son after the disastrous ending to lunch. But he didn't know what.

He had such limited experience with women and none with the proper way to court one. And part of him still had trouble believing that someone like Penny could be interested in someone like him.

How could he encourage Maxwell to pursue the grocer's daughter with the disparity of their circumstances?

Surprisingly, it was Sam who broached the subject as they took a break around the water bucket.

Jonas didn't catch all of the teen's statement as he dumped a dipper of water over his head to cool off, but heard, "…if she doesn't come around, there are other girls out there, ya know."

Maxwell frowned, but nodded silently, crinkled eyes telling more than his stoic expression did.

"Plus, I'm sure my sister isn't done trying to interfere on your behalf," Sam said with a slap on Maxwell's shoulder.

At that, Maxwell gave a half smile. "She doesn't give up easy, does she?"

"No. And if that still doesn't work, you can impress Emily with your riding in the Round Up."

Jonas shook his head as both boys laughed and Maxwell's spirits seemed restored.

What did Penny's stubbornness mean for Jonas?

Shoulders aching from toting dishes to the stream and helping wash them, a task Penny felt comfortable she wouldn't mess up, she couldn't wait for the waning sun to finish its descent behind the mountains in the distance.

She was exhausted, both from the work and from worrying over Maxwell. Lunching with Emily and the other boys hadn't turned out well at all. The girl continued to speak kindly to Penny when they passed each other, but Penny sensed that the young woman was now holding back.

However, even with all that going on, Penny had never felt so content in all her life. She'd been a part of helping the Smith family getting settled, *and* Penny had felt a part of Jonas's family.

She sincerely hoped she hadn't ruined Maxwell's chances with Emily. She *was* a sweet girl. Then again, it would take someone with a strong backbone to survive around the White boys and their propensity for mischievousness. And yet, Penny felt right at home among them.

And Breanna's crying jag kept Penny alert. She was concerned the girl's out-of-control emotions might trigger a seizure, although nothing had happened yet. Penny had reassured the girl that the stain could be removed—she hoped—and if not, that she would sew the girl a new frock. She'd also made Breanna lie down on the quilt beneath their unhitched wagon and take a nap, hoping the rest would restore the girl's cheerful spirits.

Finally, the men seemed to be wrapping things up. Penny watched with a hand shading her eyes as Jonas and Oscar climbed down from the barn roof, relieved when they set foot on the ground again. She'd been a little worried about them being so high up all day.

She set about rounding up the younger boys and Breanna, most of whom appeared exhausted but whined that they wanted to play for a little while longer. She took a stern tone with them and received a grudging acquiescence.

She was saying goodbye to the new acquaintances she'd

made when a hard grip on her elbow jerked her head up in time to see the one face she did not want to see.

"Hello, darling. I'm surprised to see you at a gathering like this."

"Mr. Abbott." She hated the way her voice wavered and worked to steady it. "What are you doing here?"

She allowed him to pull her away from the curious stares of the remaining women. She suspected he might make a scene and she didn't want anyone to see it if he did.

"The question is, what are *you* doing here? This common event certainly doesn't seem your style."

"I'm visiting my grandfather," she said with a raise of her chin, trying to disengage her arm from his hold. "I'm surprised my father didn't tell you."

"Where is your grandfather? I'd love to meet him and say hello."

"He isn't here, actually. He's been a bit under the weather, which is why Sam and I traveled to be with him and help out at his homestead."

Mr. Abbott's intense eyes narrowed and she regretted her impulsive comment. She'd made it sound as if she was here on her own, without anyone watching over her.

Where was Jonas or one of the other boys?

"It is time for pretenses to end," Mr. Abbott said. "I want you to return to Calvin with me so that our courtship can proceed. I'm sure your brother can help your grandfather with whatever he needs."

"I have responsibilities that I won't shirk." Penny tried again to disengage her arm from his hold. "I'll return to Grandfather's homestead until he doesn't need me anymore." And she had no intention of courting with Mr. Abbott in any case.

"While your independence is admirable, my dear, it is unnecessary. Your father has agreed to the match, and you'll soon bend to my will."

She struggled against his hold. "Your highhandedness does not put you in my good graces."

He chuckled, a sinister sound that had her glancing around for any source of help. Why had she moved away from the crowd? It would have been better to be embarrassed than to be alone with Mr. Abbott. She was certain her father had never seen this side of the man, a calculating, controlling side.

How could she escape his attentions?

Chapter Fifteen

Jonas's continued awareness of Penny all afternoon kept him from his very best work, but the Smiths' barn would be water tight, at least. From his high perch, he continued to catch glimpses of her fluttering around the gathering, washing dishes in the stream and chattering with the women.

She and Ricky brought water a few more times, Penny always gifting Jonas with a beautiful, warm smile he couldn't fully interpret. Was she...*glad* to be here with him?

To his relief, she didn't seem to hold Ricky and the other boys' behavior against them, though he felt sure she was going to give Jonas an earful later. He couldn't say how he knew it, but he did. But she treated the boys as always, often ruffling their hair or giving impromptu hugs.

Again, acting like a mother might do.

Not his mother, but the way he'd seen other mothers act with their children.

Hope bloomed and ached in his chest at the same time. He knew how dangerous hope could be.

They'd mostly finished the structure and Jonas had visited the water trough again to wash the worst of the dirt off his face before heading to the wagon, when he saw a gentleman in a dark suit approach Penny amongst a gaggle of women.

Had the good-looking man been present the whole day? Jonas couldn't say for sure. Jonas's attention had been caught on Penny and he'd only been peripherally aware of the other projects and men working.

The man tucked Penny's arm through his as if they belonged together. Jonas watched, unable to help himself, as she said something to him and allowed herself to be led away from the other women, around the corner of the brand-new structure.

Who was the dark-haired man? Someone Penny had met today? The familiarity of his actions disputed that notion, but…she hadn't mentioned a beau, someone that would miss her in the weeks she'd been gone from her home in Calvin.

Jonas turned for his wagon, half-numb, blinded by emotion that hit him square in the chest. Every thought he'd considered today about Penny belonging with *him* seemed to mock him now.

He'd *known* she was meant for a high-society fellow. Known she wasn't for him, but seeing her with this other man burned a hole in his chest.

"Pa, Pa!"

Matty approached at a run, his urgent shout bringing Jonas's head around. Had one of the children been hurt? Where was Breanna?

"What's the matter?"

"Penny—" Matty's gasp surprised Jonas and he forced his face to blank.

"—talkin' to fella—"

"She can talk to whoever she wants," Jonas reminded his son, trying to keep any bitterness out of his voice. *How* had he let himself fall in love with her?

"—he grabbed her—"

What? Matty now had Jonas's full attention. His son gestured in the direction Jonas had seen Penny and the stranger go off in, still gasping for breath.

"She tried to get away from him."

Finally, a full sentence from the boy. Jonas didn't waste any more time. He hurried toward the side of the barn, Matty on his heels. When he rounded the structure, he saw that Penny was indeed in a struggle with the taller man.

"Let go of me!" she hissed.

"Now—"

"She said let her go!" Matty exclaimed before Jonas could react, racing past Jonas.

The man looked up, caught sight of Jonas, and released his hold on Penny's arm. She didn't move away from him, though, only stood there in the deepening shadows rubbing her wrist.

"I'm afraid you've wandered into a family squabble," the man said, voice even. With the sky darkening even further, Jonas couldn't make out his expression, but he sensed waves of menace radiating off the man.

"Family? You ain't Miss Penny's family," Matty spat.

"As a matter of fact, I'm her fiancé."

The words stunned Jonas. He reached out to grab Matty's shoulder and guide the boy away. This was obviously a personal matter.

"You are no such thing, Mr. Abbott." This time Penny's voice rang with vehemence and she moved away from the man, rushing to Jonas's side and slipping into the circle of the arm he'd outstretched to grab hold of Matty.

She was shaking, and his arm naturally curled around her trembling shoulders.

Fiancé or not, Jonas couldn't leave her this upset. He would bring her home and deliver her to her grandfather. Let Walt sort out whatever mess she was in.

"Your father sent me to bring you back to Calvin—"

"My father isn't here," Penny interrupted. Her words didn't fully refute whatever this Mr. Abbott was saying, though. Jonas still felt as if he'd been bludgeoned.

"I don't want to go with him. Please, can you take me home?" Penny whispered, lifting her face to Jonas's.

He couldn't respond over the blood rushing in his ears, but Matty said it for him.

"Yeah, Pa, let's git outta here."

"Penny!" Sam rounded the structure at a run, and joined the group as they moved away from Penny's suitor, who said nothing more. "You all right?" he asked his sister in low tones.

Jonas allowed Sam to assist Penny onto the wagon seat as he gathered up the rest of his sons and Breanna.

The uncomfortable feeling of being watched didn't fade as Jonas guided the wagon away from the Smiths' new barn.

Penny held the quilt around her shoulders, still shivering. The same blanket on which she'd shared a meal with Jonas and his family and that he'd pushed into her arms when they'd reached the wagon.

She couldn't get warm, not after that slimy Mr. Abbott had had his hands on her. She tried to focus on the sensation of Jonas's strong arm wrapped about her shoulder. What she'd really wanted was to feel both his arms around her, offering her comfort.

But he hadn't said one word to her since coming upon her and the awful Mr. Abbott.

Surely he didn't believe the other man.

A glance at his stern profile told her nothing, other than he was probably upset. Or tired.

She wished she knew which it was. Her experiences with her father had taught her not to push with too many questions when he was in a foul mood, but she'd never seen Jonas lose his temper before.

Perhaps if she explained things. "Jonas, I—"

He sent her a quelling look. Even with his face in shadow, in the darkness, she could feel that he didn't want her to speak.

"Please, if you'll let me explain—"

"Not now," he said, in a quiet, insistent voice. He glanced over his shoulder and she followed his gaze, realizing that although the children had been quiet in the wagon, they weren't asleep, but attuned to everything passing between her and Jonas.

"Then when?" she whispered.

He shrugged and she knew he didn't intend to hear her explanation at all. He probably thought she had encouraged Mr. Abbott's attentions, even welcomed them. How little he must think of her!

That realization hurt.

She wanted him to think highly of her. To admire her, as she admired him. Maybe she was even falling in love with him.

But how could she love someone who wouldn't let her speak her piece?

"I listened to you," she almost blurted *talk about the boys* but stopped herself with a glance at the curious, shadowed faces behind her, "after the rainstorm," she continued.

Jonas stiffened beside her.

"Without judging," she added. "In fact, what you told me made me admire you." Perhaps she shouldn't have admitted that, but her emotions had gotten the better of her and she'd blurted it out.

"The least you could do is listen to me—"

"Fine," he said grudgingly. "We'll drop the children at

home and then I'll take you to Walt's place. You can *explain* on the way."

It would have to be enough, because he wasn't offering more.

They rode the rest of the way in silence. Even the children remained quiet. Only the occasional jingle of the horses' harness interrupted the peacefulness of the night.

The irony mocked Penny's chaotic heart.

Jonas didn't want to hear Penny's explanations. He wanted her to go away, go home to her beau in Calvin, and leave him to his life with his children.

But he'd told her he would listen, and so he would.

Then he'd ask her not to visit anymore. He'd figure out a way to get through the summer without her and hopefully she'd return to Calvin, where she belonged.

And then maybe he could get his dreams of having her as part of his family out of his head.

As soon as the wagon pulled into the yard, Oscar was at his shoulder, a fresh horse ready to head to Walt's place. Jonas almost asked for a second mount, not wanting the closeness of Penny riding behind him. Almost. Sam had mounted up and ridden ahead after Penny had quietly told him she wished to speak to Jonas. He was already across the yard and would outdistance them quickly.

Jonas and Penny were barely past the barn when she started speaking, as if she'd held the words in during the wagon ride and couldn't bear it any longer.

"My father wants me to make a good match. That's why he sent me away to finishing school and when that didn't take, he has now apparently chosen Mr. Abbott for me to marry."

This was the explanation that was supposed to reassure him? That her father wanted her to marry well?

Jonas would never be considered a good match.

"I tried to talk to my father, tell him that Mr. Abbott and I don't suit. We don't," she said when she must've felt Jonas's muscles tense. "He's… I can't explain it any better than there is something disturbing about him. He looks at me as if I was a breeding mare—as if, as if he only wants one thing. We've barely spoken but I have no desire to be married to that man."

She took a breath, he could feel her huffing as if her emotional words had taken a toll on her.

"I tried to talk to my father. I even tried to bring my mother into it. She understands that I don't want anything to do with Abbott but she won't stand up to Father."

"What do you mean?" He hadn't meant to speak at all, but she'd started talking about her mother and his curiosity overtook him.

"My mother…isn't happy. I have no remembrance of her being completely happy with my father. Never. He is…a hard man, much of the time. I don't know if she thought she was in love with him in the beginning, but the marriage they have is nothing like…"

She stopped speaking for a moment and when she continued, he could hear the tears in her voice.

"You knew my grandmother before she passed. You couldn't have seen her and Grandfather together and not seen how in love they still were, even after all those years together."

He nodded, unable to deny it. He'd been envious of the obvious love between Walt and Peg. He'd never seen anything like it, not between his parents or anyone else.

"*That's* the kind of love I want to find. I won't marry without it. When you arrived in Calvin and brought Grandfather's letter, it seemed too good to be true. I thought if I could get out of town for a little while, perhaps Abbott would forget about me, but he's obviously followed me here."

Jonas could understand why the other man didn't want to

let her go. A vibrant, beautiful creature like Penny Castlerock was special. Based on Penny's description of their true relationship—not really knowing each other, an agreement with her father—the other man's proprietary behavior *did* seem out of character.

But it wasn't Jonas's place to intervene. He would let Walt handle things or make the choice to send Penny back to Calvin.

She quieted as they rode into Walt's yard.

"I suppose you think I'm foolish for trying to avoid my problems, only you don't know my father."

No, but based on their two meetings Jonas could understand that perhaps the man wouldn't accept anything other than total obedience from his daughter.

"And if you found this person that you loved, would your father accept your decision?" he asked, because he couldn't contain the question.

"I don't know." Her voice was hesitant.

They drew near to the porch and Jonas helped her off the horse but maintained his seat. He looked down on her earnest face and his stomach clenched.

"I suppose if I truly fell in love the way my grandparents felt, it wouldn't matter what my father said. I would choose to be with that man."

He couldn't voice the question deep in his heart. *And what if this person was poor? Would you go against your father for someone like me?*

His questions remained unasked as he said goodbye and made sure she got inside Walt's cabin all right.

But they remained in his heart as he wheeled his mount and cried out to God. *Will I ever be enough for someone to love?*

Chapter Sixteen

Penny woke early, her most recent conversation with Jonas still fresh on her mind. He'd seemed to hold himself back, especially at the end.

He was naturally quiet, but this was more than that. As if he'd wanted to say something or ask something but he hadn't. The direction their conversation had taken made her question things herself.

If she *was* developing feelings for Jonas, would she go against her father's wishes to marry him?

She was still unsettled in her own mind about whether she could be happy living outside of town. And in a poorer financial situation than she was used to.

If she couldn't answer those questions for herself, how could she go against her father?

She pushed herself out of the warm bed, shivering when her feet hit the cool plank floor. The cabin was quiet. Had she managed to wake before her grandfather and Sam?

She'd spent so many mornings rushing through her ablutions to get over to the Whites' homestead. Perhaps today she could take a few moments for herself and try to work through her muddled feelings.

Penny took several minutes to brush out her hair, enjoying

the feel of the soft strands against her now-calloused fingers. Before she'd come to visit her grandfather, the state of her hands would have bothered her. Her mother would likely have a conniption if she saw them now. But Penny didn't mind.

Each blister served to remind her of working with Breanna or one of the boys. Actually accomplishing things on their homestead, instead of sitting in a room looking pretty.

Penny fumbled when putting her hairbrush down on the dresser, and a small wooden box tumbled to the floor, scattering its contents. Bending down to gather them, Penny realized it was the recipe box of her grandmother's that she'd moved to her room after the kitchen fire. She'd meant to look at the recipes in hopes of finding something she could try her hand at. Something simple.

Sitting on the edge of the bed, Penny spread the cards out on the bedcover to try and put them in some semblance of order. Some were just small scraps of paper, but all bore her grandmother's handwriting, its familiar scrolls and loops.

Seeing the familiar, beloved script brought on tears, and Penny had to blink them away before she could continue. She picked up the nearest recipe and traced the scrawling writing. *Carrot Jam.* She'd loved her grandmother's jams and jellies, could remember shelves full of the delicious preserves. Shelves now bare.

She'd spent so many hours in the kitchen with her grandmother. Sometimes watching the older woman cook, often peeling potatoes while her grandmother prepared the meal. Sometimes doing chores together.

Her grandmother had been happy living on this homestead with her grandfather. Penny knew it, deep in her bones. Her gran hadn't needed frilly dresses or to attend fancy parties to be happy. Her gran's peace had come from within.

Could her grandfather and Jonas both be right? Did her

gran's faith have something to do with her peace and the love she shared so freely?

Penny tucked the recipe cards back into their box, then reached for the worn Bible her grandfather had allowed her to borrow. A memory surfaced, another time with her gran, sitting at the kitchen table reading this very book together, heads bowed.

Penny flipped open the cover and began to read.

Nearly a week after the barn-raising, Penny bounced on her toes in excitement as Jonas and his sons returned from the fields. Flushed with success and from standing over a hot stove most of the day, she rewarded Jonas, first in the door, with a sunny smile that seemed to stop him in place before he reached the water basin.

"Pa!" someone grunted from behind him, shoving him into the room and severing the invisible connection between them.

"Sorry," Jonas muttered, bending over the basin to splash his face. He quickly moved aside, rubbing his face with a towel and then flipping it over Ricky's head. The boy's exclamation brought another smile to Penny's face. She couldn't contain her joy.

"Somethin' smells good," Edgar said, entering behind the other boys.

"Penny made carrot jam!" Breanna announced from her place at Penny's side.

"My gran's recipe," Penny told the surprised faces looking at her. "And I didn't even burn down the kitchen."

The boys' exclamations and Jonas's unreadable gaze were interrupted by a distressed cry.

"Pa—"

The door banged open and Oscar shouldered through the opening, supporting a white-faced Maxwell.

"What happened?"

"He hurt?"

Jonas immediately moved to Maxwell's other side, holding his son's weight. Through the chaos, Penny saw the teen's lower leg was bent at an unnatural angle. She moved to intercept the trio and met them as they lowered Maxwell to one of the benches. Jonas knelt at Maxwell's side and began to gently work his boot off.

"Matty, pump some cold water from the well," Penny ordered. "Ricky, bring some towels." Cooling the affected area was the only thing she could think of.

"I'll ride for the doc. Pa?" Oscar looked to his father for approval, his face etched with worry.

"Yes, but be careful. It's cloudy and getting dark and I don't want your horse stepping in a hole."

Oscar nodded gravely, already moving to the door.

"I'm all right," Maxwell said through clenched teeth.

For a moment, Penny thought the boy was talking to her, but then she realized Breanna had followed and now stood half behind Penny, clutching her skirt and staring at her injured brother with wide eyes.

Penny stooped and put her arm around the girl's shoulders. "My brother broke his arm once when we were younger. He tried to climb an apple tree in the neighbor's yard and fell right out of it. Once the doctor came and fixed his arm, he was just fine."

"He was?" The subdued whisper from the usually exuberant girl told of her fear.

"Yes. I think Maxwell will be all right. We should pray for him, though."

Penny moved Breanna a little ways away, turning the girl so she wouldn't be able to see her brother's injury quite so well, and said a short prayer for Maxwell's healing and that the doctor would arrive quickly.

Matty banged inside with a pail of water splashing all over his pants, just as Ricky screeched into the room with an armful of worn towels.

"We should move him to his room so he's more comfortable 'til the doc gets here," Jonas said, and it took Penny a moment to realize he was speaking to her.

"Of course." She moved to Maxwell's side, averting her eyes from his leg but being careful not to bump it. Jonas heaved the boy to his feet and Penny accepted part of his weight, her arm wrapped around his waist.

"Breanna and Seb, why don't you make sure the table is set and get everyone else to sit down and eat?"

Penny shot a questioning glance at Jonas as they maneuvered Maxwell through the other room, painful step by painful step.

"Good for them to have something to do instead of just worrying," he muttered.

"What happened?" Jonas asked as he shifted Maxwell onto the bed. Penny's heart clenched at the boy's smothered groan.

"Thought I heard kittens mewling in the barn loft," Maxwell said through heavy breaths, obviously in pain. "That barn cat's been missing for a few days. Thought she might've had her litter up there."

Jonas nodded. "I'm going to take his pants off," Jonas told Penny, and she obediently turned away, catching sight of Matty and Ricky at the door. She accepted the water pail and towels from them and shooed them back into the dining room when they wanted to watch with craned necks.

"Didn't think the ladder was that rickety," Maxwell continued, "but something broke and I fell. Landed funny on the leg."

Suddenly, he cried out and Jonas muttered, "Sorry, sorry."

"Do you need help?" Penny asked, still careful to keep her back turned.

"It ain't that bad. I've had worse." Maxwell's terse statement did not comfort Penny, only made her heart squeeze for his broken childhood.

"We've got it—you can come back now," came Jonas's strained answer.

When she returned to the bed, both he and Maxwell were sweating, but Maxwell now had a blanket draped discreetly across his middle with the injured leg exposed. She squeezed Jonas's knee briefly, knowing he hadn't wanted to hurt his son.

Penny set about wetting some of the towels and draping them carefully over the injury. "This should help keep the swelling down. I hope."

"How d'ya know?" Penny could tell Maxwell was trying to put on a brave face. She gently brushed the damp hair off his forehead.

"I found some medical books in my mother's old room over at my grandfather's. I guess my mama might've wanted to be a nurse…or something…before she met my father." She honestly didn't know how the books had come to be there, but she'd read snatches of some of them in the few moments she'd had to herself in the last few weeks.

"Used to think about being a doctor some…" Maxwell said.

"I didn't know that," Jonas said quietly, kneeling beside the bed at Penny's elbow.

"You should get something to eat and rest for a bit," Penny told Jonas. "You were already gone when I arrived this morning and you've been working hard all day." As evidenced by the layer of dust on his clothing and in his hair. When had his hat gotten knocked off?

"Maxwell needs—"

"Someone to stay with him, I know. I'll sit with him for a bit while you rest, and then if the doctor isn't here yet, you can take a turn."

Jonas agreed grudgingly, after Maxwell insisted he go eat something. He left with another indecipherable look at Penny, but she chose to ignore it and focus on the teen in front of her.

"I don't see any reason you couldn't be a doctor," Penny told Maxwell just before she heard Jonas's bootsteps fade away.

"I cain't read."

"Yet," she told the boy firmly. "You can't read *yet*. You're doing very well so far."

He rolled his head to the side and remained silent. She dipped the corner of one of the towels in the water pail and dabbed his face, removing some of the day's dust.

"It takes money to go to medical school," Maxwell said softly, still looking away.

"Mmm," Penny agreed. "But you're a hard worker. I know you could find a way to do it if that's what you truly want to do. You might even be able to find a benefactor who would help pay for some of your expenses."

"How?" His brows creased and he looked right at her, the word spoken almost angrily. "Who'd want to help *me*?"

"I would," she replied in the same even tone she'd been using. "I could write a few letters on your behalf. My father also has some contacts back East." Although her father might not be too pleased with her once she returned home.

Maxwell looked away again, as if he was afraid to hope in her offer.

"I cain't believe someone would just give me money for schooling. It don't make sense."

What didn't make sense was that someone—his mother?—had stolen this boy's hope. "Maybe they wouldn't. But it couldn't hurt to ask. And I'm happy to do that for you, if it's what you want." She paused. "You can do whatever you set your mind to, Maxwell. Your father is an example of that. He had no family, an uncertain future." She purposely left things vague as she didn't know how much of his past Jonas had revealed to the boys. "But he's built this homestead, made a family with Breanna and you boys. He's created something to be proud of."

Maxwell nodded slightly but didn't say more. Penny knew he was in pain and this wasn't the time to push him. She simply took his hand and waited with him, praying that he would find healing for his leg. And his heart.

After a long night, Penny blearily made her way to the Whites' homestead before it was even light.

She found the house dark, and a bent-shouldered Jonas sitting on the porch steps. The lightening sky provided enough light to see his head held between his hands. Was he sleeping?

"Jonas?" she called softly and his head jerked up. Not sleeping, then. "Everyone all right?"

He stood and raised a hand to the back of his neck, half-turning from her so she couldn't see his face.

"Yes. The doctor arrived just after you left—"

"After you made me leave."

"—and set Maxwell's leg. It's splinted now with a plaster cast. He's supposed to stay off it for a few days. Or as long as I can keep him down."

"Did he get any sleep last night?"

"Doc gave him some pain medication, knocked him right out."

She couldn't resist reaching out to touch his arm. He jumped at the contact but didn't pull away.

"And you?"

He shook his head, ran his other hand down his face.

"Couldn't get my mind to quiet. We're already behind on the haying, and with the Sumners' fields to cut, too…without a driver, without Maxwell, I don't see how we'll finish."

"Can you hire someone else?"

He was shaking his head by the time she'd finished her question. "Everyone's hired out for the season."

"Well, what about my grandfather?" As she said the words, she thought about her grandfather's continuing exhaustion, though he'd been trying to hide it from her. "No, he probably shouldn't be out in the sun all day."

"There's no one."

She'd never heard Jonas so disheartened before. She knew part of his defeated attitude was because of his worry for Maxwell and loss of sleep. Maybe that's why he'd overlooked the last obvious answer.

"What about me?"

Now he did turn to her, the rising sun illuminating the disbelief on his face.

"You think you can drive a team all day?"

"I'm stronger than I used to be." She was, from hauling all those water buckets and chasing chickens, pulling potatoes.

"If you'll teach me, I know I can do it. Breanna can ride along." She spoke aloud as she thought through the idea, liking it more and more. "You'll have to bring your lunch along, won't have us to bring it to you fresh."

He shook his head again. "You can't—"

"Why not?" Couldn't he see she wanted to help? "Maxwell isn't full grown yet. He's not much taller than me. If he can handle the team, then surely I can."

"Yes, but it makes for a long day and you'll be sitting in the hot sun—"

"And I want to help, all right? Why can't you just *let me,* you stubborn man?"

"I just don't understand why you're always over here helping."

Because my heart is here. She couldn't say the words. Not yet, not when the emotion was so new and overwhelming.

A light went on inside the kitchen, throwing yellow beams onto the porch between them.

"If I can't get the hang of driving the team in a couple of hours, you can fire me," she offered.

"Fine."

It wasn't the enthusiastic answer Penny had hoped for, but she would take what she could get.

Chapter Seventeen

Jonas never imagined a haying crew could be so giggly. He guessed he should be grateful that Penny was able to keep Breanna occupied during the long days, but after two days of her constant presence, all those smiles…

He felt a bit like Maxwell did being confined to bed. Cranky.

Thankfully, today was almost over. He didn't know how much longer he could hide his feelings from Penny, not with her close all the time. He appreciated her help with the haying, even if he didn't understand why she offered it. They'd struck a deal regarding Breanna, but how would he repay her for this?

Settling in the back of the full wagon along with Sam, Jonas prepared for the ride back to the barn. The last load for today.

"You all right back there?" Penny hollered back to them.

"Yep. Go," he called up to her. The sooner they got home, the sooner she could go back to Walt's place.

"They're having too good of a time for this to be considered work," Sam muttered, throwing his arm over his eyes and leaning his head back.

Jonas was proud of the boy. Sam had been taking it upon

himself to come over in the afternoons to help with haying, once his chores at Walt's place had been completed. Without being asked, he'd begun to act responsibly, like a real neighbor, a real man.

Who now dozed in the hay, snoring slightly.

Words passed between the two females on the wagon bench and Breanna giggled again.

The close relationship Penny had developed with his daughter was another cause of concern for Jonas. What would Breanna do when Penny had to return home to Calvin? He knew now that she needed a woman's presence in her life, but how could he make that happen? Especially when his heart was knotted over the banker's daughter?

His thoughts distracted him and the wagon was slowing to a stop near the barn before he even realized it.

"Pa, you asleep back there?"

Breanna rounded the back of the wagon and he tried to force himself into a better state of mind. No need to take out his worries on his precious daughter.

"No, not asleep."

"Good." Penny approached, rounding the wagon from the other side. "Breanna and I want to play a little trick on Davy and we need your help."

"What?"

Sam roused and jumped out of the wagon with a quick, "Leave me outta this."

Penny lifted Breanna to sit next to Jonas on the wagon bed. Both girls' faces shone with mischief. He vowed he would never forget Penny's sparkling eyes, not after she left, not ever.

"I didn't mention this before, but last week Davy put a frog in one of the cooking pots and it jumped out at me and Breanna."

"Scared us *real* bad," his daughter confirmed.

"And Breanna told me he's deathly afraid of snakes..."

Jonas nodded, wary, not sure where this was going.

"Well, I ran over this earlier today." Penny held up a large black snake, making Jonas yelp and jump off the back of the wagon.

Breanna dissolved into giggles and Penny's hearty laughter rang out over the quiet yard. Heart thudding in his ears, Jonas realized the snake was decapitated. It must've been run over by the wagon wheel.

"Guess Davy's not the only one afraid of snakes," Penny murmured, eyes glowing with mirth.

He shuddered theatrically, cracking a smile when Breanna laughed again. "Just what are you planning on doing with that?"

"Tricking Davy!" Breanna exclaimed gleefully.

Jonas just shook his head. He knew his sons had a propensity for playing practical jokes, but he never would have guessed it of Penny, and now she'd roped Breanna into helping.

She'd melded with his family. He couldn't deny it. Desperately wanted to stop fighting it, but he was afraid...

"You do know Davy will just retaliate, don't you?" he asked, eyebrows raised.

"Oh, I've got lots more tricks up my sleeve," Penny confided, her eyes drawing him in, drawing him closer, though he stayed on the side where she *wasn't* holding the snake.

"'Sides, Davy needs some of his own medicine," Breanna added.

"What do you want me to do?" He wondered if this was a mistake but was curious to see where they were going with it.

"I'm going to distract the boys and Breanna's going to sneak into Davy and Edgar's room to open the window. We need you to go around back and pass Breanna the snake."

"You're going to put it in their room?" Jonas was suddenly glad he hadn't played any pranks on Penny.

"Worse. In Davy's bed."

Penny stretched her legs out in front of her, settling her skirt modestly. She rested her aching back against a gnarled tree trunk and watched the children frolic in the little tree-lined stream she hadn't known ran through both Jonas's and her grandfather's properties until just this morning.

They'd finished harvesting the last of the Sumners' hay fields yesterday and she'd thought they would start on Jonas's crop today, but this morning Jonas had declared they were taking a day off. He'd shooed everyone, including her, away from the house and yard, stating he'd catch up with them after he'd taken care of the basic chores.

The boys had unanimously declared they wanted to fish and had dragged her and Breanna along. It didn't appear they were getting much fishing done, though, with all the shoving and dunking they were doing with each other in the stream. Sam was right in the middle of the action, laughing more than Penny had heard in a while. She was glad he got along with the Whites and seemed more settled than when they'd first come to visit their grandfather.

Even Breanna was getting in on the action in her petticoat, though Maxwell was relegated to the bank with Penny, as he had instructions not to get the plaster binding on his leg wet.

Penny thought it likely any fish around had swum upstream to escape the ruckus. But she couldn't reprimand the children for their fun, not after they'd been working so hard.

With a sudden roar, Jonas appeared through the woods and attacked, sending shrieking boys and girl in all directions. He chased them through the knee-deep water, shouting and splashing as much as they were. Penny couldn't look away from the utter contentment revealed in his features. She also noticed the children seemed to allow themselves to be caught and thrown into the water. Wanting to be near their father.

She thought her heart might burst from the joy of being with this family. Was this truly love? How could it be anything else?

Finally, Davy and Edgar teamed up and jumped on Jonas's back, wrapping their arms around his neck, while Seb tackled his feet and the whole group splashed into the water. Penny couldn't help but laugh, along with Maxwell, but that drew Jonas's attention.

He emerged from the water, dripping, his shirt plastered to his broad chest. "What are you doing sitting over here? You should be getting wet with the rest of us."

"Jonas…" Penny warned, trying to gather her skirt.

He kept coming.

"The boys agreed they wouldn't splash me. Jonas—"

"Get 'er, Pa!" someone shouted gleefully. Probably Davy, who'd screamed when he found the snake in his bed.

Penny tried to scramble to her feet, but got tangled in her skirt. Before she could stand up, Jonas pounced, scooping her into his arms and holding her tight against his chest.

"You're getting me wet!" Penny shivered as a cold drop fell from his nose onto her over-warm cheek. Her clothes were damp where she pressed up against him, but it wouldn't take long for that to dry in the warm summer sun. If she got soaked, however…

"Not as wet as you're going to get." He moved toward the stream with purposeful strides.

"But the boys—"

"You might've come to an arrangement with my children, but not with me."

"Jonas!" she shrieked as he feigned tossing her into the water. Her stomach swooped and it wasn't only due to the motion—being close to him like this set her heart to pounding.

He waded into the water, still holding her. "I'll allow you to make me an offer, but I can't guarantee I'll take it."

"Do it, Pa! Throw her in!"

She glared over her shoulder at Davy, who still held a grudge about the snake prank she and Jonas and Breanna had pulled on him.

Jonas loosened his hold and Penny clutched at his shoulders.

"Wait!" she cried out in desperation.

Jonas stilled, and she looked up, realizing how close their faces were. Close enough for her to run her finger along the tan line where his hat covered his forehead most of the time. Close enough to see how his lashes spiked from the water.

His warm brown eyes looked down on her with no guile, nothing hidden in their depths.

So Penny reached up and smacked a loud, casual kiss against his lips.

He froze, eyes wide.

She cleared her throat, then said, "There. You've collected your payment. Now put me down."

He continued to hold her, unmoving. Only now his eyes had changed, shadows darkening in their depths. She remembered Jonas's words from weeks ago, *I've never kissed a woman.*

And she forgot about the kids watching them, forgot about Sam's presence, there was only the man holding her close. A man of honor who she admired and maybe even loved.

Penny reached up to frame his face with both hands, stretched a bit and their lips met, his cool against her warm. She surrendered to the moment, allowing her eyes to flutter closed. His arms tightened around her. When the kiss ended, it was all she could do to catch her breath.

Breanna giggled softly, and Penny realized the boys had grown silent, frozen and watching her interaction with Jonas.

"Now you really must put me down." Her words emerged breathless and she became aware of the fierce blush heating her face.

Silent, he set her on trembling legs on the bank, their gazes meshing and holding. Finally breaking the contact, she retreated to her blanket, flouncing down next to a grinning Maxwell.

She'd kissed him.
Penny had kissed *him*.
Jonas returned to playing with his sons, but his efforts were halfhearted as he tried to corral his stampeding thoughts.

What did it mean? Jonas couldn't fathom. He knew kissing wasn't something she took lightly, but he'd never imagined she would bestow such a token of her affection on *him*.

The boys seemed to echo his disbelief, their play subdued. They continued sneaking glances at Penny, and Oscar kept grinning at his father.

Finally, the children calmed, some of the boys jaunting off upstream with their poles over their shoulders to try to catch supper. Breanna and Seb lay on a blanket on the stream bank with their heads together, looking up at the clouds.

Jonas and Oscar settled next to Maxwell, which put Jonas crossways at Penny's feet. He didn't have to look at her to know her hair had come loose from its pins and copper curls tumbled around her shoulders, enticing him to run his hands through it. His skin felt stretched tight over his bones with awareness of her, but he couldn't make himself look at her.

What did her kiss mean?

Penny didn't seem out of sorts at all. She chatted animatedly with the boys. "Maxwell and I have been talking a little about his dreams of being a doctor someday. Oscar, what do you want to do with your life?"

His son played with the blades of grass beside his bent knees. "Git married, I guess."

"All right. What else? Do you want to have a homestead, like your pa? Open a store? Go away to school?"

Penny's bare toes crept closer to Jonas's thigh, though her skirt still modestly covered her legs. At some point, she must've removed her shoes.

Oscar shrugged again, silent, still playing with the grass.

Jonas kept his head down, but his focus didn't waver from the small, pink toes and slender ankle edging toward his leg.

"He wants to raise horses, like Pa."

Jonas's head came up, focus shifting to glare at Maxwell, who'd just revealed one of his father's biggest dreams. He hadn't known that Oscar wanted that same thing. "I'd be proud to partner with you, son."

He focused on Oscar and the lift in his son's shoulders, but a prickling on the back of his neck told him Penny was watching.

"I didn't know you wanted to raise horses," she said softly.

It was Jonas's turn to shrug as he lowered his head again, staring down at his wet trousers. "There's money in beef, but I wouldn't mind doing something like your granddaddy's done. Start with some good breeding stock and go from there."

"I'm sure he would help you get started."

Jonas nodded. "He's said as much. He's a good friend. Better than I deserve."

"That's not true." Her sharp words were accompanied by a poke from her big toe, prompting Jonas to look up. She didn't acknowledge the action, was relaxed and leaning back on both hands. "You've worked hard to get where you are, but that doesn't mean you can't accept help from the friends you've got."

"You and Walt have been *helping* so much, I don't know how I'll ever repay you."

His words earned him another poke with her foot.

"We didn't do it expecting anything back. Well, except for what you promised about getting Grandfather's kitchen and barn back in shape."

She continued nudging him with her foot and it tickled. He shifted his leg away, didn't reply.

"I can't say what his motives are for helping you out. Probably the same as mine."

Again, she scooted her foot closer although she didn't visibly shift on the blanket.

"Because he likes you."

Her words froze him for a moment. If she said her motives were the same as Walt's, did that mean she liked Jonas, too?

Oscar stood suddenly. "We're going to go check on the other boys. See if they're having any luck with the fish."

"We are?" Maxwell asked, a perplexed look on his face.

Jonas was sure he wore a similar expression. What was Oscar's hurry?

Oscar yanked on his brother's arm. "We are."

"All right already. Help me up."

Oscar nudged his father with his boot as he hefted Maxwell to his feet, winking as he and his grumbling brother walked off, Maxwell leaning on a makeshift crutch.

A glance at Penny revealed she wore a secretive smile, and Jonas felt distinctly as if he'd missed something.

She kicked his leg again, and this time her confusing words and the fact that they were alone gave Jonas the courage to clasp her foot in his hand, his thumb pressing into her arch. He hoped it was acceptable, but didn't know for sure.

Didn't know anything. Was inside out, still floating from her kiss.

He wanted to believe she'd meant it.

She wiggled her foot in his grasp but didn't pull away. "You don't have to do everything, conquer everything alone, you know. It's okay to need help sometimes."

He looked into her serious blue eyes and wanted to believe her. He really did. But his experiences had taught him otherwise. He had to be strong enough to take care of himself, of his family, on his own.

It wasn't safe to depend on others.

Except...

Penny had begun by watching Breanna and then sewed shirts for his family. Then helping driving the hay wagon.

And she'd brought light to his home. Laughter that hadn't been there before her arrival at Walt's place.

She'd even given the boys advice on romance.

What if he *did* have a chance at winning her heart?

Chapter Eighteen

The next morning, as Penny fumbled around in the semi-darkness, preparing for another long day in the hay wagon, she marveled at her actions from the previous day.

She had admitted to her developing feelings for Jonas, at least to herself.

She had acted on her feelings.

She had really kissed Jonas White.

A blaze of heat crept over her cheeks and she pressed shaking hands to her face, even though there was no one to see her. She would never have dared such a thing with men of her previous acquaintance. She had never actually kissed anyone before.

And Jonas hadn't seemed to think less of her for it. He'd seemed uncertain at first, but stayed at her side under the shade of the trees and talked for a long time, until the boys had returned carrying a wriggling, bulging burlap sack.

The fish they'd fried had been excellent. Sam seemed to be growing up, getting along with the White family and in his help with his grandfather's place. She was happy. Happier than she'd been in a long time.

She tiptoed through the kitchen, just in case her grandfather hadn't woken yet. On the back stoop, she nearly tripped over a bunch of weeds. No, no weeds. Wildflowers?

Kneeling to gather the somewhat smashed blossoms tied by a piece of string, her attention was diverted by the multiple pairs of boot prints in the soft dirt near the step. Prints of varying sizes.

What was going on?

Had some of the boys snuck over here with the flowers? It was the only thing she could think of, and the different sizes of the boots might indicate that.

Was she meant to think the flowers were from Jonas, after the children had witnessed their embrace yesterday? She would have to try to find out without letting the boys know she was on to their game. After all, leaving the flowers was a sweet gesture. And it meant they were listening to her advice on courting ladies.

Feet and heart light, she made her way toward the White homestead as the sun began to rise.

Cresting the last hill before she would catch sight of the White cabin, she was startled to see a figure on horseback, unmoving, close to a copse of trees not far away. One of the boys? But what were they doing out so early?

Unease tightened her stomach. Something felt wrong.

"Oscar?" she called out tentatively, hazarding a guess to the person's identity.

The figure turned toward her, but made no other move. Against the shadows of the trees behind him, she couldn't make out his face, only a dark outline. Goose bumps broke out along her arms, and not from the cool morning air. What if it wasn't one of the boys? Or Jonas?

Quickening her steps, Penny topped the hill and saw movement in Jonas's valley. The Whites were up and about. So who was this, half-hiding on the hilltop?

Heart pounding as she perceived the danger she'd put herself in by calling out, Penny hiked up her skirt and hastened toward the cabin she'd come to feel was as safe as her grandfather's place, or her own home.

Hoofbeats sounded behind her, echoing her pounding heart and she broke into a full run, calling out for Jonas, for anyone. She didn't dare look back.

And there was the barn, and the yard beyond it.

A tall figure turned to meet her, reached out for her. Jonas!

As if he sensed the malevolent presence behind her, he swept her into his arms, turning his broad back to shield her.

"What's wrong?" he demanded. "Is it Walt?"

"No," she gasped, resting her cheek against his muscled shoulder, clinging to him. "Someone on horseback. I couldn't see a face, but he was half-hidden behind that stand of trees on the hill." She motioned over Jonas's shoulder to where she'd seen the man. She panted, trying to regain her breath.

"I called out to him—thought he was one of the boys—he might've ridden away."

She couldn't stop shaking, thinking about the menacing presence she'd felt.

"It's all right," Jonas murmured, his mouth close to her ear. He seemed to hesitate, and then gently cupped the back of her head. "You're safe now. You're here."

"Pa?"

A voice from the porch had them both turning that direction, only to find an audience of grinning boys. But when Penny glanced at Jonas, his jaw was set, expression hard.

"Oscar, saddle up a couple of ponies. Davy, grab my rifle, will ya?"

"What are you going to do?" Penny asked as Jonas released his loose grasp on her waist.

"I'm going to ride up there and see if I can find out what someone was doing on my land."

"But what if that man—or whoever it was—is still there?"

"That's what the rifle is for." The coldness in his tone surprised her. She knew he was simply protecting his family, protecting her, but she'd never seen Jonas in that light before.

Within minutes, Jonas and Oscar rode up the hill, leaving Penny to sink down on the front porch steps because her suddenly weak legs wouldn't hold her. She wanted to call out for Jonas, tell him not to go. What if he was hurt?

But he and Oscar were already gone before she'd decided, and soon they were riding back into the yard, mouths grimly set.

"What—" Penny couldn't even force a whole question out from her parched lips. She used the porch railing to pull herself up on shaky legs.

Jonas shook his head after he'd dismounted and allowed Oscar to lead his horse away. "Nothing there except tracks. Whoever it was is long gone. I'll talk to the town marshal on Sunday, see if anyone else has been having trouble."

"But—"

He shook his head again, this time imperceptibly, and Penny forced herself to quiet.

"We need to get out in the fields. Got a lot of ground to cover today. Maxwell, can you get this herd to eating, so we can go?"

The teen shooed the other children inside and Jonas moved closer to Penny, speaking in a low voice for her ears only. "Tracks looked like that horse was standing around all night."

Her breath caught in her chest. "What does that mean?"

"Maybe he was just passing through and needed somewhere to rest his horse for the night." Jonas's skeptical expression indicated he didn't think that was likely.

"But wouldn't he have come down to the house? Hospitality and all that?" Penny asked.

"Or at least have laid out a bedroll…" Jonas's mouth continued to be set in that grim line. "He could've been watching the place all night."

Just the thought sent shivers down Penny's spine. "What—what would be the purpose of someone doing that?"

As if he sensed her turmoil, Jonas's warm hand closed over hers. "I dunno. I can't help but wonder…"

"What?"

"There've been some other things. When the cattle got loose during that storm, it looked like the fence had been knocked down by someone. And the ladder that broke when Max was climbing it…"

"You think someone purposely damaged the barn ladder?"

"I went and looked at it after Max got hurt. Someone'd loosened the boards so the whole thing would come apart."

"Are you certain?" The thought of anyone making trouble for Jonas and his boys seemed ludicrous. They might not be accepted by everyone in the community, but who would do the things Jonas had said? The cattle were the Whites' livelihood. If more of them had gotten hurt or run away, it meant less money for the Whites to survive on. And Maxwell had ended up with a broken leg. What if someone else had been climbing the ladder and been injured even worse?

Instinctively, Penny shifted closer to Jonas's warm, safe presence. Their shoulders brushed above still-clasped hands.

"The barn ladder wasn't that old. I hadn't paid attention to it specifically, but I don't think it could've come apart like it did on its own. And with someone watching the place, it makes me even more suspicious."

"Should you…perhaps you should ride into town and talk to the marshal today."

He frowned, considering her words. "I can't lose a day of haying. We're rushing it to get done as it is. Sunday'll come soon enough."

She stayed close to him, drinking in his strong, stoic presence. He didn't seem shaken by what had happened, not like she was. How did he always manage to be so calm?

He leaned his chin against her hair. They were barely touching, only their clasped palms and shoulders, but the moment seemed intimate, as if he knew the turmoil in her heart and was offering comfort.

Until Maxwell called from the kitchen, "Pa, you want a plate?"

Following Jonas into the cabin, Penny joined in the chaotic, rushed meal. It wasn't until everyone was about to spread out for the day that she remembered her flowers and turned to Jonas. "Thank you for the lovely bouquet."

He choked on the coffee he'd just swallowed, setting his cup on the table with a rattle. "What?"

Her suspicions about the boys' involvement in the gift were confirmed when Maxwell and Ricky both turned red, while none of the other boys would look at her.

Jonas must've noticed the boys' suspicious miens, as well, because he growled out a warning, "Boys…"

"Gotta get the wagon hitched, Pa," said Ricky, springing from the table.

"I'll help him—" "Me, too—" Davy and Seb were gone, too.

"I'll explain in a minute," Penny murmured to Jonas, as the other boys rushed out the door.

When the room was clear, she began stacking dishes, though Seb would be in charge of the washing today, since he was too small to do the haying work. "I found a bouquet of wildflowers on the front step this morning on my way out."

"And you thought they were from me?" Jonas's voice sounded strangled and she took pity on him.

"Not unless you wore five pairs of boots—of different sizes."

"The boys." His face showed his consternation and she laid a hand on his shoulder.

"It's actually very sweet."

"But how would they—why would they—"

He was really uncomfortable. Wouldn't look her in the eye. So Penny sat down on the bench beside him, facing away from the table while he still faced in.

"You saw their faces after they saw us kissing yesterday."

His face tinged pink as she mentioned the kiss.

"They probably started talking. You know how they are at cooking up schemes. And decided they wanted to help their father with his courting."

"C-courting?" he blurted. "But I'm not—we're not—"

She leaned back against the edge of the table and looked full into his face. "We could be."

His mouth hung open long enough that she had to hide her smile. Hesitantly, he asked, "And you would accept those kinds of attentions…you would let me court you?"

Before she could reply, he rushed on, "Because I don't know the proper way to do things. I wouldn't have thought to bring you flowers."

His uncharacteristic hesitancy, the uncertainty in his voice touched her heart. Jonas was completely different from Mr. Abbott. Jonas was someone she could trust.

"I think, for right now, we should do what we have been doing. Getting to know each other. And then…when I have to go back to Calvin, we'll see where things stand."

"What happened to your leg?"

Pausing just before the front steps of the church building, Jonas turned his head to catch sight of the speaker.

"It's all right," Penny whispered, squeezing his arm with the hand she had tucked in the crook of his elbow. "It's just Emily."

She was right. The girl Penny had invited to picnic with them at the barn-raising had approached Maxwell, who stood a little apart from the rest of the boys, his crutch supporting him.

"Had an accident in the barn. Fell off a ladder," came Maxwell's quiet answer.

The girl said something too softly for Jonas to hear over the patter of other conversations, both inside and outside the church.

Jonas watched Sam intercept Matty and Davy when they would have moved toward Maxwell and his girl. The boy was more sensitive than Jonas had originally thought. He was a good friend to Maxwell.

Jonas should be looking for the marshal, since he had to rush his family, Walt, and the Castlerocks home after services, but he couldn't ignore the tableau in front of him, not when this girl had upset Maxwell once before.

"Shouldn't we go over there?" he asked Penny. He didn't know what the proper etiquette for this type of situation was, but he didn't want Maxwell hurt again. Maybe Penny could start a conversation with the girl?

"No, no. Maxwell can handle it. I hope," the last was said under her breath.

Maxwell used his free hand to scratch the back of his neck. "Miss Emily, I...umm..." Then he seemed to freeze, looking down into the girl's pretty, upturned face. Jonas could imagine how his palms were probably sweating...heart racing... the same way Jonas felt every time the boys conspired to get him alone with Penny.

"I'm real sorry for the way my brothers acted at the picnic. They shouldn't have made fun—"

"That's all right." She shrugged her dainty shoulders. "I know siblings can be a nuisance sometimes. Mine are. I wanted to tell you, I think it's swell that you're learning to read."

"You do?" Maxwell's voice squeaked, making him sound a lot like Davy's changing voice.

Again, the girl's reply was too soft for Jonas to hear, but she came closer, raised up on tiptoe and kissed Maxwell's apple-red cheek before rushing off to join her family.

"Hmm," Penny cooed, leaning her head against Jonas's shoulder for a brief moment. "Seems like everything worked out for Maxwell." She seemed happy about it, but Jonas didn't know what to think. He wasn't good with feminine emotions or knowing what to do in those kind of situations.

And yet, Penny still clung to his arm. As if she was proud to be with him. As if she was part of the family.

His chest swelled with pride to have her on his arm. Walt's smile showed his approval, which meant a lot to Jonas, too.

And then...when I have to go back to Calvin, we'll see where things stand.

But even so, her words from the other day would play in his mind at times, always reminding him she wouldn't stay with Walt forever.

But she'd left the door open, and he couldn't help hoping that there was a future for him with Penny.

He wanted it so badly. Especially sitting next to her through the service, shoulder to shoulder. Her skirt brushed against his trousers when they stood to sing. He shared a hymnal with her, even though he couldn't read the words.

Being with her felt *right*.

After the services were over, Jonas herded his family to the wagon.

A light breeze made the warm day more bearable, but as the wagon rattled toward home, an acrid scent had the horses' ears twitching and Jonas scanning the horizon. It smelled like smoke, something any homesteader knew to fear. Especially this time of year, with the drying hay out in the fields.

When a line of smoke became visible in the direction of home, Jonas urged the horses faster. Oscar, who'd ridden ahead to check things out, came flying back.

"It's our fields, Pa! Our hay's on fire!"

Chapter Nineteen

How could this have happened?

Jonas coughed, the kerchief he'd tied over his face not managing keep the smoke from his lungs. His eyes stung, face felt seared from the roaring heat.

The fire had taken the west field, but he and the boys had formed a bucket brigade, and were doing their best to prevent it from taking the south one as well. Maxwell had been upset that he couldn't help because of his foot, so Jonas had set him plowing a break line between the fields and house that might stop the fire from reaching the house and barn. He'd let Walt help, when the older man arrived with his grandson and wouldn't leave without a job. At least Walt would be out of the worst of the smoke.

Penny and Breanna had been sent to Walt's place. Jonas wanted them as far from the danger as possible. Especially if the worst happened and he and the boys couldn't stop the fire.

He just didn't understand how this fire could've started. It hadn't taken his nearest neighbor's fields, nor had there been any lightning, no storms that could have ignited it…

Another hacking cough seized him, almost taking him to his knees.

"Pa!" Matty shouted, the next in line beside him.

Jonas waved his son's concern off, forcing his sore legs to stand, to hold his weight. He had to save the field. Needed the hay for his animals to make it through the winter.

Needed the money for Breanna's treatment.

Precious water sloshed over Jonas's hands as he accepted the full bucket from Matty and passed back an empty one. Despair seeped over him as they were forced to move back farther, as the fire continued raging, eating his crops, his livelihood.

His hope.

Penny waited anxiously in Jonas's kitchen. She and Breanna had watched from Walt's porch until the worst of the smoke had dissipated, then they'd run all the way down to Jonas's home and now waited for any report.

It had been hours. Where were the men?

She and Breanna had pulled pail after pail of cool water from the well and filled every container she could find, knowing Jonas and the boys would be parched when they came inside.

Penny's thoughts felt scrambled, as if she couldn't form one coherent thought. All she could do was pray for Jonas, her grandfather, and the boys' safety. If something happened to one of them, she couldn't bear it.

The door banged open and several soot-covered, coughing bodies came in, slumping down at the table. Penny counted Seb, Ricky, Matty, Oscar, Davy, Edgar, and Maxwell hobbling in at the rear. Sam and Walt followed them in, but where was Jonas?

She didn't realize she'd spoken aloud until Seb answered her, his voice scratchy, "Pa wanted to make sure the fire was all out."

"It isn't stopped?" she asked, anxiety breaking her voice.

Oscar gulped from one of the glasses, wiping his mouth with his sleeve and leaving black streaks across his chin. "The fire stopped burning at the creek line. Pa wanted to make sure there weren't any more embers before he came in."

Her grandfather turned serious eyes on her. "You'd best go to him. I've never seen Jonas so disheartened."

His words were all she needed. She grabbed a large pitcher she'd filled earlier and rushed out to go to Jonas. She needed to see for herself the damage that had been done, needed to know that Jonas was okay.

She stopped short at the edge of the burned-out field. Black rubble was all that was left of Jonas's previous golden crop, ready for harvesting. The choking scent of smoke still filled the air.

She spotted Jonas walking along the far side of the field, head and shoulders down as if he could barely hold himself upright. Carefully lifting the hem of her gran's borrowed dress above the ashes of the field, she clutched the water pitcher to her midsection with the other hand and started toward him.

Her boots crunching in the burned-out hay must've alerted him to her presence, for he looked up, and she gasped softly at the bleakness in his expression.

"Jonas," she breathed, letting go of her skirt and reaching out to him.

He pulled her close, and she wrapped her free arm around his neck, stretched up on her toes to be closer to him, uncaring that he was covered in dirt and soot. He buried his face in her shoulder, shuddering. Was he crying? She couldn't tell.

When he pulled away a moment later, his eyes were dry, though red. That could be from the smoke.

"I don't want to get you all filthy," he said, voice hoarse.

"I wasn't complaining," she returned, slinging her arm

around his waist even as she pushed the water pitcher into his hands. "Drink."

His eyebrows twitched but he made no other expression as he raised the pitcher to his lips and drank directly from it. He gulped it, water running down his chin and onto his shirt.

Penny stared at the devastation around them, wondering how he was going to get through this. She knew he liked things carefully planned, and that he needed this crop to make it through the winter. If he had to purchase hay from somewhere else, how would he manage to pay for Breanna's treatment?

He finished drinking and used the back of his wrist to wipe his mouth, spreading streaks of soot across his face in the same way Oscar had.

"The boys said you were down by the creek."

He nodded. "I was. Everything's out down there. I wanted to come up here and see…" He trailed off, his face set in hard lines. "Someone intentionally set this fire."

"What?"

The grim set of his lips said it all. "They spread some of the cut hay, so it would move quickly. They even left their torch behind."

Bitterness seeped into his voice. "I just don't understand why someone would do this to me."

She shook her head; she had no answer. "I don't know, either, Jonas. You've been living here for years and you've never had trouble before, have you?"

"No." His short answer, his pain, made her want to comfort him, but she didn't know how to go about it.

And then he drew away from her one-armed embrace. "I don't know how—" He cleared his throat. "Without the hay, I won't be able to make it through the winter."

"But I thought your neighbor was going to pay you for cutting his hay?"

He ran both hands over his face, smearing the soot and sweat even more. "It's not enough. I needed that money for Breanna's treatment. The doctor won't treat her unless I've got the full amount."

"I wanted to talk to you about that." She'd forgotten, in all the busyness with haying and then her developing relationship with Jonas. "I've been reading some medical journals and I'm not entirely sure this doctor is telling you the truth about a new treatment for Breanna's epilepsy. Are you certain the treatment is legitimate? Have you talked to any other doctors?"

His face hardened, lines forming around his eyes. "I've talked to as many doctors as I can get to. You know as well as I do that there's not one in every town. This man is the only one who says he can treat Breanna."

"Yes, but how do you *know?* Does he have other patients that he has treated? Has he published his findings anywhere?"

His face creased with an emotion she couldn't name. She rushed on, afraid she'd lose her courage to speak up if she didn't get it all out.

"I know this isn't the most opportune time to bring it up, and I don't mean to question you. But I'm concerned for Breanna. What if the procedure is dangerous? If you don't know anything about it—"

Now his face darkened like a thundercloud. "Don't you think I know it could be dangerous? So could the seizures. What if she had one while she was climbing stairs? Or banged her head against something sharp? Or fell in the creek? I've seen head injuries that have caused death before."

She touched his arm, wanting to share his worry and pain, but he jerked away from her and began stalking toward the house. She had no choice but to follow, but she couldn't keep quiet now.

"But what if the seizures aren't permanent? Breanna's mother didn't have seizures—"

He whirled and the storm on his face had intensified. "What of her father? Do you know he didn't have seizures? Can you be sure?"

"No, but I've written to Millie—"

"You *what?*" he thundered, his face turning red.

"I remembered her saying something—at least I think I remembered, about having some kind of episodes when she was a child, but I never knew her to have one—"

His face shuttered and he turned away from her again. "We should return now and check on the boys."

"Jonas, please, will you listen to me?"

He didn't respond, just marched toward the house, his shoulders no longer bent but now stiff with tension.

"Jonas—"

"I'll have one of the boys take you and Sam and Walt home. I don't think you should come back."

Her breath caught in a tight knot in the center of her chest. "But there are still things to be done—the harvest—"

"We've managed without you for five years. I'm certain we can keep on."

His cruel words hurt, sounding more like her father than she could bear. She quieted and trailed him back to the yard.

She knew it was her fault for bringing up Breanna's condition when Jonas was so weary and upset about the fire. Maybe in a few days he would calm down and listen to reason. Perhaps then she could try speaking to him again about Breanna's condition. Perhaps by then she'd receive a response from Millie.

But she so hated waiting.

Jonas sat at the long dining table, head in hands, long after the boys and Breanna had settled for the night, something that had happened far later than usual because of their subdued excitement from the fire.

He should be in bed himself, but he doubted he could sleep. Besides, he didn't have to be up early tomorrow. There was no more hay to bring in.

He supposed he should be thankful that the hay already gathered near the barn hadn't been ignited, but all he felt was numb.

How was he supposed to get his family through the harsh Wyoming winter with only half the hay crop?

He hadn't been able to eat supper, still felt as if he would cast up his accounts at any moment. Sick in both body and heart.

He'd sent Penny away.

All he had to do was close his eyes to remember the feel of her arm clasped around his neck, her body pressed against his in comfort. For a scarce few moments, he'd felt like never before. He hadn't forgotten about the devastation of his burned fields, not exactly, but the pain and despair had faded into the background. At the time, he'd felt as if he could conquer anything, as long as she was by his side.

But then she'd mentioned Breanna's treatment and her letter to the Broadhursts, and Jonas hadn't been able to see straight for his anger. He'd told Penny on that first wagon ride to Walt's house that he didn't want any contact with Breanna's mother or grandparents. And she'd gone against his directive. Why had she done it?

Even if she meant well, what if her letter caused trouble for him? He remembered signing a bunch of papers when the Broadhursts had turned the infant Breanna over to him, but since he couldn't read, he had no idea what he'd signed. They'd told him he would have complete custody of Breanna, and that he couldn't contact them for more money, that the stipend they'd given him would be everything. That had been fine with him. After months in the presence of the stuffy, overbearing family, he'd wanted only to take Breanna and get away, to find a place where they could make their own family. And they had.

And now it was possible Penny's letter had ruined all of that. He couldn't lose Breanna.

Jonas closed his eyes, seeing again the hurt expression crossing Penny's face when he'd told her it would be best if she returned to Calvin.

He'd been in a temper in that moment, hadn't meant to push her away. But maybe it was for the best.

She'd started to become a part of his children's life, of his life. And he wanted to believe she would stay, but how could she, when he had nothing to offer her?

His own parents had abandoned him, so had Pete when appearances dictated that Jonas had behaved immorally.

He wanted to believe Penny could really come to care for him, but he just couldn't.

He was still afraid she would return to Calvin and find a husband that matched her society hopes. Someone wealthier than him, who didn't have to worry about making a crop each year just to survive.

Maybe it was good he'd pushed her away. It would be safer if his heart didn't get any more involved. Better for the children to get used to the separation now, instead of when she left later.

The problem was, the children were already attached to Penny.

And so was he.

Chapter Twenty

Penny's hopes that Jonas would reconsider her banishment from the homestead went unmet. Her only contact with the Whites was Oscar, who Jonas sent over faithfully each afternoon to finish the repairs in the kitchen and bring food. Maxwell was still recovering from his leg injury, and she missed the quiet boy.

Penny missed the children's chatter, missed Breanna's constant hugs.

Missed Jonas's steady presence.

And the repairs were almost complete. Which meant she and Sam didn't have a reason to stay on with their grandfather much longer.

She didn't want to go back to Calvin without fixing things with Jonas. She valued his friendship and had thought there was something more between them.

She'd considered going over to his home and *making* him speak to her, though she knew it was against his wishes. But with all her spare time, she'd gone back to the medical journals and still couldn't find any evidence that there were successful treatments for epilepsy, other than the bromide Jonas had told her affected Breanna negatively.

She didn't think she could hold her opinion inside if she

saw Jonas again. She loved Breanna too much to allow the girl to have a risky treatment without proof that it would heal her.

But with the information she could wrangle out of Oscar, she knew Jonas was still distressed and hadn't figured out a way to find the money for Breanna's treatment.

"Max won't be able to ride in the Bear Creek Round Up, but Edgar and I are still planning on entering. Roping and bronc riding."

Penny shook herself out of her musings and turned her attention to Oscar, who spoke quietly to Sam as they patched the wall behind the stove where she'd burned it all those weeks ago.

"We all talked about it and if we win, we want to give the money to Pa to help pay for Breanna's medicine. He's been real down since the fire…"

Oscar glanced over his shoulder, almost as if to make sure Penny heard him.

"Do you think you can win?" Sam asked, even as Penny's mind raced ahead.

She'd been too wrapped up in her own misery lately and forgotten about the cowboy exhibition. She'd been clinging to the promises found in her gran's Bible, but found it hard to trust the words when her heart seemed to be tearing in two.

"Pa says a lot of cowboys'll be there from all over." Oscar scowled, and Penny saw it even though she only had a view of his profile. "I dunno. Ed's not near as good as Max with a rope. But if I can draw a good bronc and stay on…maybe."

"Aren't you afraid of getting hurt?" Penny blurted, unable to stay out of their conversation.

"Naw." But a subtle quirk of his jaw told her he might not be telling the full truth.

"And Jo—your father's all right with you entering the events? Edgar's not even fifteen…"

He shrugged. "Pa says it's all right. We both been riding since we was Seb's age, ya know."

"I know." She did, but she also knew the cowpokes they'd be challenging were rough and tough, and they were just boys…

"Pa don't know what we want the prize money for. You ain't gonna tell him, are ya?" He glanced anxiously over his shoulder and met Penny's eyes.

"No." She doubted Jonas would even talk to her. She swallowed the lump in her throat.

"But you're comin' to watch, right?"

She had to clear her throat before she could speak. "Yes, we'll be there." Even if she had to saddle a horse and go by herself, she wouldn't miss it if the boys wanted her there. There would be enough of a crowd that she could stay away from Jonas and still support the boys.

But what she really wanted was to load up in the Whites' wagon and attend as a family, the way she would've before the fire had ruined everything.

Jonas spotted the familiar copper hair tucked into a braid down Penny's back and started toward her before he realized what he was doing and stopped.

But it was too late. Breanna, clinging to his hand in the pressing crowd, had seen her, too, and cried out, "Miss Penny!"

Whirling, Penny's face lit and she hurried through the jostling mass, bumping people out of her way. Breanna released Jonas's hand and threw herself into Penny's embrace, almost knocking the slender redhead off her feet.

Penny didn't seem to care. She buried her face in the crown of Breanna's head and hugged his daughter.

"I've missed you, darling girl," she murmured.

Breanna sniffled as she drew away. "Me, too. I've been practicing my manners."

"Have you? That's wonderful." Penny looked up at Jonas, their gazes connecting over his daughter's head. He felt almost as if she'd reached out and touched his chest with her palm.

"Hello," Penny said softly.

Chest tight, Jonas couldn't return her greeting.

"Maxwell's been helping me practice my reading, too, and I've even been trying to make the boys do better, especially when they're eatin'."

Penny looked down at Breanna, breaking the invisible connection and allowing Jonas to breathe again.

"Where are your brothers? I expected to see them with the prettiest girl in the whole crowd."

Breanna smiled prettily at Penny's compliment, twirling side to side so that her dress, the one Penny had made, swished around her ankles. "Me 'n Pa are s'posed to save some seats. Oscar 'n Edgar had to go get ready for their events and t'others wanted to look at the broncs."

Just then, Walt and Sam approached from behind Penny. The older man spoke. "Well, hello, young man. You've been scarce lately."

Jonas glanced at Penny, unsure if she'd told the older man what had happened between them. She shook her head slightly.

"I'm sure Jonas has been trying to get things back in order after the fire," Penny murmured.

Someone in the crowd jostled Walt, and Penny took his arm, giving the older man a concerned look. Jonas looked closer at his friend. Walt appeared healthy, color in his cheeks. But he was a little more bent, seemed a little older than he had at the beginning of the summer. Even with Penny and Sam around, he seemed to have aged. What would he do after they went home?

What would Jonas do?

Guilt surged through Jonas. He should've been better at checking on Walt more often, should've seen to the repairs on Walt's place himself. But he had been too afraid to see Penny.

He'd failed his friend. Just like he'd failed Breanna, though she didn't even know it yet. No wonder everyone abandoned him.

"Why don't you join us?" Walt asked.

Breanna jumped up and down. "Oh, Pa, please! Can we sit with Miss Penny and Sam and Poppy Walt? Please, please, please?"

That was the last thing he wanted—to be near Penny with the unsettling feelings still between them.

But then Breanna turned her pleading brown eyes to him. How could he deny his daughter this request when it might be the only thing he could do for her?

It might be the last time he saw Penny Castlerock.

He agreed and followed as Breanna clung to Penny's waist while they made their way through the crowd to the grandstand. Jonas steadied Walt with an unobtrusive hand under his arm as they found a location in the middle of the grandstand with enough empty seats to accommodate his large family.

Breanna wiggled around and things got confusing when Seb, Matty, Maxwell and Davy joined them and greeted Sam and Walt boisterously, and somehow Jonas found himself wedged in next to Penny. Exactly where he didn't want to be.

"Where's Ricky?" he asked, hoping to be distracted from the feeling of Penny's shoulder pressing into his.

"He had a nickel and went to get some taffy," Davy responded, eyes on the first pair of riders who darted into the arena, chasing after a calf with ropes flying above their heads. "Here he comes now."

The group shifted on the bench seat to make room for Ricky, and Jonas ended up pressed even closer to Penny. They were thigh to thigh, elbow to elbow. He couldn't ignore the faint scent of flowers wafting from her direction, nor the strands of hair that had escaped her braid and tickled his cheek.

"Whew, they're fast!" Maxwell commented as the first pair finished their ride, fists raised in the air to the crowd's applause.

"How've you been?" Penny slanted a sideways look at Jonas.

"Fine." He didn't mean to be short with her, but the less spoken between them, the better. Even so, he couldn't not reply. "And you?"

She tilted her head to one side and he felt her eyes on him, but forced his gaze to remain on the next team racing into the arena.

"It's been quiet." Did her voice sound sad? Surely not. He must be mistaken. She went on, this time louder and her voice more cheery. "Oscar finished getting the kitchen back in working order and I thought I might try another of my Gran's recipes since Breanna and I did so well with the carrot jam."

Penny leaned away briefly, bumping Breanna's shoulder and making his daughter giggle.

One of the riders in the arena wheeled his horse sharply and the animal rebelled, rearing and throwing off his rider. The crowd gasped; Jonas winced.

"Are you sure the boys will be all right?" Penny asked, voice low for his ears only. Her concern twisted the knot in his stomach even tighter. She sounded like a mother, worrying about her own kids. Like she cared about them.

Something she'd proved over and over.

"Oscar and Edgar have been roping during branding season for years. They've also been bucked off a time or two. They'll be all right."

He felt her eyes rest on his face for a long moment. Heat rushed to his neck at her scrutiny.

"I forget they've been working with you for so long. They seem so much like Sam and his friends that it's hard to think about what they've come through."

Another team came out and had a bit more flair with their ropes, whooping and getting the crowd riled up.

"I think Oscar and Edgar are next," Maxwell said.

Sure enough, Jonas recognized Oscar's distinctive tan Stetson just outside the arena. Edgar was mounted up next to him, though the distance was too far for him to see the boy's features. Edgar's horse danced beneath him. Was the animal responding to his son's nervousness?

Jonas gripped his knees, knowing how important this was to his sons.

Penny tensed. Holding her breath?

The gates opened and the calf shot forward into the arena. The boys' horses quickly followed. Lariats flew overhead and Edgar jumped from his horse to tie the calf's hooves, quickly raising his hands in the air when he finished.

It was over.

The crowd erupted with cheers and applause, but Jonas was so focused on the woman beside him that he heard her quiet exhale and the softly spoken, "Thank you, Lord."

The heartfelt prayer of thankfulness struck Jonas like a fist to the chest. He couldn't breathe.

He wanted her in his life, in his boys' life.

"Didja see, Miss Penny? Didja see, Pa?" Breanna's excitement spilled over as she jumped up and down, wobbling the entire grandstand row. Jonas didn't have the heart to correct her, though Penny quickly reached out and settled the girl with a hand on her shoulder.

"They were fast!" Davy exulted.

The other boys were chattering, too, excited, thrilled.

Only Jonas was silent, consumed with misery but not knowing what he should do. He just wanted to escape.

Penny sensed Jonas pulling away as he went quiet. Luckily, the children were so occupied with excitement for Oscar and Edgar's performance that they didn't seem to notice their father's lack of reaction.

She'd tried her best to reach out without saying anything directly about Breanna or money, but each of his answers had been subdued, even for the usually quiet man. It was obvious he didn't want to be sitting next to her. Didn't even want to speak to her.

Tears pricked the back of her eyes, but she put Mrs. Trimble's training to use and resolutely pasted a smile to her lips and did her best to respond to Breanna's excited statements.

A few moments later, shouts from the crowd milling behind the grandstand began causing a stir; heads turned.

"Miss Penny." Maxwell caught her attention from Jonas's other side, pointing to the disturbance: a hat waving frantically above the milling crowd.

Penny stood and shaded her eyes to try and see what was going on. It was Edgar, waving and calling out to her.

"Excuse me," she murmured, grateful for the chance to escape Jonas's presence, even for a few moments.

"Should I—" Jonas started to ask something and she was afraid he was about to offer to escort her down to meet his son. She needed to get away before he saw her tears!

"I'll see what he needs and be right back," she interrupted, and edged over the people sitting down the row, stepping on toes as she tried to move quickly.

She met Edgar at the edge of the crowd and immediately noticed his hobbling gait.

"What happened?" she demanded, taking hold of his arm to support him.

"Jarred my ankle when I came off the horse, that's all."

"Are you all right?" She pulled off the hat he'd jammed back on his head when he'd seen her coming and brushed a hand through his sweat-matted hair, looking him straight in the eye so he wouldn't be able to fib to her.

"Yes'm," he said, eyes shining in response.

"You and Oscar did a fine job."

He reddened under his tan. "Thanks." Then he ducked his head. "I gotta question for you, Miss Penny. You c'n say no if ya need to."

"What is it?" Did he want her to inform Jonas about his injury? Did he hope she could smooth things for him? If only the boy knew...

"Oscar's real upset that I'm hurt. He don't want me to take my turn on the bronc since I twisted my foot. And with Maxwell not able to ride on account of his broke leg..." He inhaled quickly. "It's real important for us to win this money. For Breanna."

His eyes pleaded with her. For understanding, or something else?

"Would ya ride instead o' me? In my place?"

She thought she'd heard him wrong, both because it was loud with the crowd around and because he whispered.

But the pleading, hangdog look on his face—as if he expected her to say no—convinced her she hadn't misheard.

I can't. The words stuck in her throat. Edgar had been the only one of Jonas's children who hadn't responded to her at all since she'd arrived at Walt's and begun helping out at the White homestead. The fact he'd asked her showed his attitude about her had changed. She didn't want to disappoint him, but...

"It wouldn't be proper for me to ride," she said softly, putting a hand on the boy's shoulder.

"But you tried to help Oscar break that filly. And we all saw you ride the day the cattle got loose. You're even better than Oscar. Pa said so himself. You're the only chance we have to win!"

"Yes, but that was different. That was to help your family." She motioned her hand to encompass the crowd around them. "Look how many people are here."

Though the women in the crowd might not dress as fancy as her mama, she knew it would cause a stir if she rode in a men's competition. Word might even get back to her father in Calvin.

"It's not proper," she repeated, trying to convince herself.

Edgar's disappointment was palpable. His shoulders slumped, chin lowered to bump his chest. "It's all right."

She hated disappointing him. Knew how much the boys wanted to win some prize money and use it to help Jonas. The same man who'd instilled the courage in them that they needed to do it.

The same man who'd taught her what it meant to open her heart. And that real love made sacrifices.

And she loved these boys. She couldn't let them down.

"Wait!" she called out, reaching for Edgar as he shuffled away. "I'll do it."

"Really?" He gaped at her, eyes taking on a shine.

She looked down at the calico dress she wore. "But I won't be able to stay on long dressed like this."

"You can wear my pants and shirt. I'm wearing my long underwear. Thought it might give me some extry padding in case I fell off the bronc." He spoke quickly in his rising excitement. "There's a changing room in the general store. But you gotta hurry!"

Chapter Twenty-One

She shouldn't be doing this.

Of all the things Penny had ever regretted because of her impulsiveness, this decision topped the list.

She couldn't stop shaking as she waited outside the arena, Oscar at her side. She kept her head down, hoping no one could tell there was a woman hiding under Edgar's shirt and trousers. She'd tucked her braid up into the hat, praying it wouldn't be knocked off during her ride.

She felt sick.

For Breanna, she reminded herself silently.

Oscar's turn came and he left her with a final squeeze of her hand. She focused on her boots, unable to watch him ride the bucking horse while knowing she would be next.

The crowd went wild during Oscar's ride, cheering and clapping. Perhaps he'd done well and she didn't have to ride, after all—

And then a shove to the middle of her back sent her reeling up to the prep stall and she was boosted onto the back of a sweating, snorting animal.

"I can't—" She started to gasp, but a grinning, snaggle-toothed cowboy slapped her on the shoulder.

"Have fun, young'un."

"But—"

She swallowed her words as the gate swung open.

For Jonas.

Penny forgot about showmanship and everything else as she clung to the animal's back. The bronco bucked and see-sawed, whirled and wheeled. She thought once that all four of its feet left the ground.

All she could think about was those feet landing on *her* if she fell off.

"That's not Edgar," Maxwell murmured as the rider took to the ring.

Jonas squinted in the midday sunlight, trying to see the rider's features while the animal bucked wildly. Maxwell was right. The figure was too slight, too pale to be his third-oldest son.

"Look at Edgar go!" Breanna cheered from Jonas's other side. The side that felt Penny's conspicuous absence.

"It's Miss Penny." Maxwell breathed the words.

"What?" Was that his voice, sounding strangled? It couldn't be her.

But it was. He caught a flash of copper hair beneath Edgar's hat, caught a flash of those piercing blue eyes he would know anywhere.

"What is she *thinking?*"

"Shh," Max shushed him absently, absorbed in watching Penny's ride. "Don't let Breanna hear," he added.

Probably a good idea.

"Whoohoo!" Ricky shouted from Maxwell's other side. "Ride 'em, Ed!"

"What is she *doing?*" Jonas mumbled, heart in his throat as Penny almost took a spill. By some miracle, she managed to stay on the horse's back.

The crowd roared.

"She's riding."

He could see that, with eyes that would never forget the sight of her clinging to the back of that monstrously large animal.

What he didn't understand was why. Why would she do such a thing? Such an *improper* thing? This was the same woman who'd been ashamed to wear a simple calico dress to church, because it wasn't fancy enough for her tastes. Who couldn't cook a lick and could barely gather eggs. Prim and proper Penny Castlerock was riding a bronc.

Why would she do this?

Jonas watched with bated breath as Penny's ride finished, the horse finally settling after several heart-pounding minutes. The crowd went wild. It was the longest, most action-filled ride so far. There weren't many riders left.

He couldn't wait for the other rides. He had to see Penny now.

He needed to see for himself that she was all right. He stood, receiving an angry grunt from the person behind him, and began edging his way over his children, who were riveted to the next rider in the arena.

"I'm going to go," he coughed, "check on the boys."

Penny braced her palms on her wobbly knees as she tried to catch her breath. Oscar and Edgar hopped and hooted around her.

"I think you won!" Edgar cheered.

"She did," Oscar echoed. "There's only two more riders and they don't look so good."

"Shh." She shushed them. The last thing she needed was for anyone to recognize that she was female. Or worse, to recognize her. She was half-afraid that her grandfather had seen her face while she'd been in the arena.

"What were you *thinking?*" A familiar voice hissed.

Penny looked up from her bent position, right into Jonas's furious face.

"You could've been *killed!*"

The crowd cheered again. One more rider finished. One left.

Jonas grasped her upper arms and pulled her upright, where she couldn't avoid looking him right in the face.

"Edgar needed me," she whispered.

"What if you'd fallen—"

The boys' whooping and hollering interrupted him. Edgar chattered at his father about his ankle getting twisted while Oscar pumped both fists in the air.

"That was the last rider," Oscar crowed.

Someone shouted that "Edgar" had won the bronc-riding contest. Penny was still caught in Jonas's intense gaze, but she was pulled away and pushed onto a platform, presented with a heavy, fancy saddle and a wad of cash. She waved to the crowd, everything a blur until she got off that platform and was surrounded by Oscar, Edgar and Jonas once again.

Oscar relieved her of the saddle that tilted her awkwardly to one side.

She shoved the pile of cash at Jonas. "This is for you."

He recoiled, shaking his head. "You rode. It's your money."

"I'm giving it to you."

His brows furrowed and a look of suspicion crossed his features.

"Take it." She picked up his broad hand and placed the stack of bills in his palm, forcing his fingers to close over it. "It's for Breanna. Because I love her." *And I love you, too.* A sudden lump in her throat kept the words from emerging. He wouldn't want to hear them, anyway.

"Whoohoo!" A familiar young voice cheered. Over Jonas's shoulder, Penny saw the rest of his family approaching.

"I need to go change back into my clothes."

Penny started to move away from Jonas when a cold hand clamped onto her shoulder. A hulking shadow fell over her.

"I can't believe what I've just seen."

She knew that angry, terse voice.

"F-Father?" Penny looked up into her father's furious, purpling face. Standing right behind him was Mr. Abbott, whose weasely features were set in a look of satisfaction.

"Your mother assured me that you would be safe with your grandfather, but *this* is what I find?"

At the same moment, her grandfather and the boys and Breanna swarmed around them, oblivious to Penny's turmoil. She could feel Jonas watching her but he made no move to step between her and her father.

"What did you think you were doing? You've humiliated yourself in front of all these people—"

"She was helping us. We needed the money for Breanna," Edgar explained from Penny's elbow.

Sam and Maxwell stepped closer at the same moment, their shoulders nearly touching, forming a wall of solidarity for her, though they didn't say anything.

Her father glanced over the gathered group, and Penny saw them as she would have in the beginning: worn but clean clothes, some of the boys' faces unwashed, a group that didn't look as if it belonged together.

But now that she knew them, she knew the love that held their family together, the work they'd done together. All because of Jonas and his honor. That was how she wanted her father to see them, but would he listen to her?

"I'm certain you *do* need the money," Mr. Abbott said snidely, turning toward Penny's father and away from the Whites, as if to dismiss them. As if they were beneath his notice.

"Father, the Whites are not only Grandfather's neighbors,

but his friends, and mine as well. They've helped Sam and me get Grandfather's place back in shape."

"I don't care what they've done; that is not the issue here. The issue is that you have brought shame on your family—"

"Now, George, I don't think you need to take that tone with the girl—"

"Stay out of this, old man," her father interrupted her grandfather. "This is not your concern, not after you let my daughter humiliate herself."

"He didn't *allow* Penny to do anything," Jonas interrupted, taking up for him. The scorn in his voice brought tears to her eyes, though. "She does what she wants."

Her father turned on him, too. "I'll thank you to stay out of this. This is not your affair."

"Father—" Sam started, but quieted when his father sent him a scathing glance.

Mr. Abbott moved closer to Penny, partially blocking her view of Jonas and his family. "Perhaps you should advise your farmhand to stay out of this." His voice was a near whisper and with his back to the group, Penny doubted anyone else could hear him. She started to move away, but his next words froze her in place. "I would hate for anyone else to *get hurt* or for any more *disasters* to befall him or his family."

An awful suspicion took root. Penny scrutinized his hateful countenance. "You started the fire in Jonas's fields. And the rest of it."

He didn't deny it; an ugly, prideful smile spread across his face. Penny hated him more than ever.

"How could you do such a thing? Father—"

She started to turn to her father, but Abbott's pinching grip on her forearm caught the words in her throat.

"If you want to ensure nothing else happens to them, you'd better accompany your father and me back to Calvin."

The soft-spoken threat curdled her stomach. She glanced

at her father to see if he'd heard, but he was barking at her grandfather again. She would refuse. Abbott couldn't force her to go with them, not in such a big crowd.

But then she imagined Breanna, little innocent Breanna, injured at Abbott's hand, and she couldn't do it. Couldn't risk them.

"—believe what you want, Walt, but my daughter is coming home with me this instant." Her father turned and the thunderous expression on his face almost made Penny cringe.

Her conversation with Jonas flashed through her memory. This was her moment. She loved Jonas and she loved his family. Without a doubt, she loved them. She wanted to tell her father that she was staying.

But one look at Jonas's closed face and the memory of how he'd turned her away was just as strong.

She wanted to stay, but if she did, would he forgive her for writing to the Broadhursts?

She knew it was impossible to get a moment alone with Jonas, but if she could just see a hint of reassurance in his face. "Jonas—"

The pressure of Abbott's hand on her elbow increased and she turned to him briefly. "Release me at once," she ordered.

He did, but when she turned back, Jonas's face was tilted away.

"Penelope, enough. We're going home. Sam, come along."

How could she refuse? If only Jonas would glance at her and she could determine his feelings…

But it was not to be. "I'm sorry," she said, rounding on her grandfather and embracing him tightly. "I've got to return with my father."

Her grandfather's withered arm came around her. "I'll miss you, girl."

With her chin still tucked against her grandfather's shoulder, she addressed Jonas. "Will you see that he gets home?"

He nodded, expression closed off as if he'd already dismissed her. "I'll take care of him."

She knew that he meant for more than just the ride back to her grandfather's homestead. Jonas would watch out for him.

Just like he did for all those around him—the children, even her.

But no one could get her out of this mess except herself.

Chapter Twenty-Two

Jonas took refuge in the barn, pulling the milking stool into Molly's stall and leaning his head back against the placid animal.

He felt silly hiding from his own children, but he couldn't bear hearing any more comments about Penny.

"I miss her laugh."

"She was helpin' me read."

"She liked to have fun."

"She played awful mean tricks on a body!"

"I miss her hugs." That had been Breanna, accompanied with an overdone sniffle.

With no more haying to do, he'd been stuck inside canning all the vegetables, fruits and berries that were ripening daily. Unable to escape from the kids' chatter, which happened to be full of reminiscing about Penny.

Problem was, he missed all of those things about her and more. He felt like he had a gaping hole in his chest where his heart had been.

After the barn-raising, Penny had been adamant that Abbott wasn't courting her, but when the suitor and her father had shown up, she'd barely said anything at all, which wasn't like the outspoken gal he knew. If she'd wanted to stay with Walt, she would've fought harder, wouldn't she?

Was she even now preparing for a wedding?

The thought created a burn in his gut. He didn't want to believe she'd marry that man, almost as much as he'd wanted to believe she would consider marrying *him*. But he'd ruined the chances of courting her when he'd pushed her away after the fire. Hadn't he?

One niggling doubt kept pressing on him like a headache just behind his eyes that he couldn't get rid of.

Why had Penny really ridden in the bronc contest? She'd said the money was for Breanna. If he sold the fancy saddle, he could probably get another fifty dollars. It would make up the difference he needed to pay for Breanna's treatment. Although now...after he'd thought about Penny's questions mighty hard, he wanted to find out more about the doctor in Cheyenne before he committed to anything. He wouldn't do anything to endanger his daughter.

His thoughts tracked back to Penny. Had she really ridden in the bronc contest, risked being thrown off, risked her identity being revealed in front of that large crowd, for Breanna's sake? If so, did it mean that she really loved his daughter?

And if she loved Breanna...could she possibly come to love *him?*

He wished he knew the answers. Wished he had confidence that she'd meant it when she said she would consider courting him.

The barn door opened and Jonas hunched down even farther next to Molly. Couldn't he have a few minutes alone to lick his wounds?

But no one called out for him. He didn't hear any sounds of footsteps on the packed-dirt floor or any stall doors opening as if someone was searching for him.

"We've got to do something." Maxwell's voice was pitched

low, but with most of the horses out to graze, the barn was quiet enough for Jonas to make out his son's words clearly.

"I know." That was Oscar. What were the two up to? "We're all miserable without Penny around. Pa most of all."

What? How could they tell? Jonas had been doing his best to act normally, even playing games and joking around with the boys after supper most nights. He hadn't wanted them to know the depths of his sorrow since he'd sent Penny back to Walt's place the night of the fire.

"I thought for sure she'd come back." The third voice belonged to Edgar, which surprised Jonas, as he'd been the one most reluctant to let Penny get close. "Maybe that creepy friend of her pa's kidnapped her or somethin' and she can't get loose of him."

Jonas had a hard time believing anyone could keep Penny against her will. She was strong. Strong enough to gain his entire family's trust. Strong enough to worm her way into their lives.

"I dunno," Maxwell replied skeptically. "What if she thinks we don't want her to come back?"

"Pa don't seem to be catching on to our hinting about her."

So *that* was the purpose of their continued remarks about Penny? To convince him to…what?

"We could write a letter, maybe pretend it's from Pa, and ask her to come back."

"What if she *does* come and asks him about the letter—and he don't know anything about it?" That was Maxwell. His son that considered every angle carefully before making a choice.

He needed to put a stop to their finagling, though, before they got themselves—and him—in a spot of trouble.

He stood up from his hiding place beside Molly, his head clearing the edge of the stall, and cleared his throat. Loudly.

All three boys jumped and whirled toward him, the guilt

on their faces speaking more than words. Jonas let himself out of Molly's stall and joined them in the open area just inside the barn doors.

"I guess you heard all that." Oscar was the first to speak, but didn't look particularly apologetic.

"I heard. What makes you all think I've been missing Miss Penny? I've been acting happy, haven't I?"

Edgar answered, "That's the thing…we can tell you're fakin' it." He shrugged. "We figured if we was missing her then you was prob'ly hurting even worse, since you're sweet on her and everything."

Jonas couldn't deny his feelings for Penny.

"And you thought that if you all talked about her enough I'd do what? Ride down to Calvin and ask her to marry me?"

"That sounds like a good plan, Pa. Better'n ours." This from Maxwell. Jonas's usually reserved son said it with dancing eyes.

"You want me to saddle your horse?" Edgar asked, bouncing on his toes.

"You should probably change first. Maybe wear your Sunday suit?" Oscar offered.

Jonas blew out an exasperated breath and sat down on the nearest hay bale. "I'm not going to go to Calvin. And I'm not going to ask Penny to marry me."

The three boys deflated.

"Why not?" Oscar asked.

Jonas took off his hat and ran his hand through his sweat-matted hair. "She would've come back if she wanted to. She's the kind of person who does what she wants." Up until her father had come, anyway.

"What if she can't?" Edgar asked. His earnest expression wasn't hiding any ulterior motives. He was honestly concerned for Penny.

Jonas shook his head.

"Miss Penny told me not to be afraid. That if I wanted to be a doctor I should try." Maxwell sat down next to Jonas and stretched his still-casted foot out in front of him. "Are you afraid if you ask, she'll say no?"

His son's question hit a little too close to home. Jonas didn't want his boys to see him as weak, couldn't admit that he was afraid Penny would find him lacking and leave, just like his parents had.

"She doesn't belong here," Jonas insisted against both his sons and the voice in his head that was starting to take their side. "Do you really think someone like her, someone fancy, could be happy on this little homestead?"

Do you think she could really love me?

He couldn't voice the words, couldn't give them life.

Oscar shrugged. "She seemed happy enough when she was here before."

"That was for a few weeks. A little over a month. If we got married—" Just saying the words sucked all the breath from him and he had to start again. "If we got married, she would be here for good. You know everyone has to pitch in around here. She couldn't do fancy tea parties or the like."

"She seemed to like the barn-raising well enough," Maxwell offered.

"Yeah, she was making friends with all the women. And at church, too," Edgar said.

"She knows how to drive the wagon now, so if she really needed to visit, she could jaunt off to town," Oscar said.

They had an argument for everything!

And the voice in Jonas's head was agreeing with them. Penny *had* seemed happy here, with them. She'd filled their lives with joy and laughter.

It was *Jonas* who'd gotten scared and sent her away.

"I need to think this through. Pray about it." Jonas stood

and moved out of the barn. What he needed was a long walk and time to figure things out.

Dear Penelope,
How delightful to hear from you after all these years! You didn't mention a husband in your letter. Are you still single?

I've been married to my dear Mr. Kenneth for these past three years. He has many investments in the railroad and we are blissfully happy together.

It seems a fortuitous coincidence that you came across the situation addressed in your previous letter. I've often wondered what happened to the child from so long ago.

And yes, you were correct about my childhood episodes. They abated shortly after my fourteenth birthday.
Do stay in touch.
Millie

Exultant, Penny refolded the letter and slipped it back into the thick cream-colored envelope. In her hands, she held the proof that Breanna didn't need an expensive and possibly dangerous treatment to correct her epilepsy. Along with the two other letters Penny had obtained from respected physicians, she hoped to put Jonas's mind at ease. If she could just get back to his homestead.

She needed to tell him her news, as quickly as possible. But Penny settled back onto the settee in her parents' parlor to wait for her father to arrive home. She'd promised she wouldn't run off again, and she would keep that promise. She just needed to find a way to convince her father to take her back to Bear Creek. And Jonas.

She and her father had come to a tentative agreement

about Mr. Abbott, and she didn't want to do anything impulsive to ruin their accord. Sam, too, had settled since their return home. He'd apologized to their parents for his previous pranks and irresponsible behavior, and even taken a job at the livery, working with horses all day. Yes, Sam was growing up and becoming the man she'd known he could be.

Her former friend Millie's veiled reference to Penny's unmarried state had barely registered. That might've bothered her before, but not now that she knew the White family, and loved them, she couldn't be disappointed in her circumstance.

If only she could convince Jonas that they belonged together. She'd gone with her father, but after a week away from the Whites, she was desperate to see them again, desperate to tell Jonas how she felt about him. She should have done so before she left, but she'd let fear get in her way.

She'd spent two days convincing her father that she would never consider marrying Mr. Abbott. He hadn't believed her about Abbott sabotaging Jonas's farm, but after a lot of blustering, he finally came to accept that a wedding was not in the future.

He'd said he would take care of things with Mr. Abbott, and Penny hadn't seen hide nor hair of the man since.

She'd gone to Calvin's town marshal to explain about what had happened at Jonas's homestead, but been disappointed that Marshal Danna Carpenter couldn't do more. Without firm evidence against Abbott, it was Penny's word against his. And although the marshal had said she would question Abbott, Penny knew the man wouldn't admit to any wrongdoing.

Penny wished she'd gotten a better look at the figure on horseback she'd seen that morning while walking over to Jonas's homestead. If she'd seen Abbott's face clearly, maybe then the marshal would have believed her.

The front door opened and closed. Finally, her father was

home. She rose and smoothed the skirt of one of her simpler frocks. Wearing the fine silks and satins she'd enjoyed before wasn't as important to her now.

"Father? I need to talk to you."

The floor in the hallway creaked as her father drew near, but he didn't respond to her greeting. She took a deep breath, prepared to explain all her reasons for visiting the Whites.

"I've just received a letter and it has some very important information that I need to share with Grandfather's neighbors. It's about the little girl, Breanna."

"I'm afraid you won't be going anywhere near that farmhand, my darling."

The unexpected voice preceded Abbott's appearance in the doorway. Penny glanced behind him, expecting to see her father, but the hallway was empty.

"I'm afraid your father has been detained at his office."

Penny backed around the sofa, putting it between herself and the man she hadn't wanted to see ever again. What was his purpose here?

"I have to admire your independent spirit, my dear. It will make settling you more enjoyable for me. I'm not sure how you convinced your father to discourage my suit, but I'll have my way in the end."

She suppressed a shiver at his sinister words, but forced a brave face.

"Mr. Abbott, as you said, my father is away. It's not appropriate for you to be here, so I'll ask you to leave."

Abbott slipped a derringer from the inside of his vest and pointed it at Penny. "I think not. You're coming with me."

"I won't." Somehow, she kept her voice from shaking, but the sight of his weapon unnerved her. Would he really shoot her if she didn't do what he wanted?

"You're questioning whether I'll fire on my intended bride. Your face is so delightfully expressive, my dear." He inhaled deeply, his eyes closing momentarily. "Yes, breaking you will be ever so enjoyable."

"I'll thank you not to call me *my dear*. I'm not *your* anything." Penny backed farther away, frantically trying to figure out a way to escape the man. She had no intention of accompanying him anywhere. She ran into the writing desk in the corner, bruising the back of her legs.

"Oh, you will be. I've a preacher waiting in Cheyenne to marry us. Now come along, I've got the train tickets here." He patted his breast pocket with the hand not holding his gun. "We'll be off immediately."

"I won't marry you. I don't want anything to do with you." Her hand closed over a letter opener on the desk. Did she have the fortitude to use it as a weapon?

Chapter Twenty-Three

Jonas adjusted the tie Oscar had talked him into. It felt like it was strangling him.

He strode down the boardwalk in Calvin, the same way he had over a month ago, with the same destination in mind. The bank. Only this time his purpose was completely different.

He'd come to ask if he could court Penny.

The boys had voted for him to ask for her hand, but he thought he might have better luck if he started slowly.

He tried to swallow, but his mouth was drier than his burned out fields. What if her father denied him?

What if *Penny* denied him? What if she couldn't forgive him for sending her away?

He blew out a shaky breath. He'd spent two days thinking and praying after his conversation with his three oldest sons. And he'd finally decided they were right. He couldn't let fear rule his life.

He had to know if Penny could accept him. He prayed it was so.

Another deep breath and he was there, just outside the gilt glass doors of Mr. Castlerock's bank. He pulled, but nothing happened.

Locked.

Pulled again, and the door rattled. Definitely locked. Was he too late to catch Penny's father at the bank?

A sound from inside had him shading his eyes against the late-afternoon sun's glare on the windows. Was someone still there?

After a glance around and noting that the dirt-packed streets were nearly empty, Jonas decided to try one more time.

"Hello?" he called through the doors. "I need to see Mr. Castlerock!"

This time, he definitely heard a noise from inside.

A moan.

"Is someone there? Do you need help?"

Jonas leaned closer to the glass-plated door, but couldn't see enough of the inside of the bank to determine if anyone was in there. It was too shadowy inside.

He moved to a large window that took up most of the building's outer wall and peered inside. There! It looked like someone was lying on the floor half-behind one of the desks.

Jonas glanced around again, but there was no one around, no one he could ask for assistance.

"Do you need help?" he shouted, hoping the person could hear him through the window.

He leaned his head close to the glass and heard a soft, "Help."

But looking at the window, there was no latch, and the sill looked solid.

"I can't get in the front!" Jonas shouted. "I'll have to break the window!"

He only hoped the glass wouldn't fall on the person lying prone inside.

"Can you move away?" Jonas called through the window. He listened for a response and heard a faint, "Back...door..."

There was another entrance? Jonas hurried around the side of the building, until he found a rear door, this one nothing like the fancy facade at the front, and pushed inside.

He made his way to the lobby, where it appeared there had been a brawl. The interior looked nothing like the organized office he'd seen when he'd visited during his previous trip to Calvin. Desks and chairs were shoved into odd configurations. Papers were strewn across the floor.

Jonas moved to where he'd seen the figure on the floor, mouth opening in surprise as he knelt next to Castlerock himself. The man's hands and feet were bound. There had been a handkerchief twisted around his face as a gag, but he'd managed to wiggle it off.

Jonas quickly moved to untie the knots binding Castlerock's hands. "Sir, are you all right?"

"Of course I'm not all right. Look at me!" the older man blustered.

Jonas freed Castlerock's hands and helped the man sit up, before scooting down to untie his feet. "Were you robbed? Should I try to find the marshal?"

The older man rubbed his wrists, appearing agitated. "I was trying to tell that fool Abbott my daughter wants nothing to do with him and he went raving mad. Knocked me around before I could reach the pistol I keep in the bottom of my desk and then tied me up."

Jonas's heart thudded at Castlerock's mention that Penny had refused Abbott. She wasn't marrying the other man. Relief roared through him, and leaving him momentarily feeling weak.

Then he heard the last part of Castlerock's sentence and went cold.

"—she tried to tell me there was something wrong about him but I thought she was just refusing on principle. I'd never subject my daughter to a madman."

Finally loose, Castlerock shifted his legs a bit—shaking blood back into them, Jonas imagined—and used the nearby desk to lever himself up.

Jonas rose from his crouch. "If he's angry, might this man go after your daughter?" What if Penny was in danger this very minute?

Castlerock's face paled. "D'you think—? I've got to go for the marshal."

Remembering the broken barn ladder and the fields burned with no regard for human life, Jonas began to tremble. "It might be too late. What if he's already got her?"

Castlerock shook his head, moving to the outer doors and unlocking them. "As you can see, I'm no match for Abbott. Better to let the marshal and her deputies get involved."

Maybe it was better for the gently bred man, but Jonas's woman was in danger! He didn't wait for Castlerock, but brushed past the older man and took off down the boardwalk toward the stately home farther in town.

"Wait—"

Jonas couldn't wait. He had to get to Penny, now.

"I *said* I won't go with you, so you might as well just leave now."

Still clutching the letter opener amongst the folds of her skirt, Penny didn't dare turn her back on the lunatic holding a gun on her.

She'd known there was something off about Abbott from the beginning, but she'd never imagined he was actually insane. And it must be insanity that made him imagine she would marry him after everything that had happened. Did her father know?

Abbott moved farther into the room, leering at her. "While I'm certain I would enjoy the struggle you would put up, *my dear,* I'd prefer you not be too mussed for our little train ride."

Behind Abbott, a shadow passed over the parlor window. Was someone coming? Penny's heart began thumping in her ears.

"I'm not going with you." Penny slipped across the room, careful to face him at all times.

"I'm afraid the business dealings with your father were just a ruse, Penelope. While I *do* have money—enough to do most anything I want—I knew from the moment I met you that I had to have you for my wife. I'll enjoy bending your independent spirit to my will. No matter how long it takes."

Penny shivered, unable to conceal the reaction from Abbott's intense gaze. How had her father ever thought this man was a good business partner? Had Abbott hidden his true motives that well?

Her over-aware senses picked up a soft sound from the front of the house. The door opening?

Unfortunately, Abbott heard it, too, because he turned toward the hallway.

"Sam!" Penny shouted, taking a guess to who was coming inside. "Watch out!"

"Why, you little—"

Penny crouched behind the heavy wingback chair in the corner, afraid Abbott would fire on her, but he stomped into the hallway. Penny craned her neck from her hiding place to see late-afternoon light streaming onto the wood floor. Someone *had* opened the front door. Had Sam heeded her warning and run away?

She waited for a shot to be fired, or shouts, or anything, but only heard eerie silence and the clamoring of her heart.

The door slammed and she heard Abbott's heavy tread indicating he was returning. "Must've been the wind that blew it open. We have no more time to waste." He waved the gun wildly at her. "Get up. We're leaving now."

"No—"

Penny's denial was cut short when a figure launched at

Abbott from the opposite direction, the back hallway, and attacked him.

A flash of blond hair glinted in the lamplight—those shoulders—

"Jonas!" she cried.

He glanced at her, and in that moment of distraction Abbott's fist connected with his cheek.

"Oh!" Penny stifled her cry by biting her knuckle. How had Jonas come to be here?

The tussle continued, fists flying. From her hiding place, Penny couldn't remove her eyes from the silver derringer as Jonas wrested Abbott's arm to one side and banged it against the wall. Abbott didn't release the gun.

The sounds of fists hitting flesh made Penny cringe, but she couldn't tell if either man was winning. It worried her that Abbott still held the gun. What if he got a shot off and it hit Jonas? At this range he likely wouldn't miss.

She couldn't let that happen.

Penny crept out from behind the chair on shaking legs. She stayed on her hands and knees, hoping Abbott wouldn't see her movement if she stayed behind the settee.

The men shifted and bumped against the wall in the hallway, sending a framed portrait to the floor with a crash.

Penny reached up and hefted her mother's heavy brass lamp from the table, then edged around the settee and put her back against the wall, standing next to the doorway. How could she be sure to hit Abbott and not Jonas?

Heart racing, her grip damp against the metal lamp, she prayed *God help me!,* raised the heavy object above her head and flung herself around the corner.

Jonas's heart nearly stopped when Penny flung herself into the altercation. He hadn't been able to take the small gun from Abbott and as far as he knew, it was still loaded.

Penny clubbed Abbott in the shoulder with a piece of furniture, and he finally dropped the gun. It skidded on the wooden floor, disappearing in the shadows.

"Please—" Jonas gasped. "Get back!"

He elbowed her out of the way, putting himself between her and Abbott. The other man swung a wild punch and Jonas dodged it, returning with a quick jab to Abbott's face that whipped his head back. He slumped to the floor as the front door banged open and two men rushed inside with pistols drawn.

"Hands up!" one of them ordered.

"Wait!" Penny exclaimed, reinserting herself into the conflict by moving in front of Jonas. She wrapped one hand over his shoulder, as if to shield him from the deputies. "That's the man you want." She pointed to Abbott lying on the floor. "Jonas came in as he was trying to kidnap me and they fought."

One of the deputies, tin star flashing on his chest, knelt next to Abbott and patted his clothing. Probably determining he didn't have any more weapons.

"He dropped his gun," Penny said helpfully, pointing down the hall.

"This the man we're looking for?" the second deputy asked. He didn't address Penny or Jonas, and for the first time Jonas noticed Castlerock standing just outside the open front door.

Castlerock nodded. "He was my business partner…" He shook his head, seemed to shake himself out of his thoughts.

Abbott began to rouse and the deputies each took one of Abbott's arms and hefted him to his feet, holding him securely between them. They ushered him out of the house, saying something to Castlerock as they went.

The older man hurried inside, reaching for Penny. "Are

you all right? Were you hurt? Oh, thank goodness your mother wasn't here. She'd have had a conniption…"

She went into her father's embrace, leaving Jonas's side. "I'm fine. A little shaken up. Thankful that Jonas arrived before that awful man could force me to leave with him." Over her father's shoulder, Penny gazed admiringly at Jonas. Or was he imagining her looking at him that way because that's what he wanted her to feel?

"Yes, we have much to thank this young man…" Castlerock seemed to take a good look at Jonas for the first time. "Say… You're Walt's neighbor."

Penny drew away from her father. "Father, this is Jonas White. I think you might've met him the night of your most recent party. He has a beautiful homestead near Bear Creek. Grandfather's going to help him get started raising horses."

The pride in her voice encouraged Jonas to extend his hand. He half-expected Castlerock to reject it, but the other man stepped forward and accepted his handshake.

"I'm grateful for what you did for my daughter this evening. Will you accept a monetary reward?"

Shocked, it took Jonas a moment to respond. "No, sir. I actually came to ask you—" He glanced at Penny, listening attentively at her father's elbow. "I came to speak to you about another matter." If Castlerock intended to deny his request to court Penny, Jonas didn't want her to know.

"Hmm." Castlerock considered him briefly. "I suppose I can spare a few minutes for you. Come into my office—"

"Father," Penny chided, interrupting. "Jonas is a little banged up from rescuing me. Can your talk wait for a few minutes? I'll see about fixing him up."

Castlerock agreed, though reluctantly, sizing up Jonas with a look. Jonas wondered if the man could sense his nervousness. Now that the altercation with Abbott was resolved and he knew Penny was all right, his misgivings were back in full force.

"Come into the kitchen." Penny took Jonas's arm and pulled him along the hallway and into a large, open room with a long table in the center. She pushed him down onto one of the stools lining the table and turned to rustle through a cupboard. "I know it's here…"

She let out a triumphant exclamation and turned back to set a glass bottle of antiseptic and a clean cloth next to Jonas's elbow. He lost his breath when she moved close, thumbing his chin to tilt his head to one side.

"You've got a scrape on your jaw…" Her breath warmed his cheek, sending goose bumps along his neck and down his spine.

It was a reversal of the few moments he'd spent doctoring her scrape after Breanna's seizure in the wagon, back when he hadn't known her at all.

With her chin just inches away, he couldn't help focusing on the sweet bow of her lips. She'd kissed him once before with those very lips.

"Here, tilt up a little more. I can't see…" She dabbed at his jaw with a damp cloth, almost businesslike in her movements. Did she not feel the bubbling current between them?

"I can't believe you just attacked Mr. Abbott like that. Did you know he had a gun?"

"Yes." It hadn't mattered to him, except not wanting the weapon to be pointed at Penny.

"Well, you could've been hurt. Or killed. Who would've taken care of your children if something had happened to you?"

Couldn't she sound a little happy to see him? "Nothing did happen."

"Shh, be still," she scolded him. "Let me finish here."

Was this his answer? Should he not even ask her father

if he could court her? She didn't seem to have any reaction to seeing him. He clenched his jaw to keep from asking her something that would embarrass them both.

He couldn't help the flare of his nostrils when she dabbed the antiseptic on his skin. It burned. Almost as much as the hand she'd braced on his shoulder.

"There. Almost..."

She set aside the cloth and her hand moved from his shoulder to the nape of his neck, her fingers sliding into his hair.

She pursed her lips and blew on his stinging skin. He needed to draw away—she was too close—

And then the pressure of her thumb and forefinger holding his chin changed and she drew his face upward. Their lips met and this time he did what he wished he'd done the first time: he crushed her to his chest, arms coming around her slender waist. He couldn't be sure which of them deepened the kiss, but it didn't matter because he was drowning in the sensation of holding her, the smell of her, her mouth against his—

She broke from the kiss, pulled away, pressing her face into his shoulder and whispering, "I'm so glad you weren't killed."

Her words doused him in cold reality. Was relief the reason she'd kissed him? He'd thought they were coming together this time out of similar emotions—because they cared for each other. Had he been wrong?

"You've ripped your jacket, too," she said, voice muffled against his collarbone. She fingered the seam above his shoulder. "Perhaps I can mend it for you after your discussion with father. It wouldn't take long."

He wanted her to mend it for him while sitting in the rocker in his cabin. A strangled "Maybe," was all he could manage to push past his suddenly stiff lips.

He wished he knew more about females. What did her kiss mean? Did she have feelings for him at all?

He released his hold on her waist, gently pushing her away. "I need to go—your father's waiting." He'd come here for a reason, and he wouldn't back out, even if he was unsure of her feelings. He'd promised the boys he would go through with it, and he couldn't disappoint them. Even if he ended up being the one disappointed.

"Jonas." She put a hand on his arm, halting him when he would have stood up from the stool. "Please, I'd like to speak to you after you and my father are done discussing your business. It's important."

It sounded as if she didn't know that *she* was the business he was here to take care of.

Still reeling from her kiss and confused by her manner— maybe he'd gotten whacked harder than he thought by Abbott because he couldn't get his thoughts to make any sense—he only nodded dumbly and allowed her to point him to her father's study down the hall from the kitchen.

Castlerock was waiting for him, sitting behind a wide, expensive-looking desk with fingers steepled above his paunch.

Jonas took a seat in the chair the other man indicated. The furnishings in this room alone were much nicer than those in his cabin. It reminded him of the Broadhursts' home in Philadelphia. He was also conscious of Castlerock's orderly appearance, while he knew his Sunday suit was rumpled from the scuffle. In the past, it might've made him feel out of place or uncomfortable, but after Penny's admiration when she'd introduced him, he felt confident. Somewhat.

"What can I do for you, son? Still looking for money?"

Jonas swallowed. So Castlerock did remember him from the evening Jonas had interrupted his elegant party, and Jonas's meeting at the bank the next morning. Jonas could only hope that those impressions wouldn't affect Castlerock's answer to what Jonas was getting ready to ask.

"No, sir. Not about money." He stopped, all the words he'd practiced on the ride into Calvin fleeing his brain. He went on, knowing he should just get this over with. "Your daughter was a big help to both Walt and me while she was visiting."

Castlerock's eyebrows rose. "I find that hard to believe. Penelope hasn't done an ounce of manual labor in her life."

"Well, maybe she wasn't so much help at first, but she learned." And she'd brought color into his life, his family's life. "The thing is, as I came to know your daughter, I started to—to care about her." He couldn't say the word *love,* not when Castlerock was staring him down so intently.

His chest was tightening up at the same rate that Castlerock's face was closing off. Jonas rushed to get the words out. "I'd like to ask permission to court your daughter. With the—with the intention of getting married. If she'll have me."

Castlerock's face was completely devoid of emotion. Jonas had no idea what the man was going to say.

"That's an interesting proposition from someone who not six weeks ago was barging in on my party and begging for money."

Jonas's face flamed. What Castlerock said was true. Although he hadn't quite begged for money, he'd been desperate to get funds to pay for Breanna's treatment.

"I have to admit I'm concerned how a man in circumstances such as yours plans to take care of my daughter. As you know, she's used to certain fine things." Castlerock gestured expansively at their surroundings.

Jonas knew that. He knew there was a chance Penny wouldn't be happy living in the conditions his homestead could support. But wasn't that her decision to make?

"Or perhaps you think if you marry my daughter, I will

support you and your passel of offspring? I can assure you that is not an option."

Anger surged through Jonas's veins, sending him to his feet, as he finally understood what Castlerock had been getting at. "I don't want to marry your daughter for money," he argued hotly. "That thought never crossed my mind. I know we come from different social circles, but I love your daughter. That's what she wants from a husband, you know."

Jonas turned to leave, pulse thundering in his ears. He knew he'd ruined his chances this time. He should turn back, apologize to the other man, but the implication that he wanted to be with Penny for her possible inheritance was too big an insult.

"Wait," Castlerock commanded.

Jonas stopped, one hand on the door, blood still boiling.

The man considered him for a long moment. "You'd better sit back down. We've more talking to do."

Chapter Twenty-Four

Penny's mother had returned from her afternoon tea while the men were sequestered in her father's study. She'd demanded an explanation for the disheveled state of her house and the broken lamp, and when Penny had told her everything that had happened, went into a swoon.

After reviving her mother and settling her in bed upstairs with a moist towel covering her face, Penny stopped for a moment in her room for a quick glance in her looking glass.

Cheeks flushed, hair wisping out of the pins she'd put in earlier, eyes shining. She looked like what she was—a woman in love. But could she convince Jonas to give their relationship another try?

Voices from below alerted her that the men had exited her father's study. She rushed into the hallway and met her father on the stairs.

"Your mother?" her father asked.

"In her room. She didn't react well to the events of the evening."

He half smiled. "I'd better go check on her. Your young man is waiting in the parlor."

Was it her imagination, or was her father's gaze a bit more considering than it had been since she'd returned home from

Philadelphia without a husband? He patted her hand and then moved past her on the stairs, leaving her to go to Jonas on her own.

She found him standing in the parlor doorway, looking anxious, bending his hatbrim in both fists. He watched her descend the last few steps without saying anything. He cleared his throat.

Suddenly nervous herself, she asked, "Should we—do you want to sit down?" Her hand flipped toward the parlor, gesturing awkwardly.

"I—" He grimaced and looked over his shoulder to the room that was still in disarray.

"Oh. There's a swing on the front veranda," she offered and he nodded, still silent.

She preceded him out the door and sat on the swing, settling her skirts around her. Jonas hesitated, but then perched beside her, dropping his hat on one knee. In the fading sunlight, she could see his hands shaking.

His subdued manner made her ask, "Did my father— did your business conclude in a satisfactory manner?" That wasn't too forward, was it?

He coughed. "Yes. At least I hope so." He shifted on the seat, angling more in her direction. "I came to ask your father if I could court you."

"You did?"

He captured her hand in one of his larger hands, then remained looking down on their joined appendages. "Is this all right?"

She nodded, dizzy with emotion, heart pounding nearly as loudly as it had when she'd been threatened by Abbott earlier.

"I told your father that I've come to care about you. And he said—your father said it was all right if you felt the same—if you agreed to allow me to court."

A slow smile spread across her face, echoing the joy in her

heart. "He did? But how did you come to change your mind? You sent me away…"

She watched in fascination as a flush spread up his neck and into his face. "I had some help."

She could only imagine. "Was it purely Breanna, or did the boys have a hand in it?"

He shook his head, responding to her smile with a tentative one of his own. "It wasn't Breanna at all. Oscar, Maxwell and Edgar concocted a plan to convince me to come after you."

"Edgar? Really?"

He squeezed her hand. "Mmm. Seems you've won him over, just like everyone else in the family."

"Even you?"

He let his gaze rest on her face, let her see the seriousness in his eyes. "Especially me. You captured my heart in Philadelphia and have kept it all this time. Only I was afraid you wouldn't be able to love someone like me," he admitted.

He lowered his face to look at their clasped hands. His thumb slowly followed the line of her finger and then back, sending shivers up her arm. "You haven't given me an answer yet."

"Hmm. Well, considering my plans from earlier this evening, before Abbott came in and ruined everything, I'd say the answer would be yes."

"What plans?"

"I'd just received a letter—a very important letter concerning Breanna's health and future prospects—and I was waiting for my father to arrive so I could convince him that I needed to visit you."

She shrugged and looked out over the dark lawn as she spoke her next words, knowing she was blushing. "I was planning to make a passionate appeal about Breanna needing a woman in her life. And something about how I've proven that I can handle myself on your homestead and that you should give our relationship a second chance."

"And if that didn't work…"

"Then I planned to just admit it outright. That I love you. And see if that worked to change your mind."

She risked a glance at him, taking in his stunned expression and slightly open mouth.

"You…love…*me?*"

"Yes—"

He crushed her to his chest, sending the swing swaying and creaking. His jaw pressed against her temple and she heard his ragged breaths and realized that it wasn't just his hands that were shaking—his whole body was quaking.

She also realized it was quite a pleasant feeling, being held so tightly.

"Penny—" The stubble on his jaw rasped against her cheek as he placed a kiss in the hair just above her ear. "I can't—"

She slipped her arm, the only part of her she could move, around his side and grasped a handful of his jacket, holding him just as tightly.

"I feel as if I'm about to burst from all the happiness inside," he whispered. "I never—I didn't really believe you could actually love me back."

"Love you back, hmm?"

He eased away, hands still locked behind her back, until she could see his dear face.

"I think I've loved you since that first day, riding in the wagon. When you held Breanna after her seizure…"

His eyes raked over her face as if he wanted to memorize every feature. Her chin tilted toward his naturally and this time *he* kissed *her,* melding their lips together the same way their hearts had just connected.

Moments later, he drew away, breathing hard, and pressed

her head against his shoulder once more. "I think I like your kisses entirely too much."

She gave a soft "hmm" of agreement, content to be close with him like this. Until she remembered his last words before the kiss.

"Speaking of Breanna," she murmured, "I have the letter here."

She touched her pocket and the paper rattled, but it was too much effort to remove it. She liked where she was settled next to Jonas.

"I can't read it," he returned. "Not until you teach me how."

She smiled against his shoulder. "Maxwell giving you a hard time about his lessons?"

He shook his head, chin brushing against her hair. "No. It's something I want for myself."

She felt another surge of joy that he'd decided to do something simply for himself. "Breanna's letter," she went on, trying to remain focused, "is actually from Millie. I was a little disappointed that she wasn't more concerned about her own daughter. She barely mentioned her, was more interested in telling me all about her own life now."

He released a breath she hadn't noticed he'd been holding. "I'm not disappointed. I don't want—I thought the family might one day try to take Breanna back."

Her breath caught. Of course he worried about that. When nearly everyone in his life had abandoned him, he didn't want to lose his beloved daughter. She squeezed his waist.

"I have my doubts. They were so worried about scandal and the circumstances of her conception would certainly qualify. Anyway, the *important* part of the letter was that Millie *did* suffer from seizures during her childhood, but they went away during her teen years. No treatments required. And I've corresponded with a couple of other doctors, well-respected ones, about the possibility that she might get better with time."

He moved away slightly and she wondered if he was still angry that she'd contacted Millie. But when he spoke, his voice was hesitant. "What do the doctors say?"

"With a condition like Breanna's, they can't say for certain that the seizures will go away as she gets older, but it *has* happened for other children. And if the condition is hereditary, if Breanna only has it because Millie had it, then it seems likely it will go away on its own."

He tensed. "I know that you care about Breanna and want what's best for her. I'd like to talk to some of these doctors myself. I'm not ready to give up on a cure for her. I love her too much."

"If you want to keep searching for a cure, we will. I love Breanna, too, you know. And all the boys. Even Davy and his mischief."

"That's good to know. They're all waiting over at the hotel to find out if you accepted my suit."

She stood up from the swing. "Why didn't you say so? Let's go tell them together."

Epilogue

"I'm glad we chose a Christmas wedding," Penny murmured, snuggling closer into Jonas's side under the heavy layer of blankets. Snow fell all around the sleigh, muffling sounds and making it seem as if they were the only two people on earth right now.

"It was a pretty service," he agreed, the words muted by the scarf he'd looped around his chin and lower face. She suspected he'd have said that if the ceremony was as simple as standing up after Sunday morning services and pledging their lives to each other.

Unfortunately, Penny's mother had wanted an extravagant affair for her only daughter. Jonas had suffered through many conversations about pine boughs and fancy dresses with good humor.

After winning over her father, Penny's mother was easy in comparison.

Jonas's initial courting had consisted of a couple of sporadic trips to Calvin, where he'd had to bring along the children because it was too much for her grandfather to watch over all of them. Finally, Penny's mother had taken pity on the pair and arranged an extended visit with Walt for herself and her daughter, to keep things appropriate.

With Penny only a short walk away, Jonas had been a frequent visitor, and she'd spent much time on his homestead with the children.

She knew Jonas had been afraid she might tire of him or change her mind about their relationship, but the more time they spent together, the deeper she fell in love with him. With some not-so-subtle urging from the boys, he'd proposed in the fall.

Now, he flipped the reins and urged the horses pulling their sleigh to move faster, probably as anxious as she was to get home. To *their* cabin. And *their* children. The animals seemed to realize they were almost to their warm barn, and they sped up accordingly.

"I am sorry we couldn't take a longer honeymoon." Jonas shifted next to her. Probably as stiff and cold as she was after the long ride. "You deserve more than two nights in Cheyenne. I'm sure there are plenty of fancier hotels back East…"

"I don't want to be back East. I'm right where I want to be." She reached up and smacked a kiss on the small patch of bare skin at his temple, quickly ducking her face back into her own scarf to escape the frigid air.

"I'm glad. Because we're about to give up our privacy for the next thirteen or so years, until Breanna leaves home."

"Hmm," she hummed, leaning her head against his shoulder. "Or longer, if we have children of our own…"

He inhaled deeply. "Hadn't thought of that—"

The sleigh topped the last rise before they'd pulled into the yard and immediately a shout rang out. "They're home!"

Chattering voices echoed across the silent, still evening. Light spilled across the darkened landscape and the family tumbled over each other onto the porch, waving and yelling wildly.

"They must've been waiting for us," Penny said, unable to

stop her smile. She raised her gloved hand and waved back, scattering snow and making Jonas chuckle in her enthusiasm.

"Pa! Ma!"

Hearing the title for the first time—Breanna had tentatively asked if it would be all right to call Penny "ma" just before the wedding—Penny's heart threatened to burst.

Yes, she was right where she belonged. Home.

* * * * *

Dear Reader,

Thank you for picking up this book! I hope you fell in love with Jonas White like I did. Jonas had strength enough to overcome his past, including being abandoned by his parents and surviving life on the streets of Philadelphia. He could have let his past turn him into a bitter, cynical person, but instead he chose to use it to help him understand the orphaned kids he brought into his life. Jonas's compassion and big heart are two of the things I like best about him.

I'd love to hear what you thought about Jonas and this book! Visit my website at www.lacywilliams.net or send me an email at lacyjwilliams@gmail.com.

Lacy Williams

Questions for Discussion

1. Jonas White is passionate about finding a cure for his daughter, if possible. He is willing to do anything to help her. What is the one thing you're most passionate about and why?

2. Why do you think Jonas's family is so important to him?

3. Penny Castlerock has dual motives for visiting her grandfather—one unselfish and one selfish. Have you ever worked on a project or helped someone with more than one reason behind your motivation? What was the end result of those actions?

4. In the beginning of this book, fancy clothes and fine things are very important to Penny. Is there anything wrong with thinking this way? What dangers could come from putting too much value on possessions?

5. Penny believes a lie about Jonas based on gossip and half-truths. Have you ever believed something and later found out the truth? How did it make you feel?

6. Jonas's daughter Breanna suffers from a disorder that causes her to have occasional seizures, but she embraces the little joys in her life. Have you ever been close to someone with a disorder or disability? What did you admire most about that person?

7. Penny worries about her brother, Sam, and tries to encourage him to behave better. Have you ever been close

to someone you thought was making a wrong decision or behaving badly? What did you do?

8. Penny and Jonas come from very different circumstances. Her family is comfortably wealthy while he must work hard to survive on his simple homestead. Have you ever known someone who was in a very different social circle than you? In what ways did it affect your friendship?

9. Penny makes the decision to write a letter to find out more about Breanna's condition without letting Jonas know about it. Have you ever done something like this without another person's knowledge? What happened in that situation?

10. Penny earns the respect of the White family by doing simple things to help them, and not because of her family's money or social standing. Describe a time when your view of someone else changed based on their actions and not on status.

11. Jonas's abandonment by his parents makes him believe that others will eventually leave him, too. Give an example of something from your past that has shaped the way you think today.

12. What do you think causes Penny to start seeing Jonas in a different light?

13. Penny rides a bronco to help Jonas's family. Have you ever done something outrageous or dangerous? What was it and why did you decide to do it?

14. Jonas must overcome his fears of being unworthy to win Penny's heart. Discuss a fear that you have had to overcome. How did you get past it?

15. What do you think was the theme message of this book?

INSPIRATIONAL

Love Inspired.

celebrating
15
YEARS

HISTORICAL

COMING NEXT MONTH
AVAILABLE JUNE 12, 2012

A BABY BETWEEN THEM
Irish Brides
Winnie Griggs

THE BARON'S GOVERNESS BRIDE
Glass Slipper Brides
Deborah Hale

A PROPER COMPANION
Ladies in Waiting
Louise M. Gouge

WINNING THE WIDOW'S HEART
Sherri Shackelford

REQUEST YOUR FREE BOOKS!

2 FREE INSPIRATIONAL NOVELS
PLUS 2
FREE
MYSTERY GIFTS

Love Inspired

HISTORICAL
INSPIRATIONAL HISTORICAL ROMANCE

YES! Please send me 2 FREE Love Inspired® Historical novels and my 2 FREE mystery gifts (gifts are worth about $10). After receiving them, if I don't wish to receive any more books, I can return the shipping statement marked "cancel". If I don't cancel, I will receive 4 brand-new novels every month and be billed just $4.49 per book in the U.S. or $4.99 per book in Canada. That's a saving of at least 22% off the cover price. It's quite a bargain! Shipping and handling is just 50¢ per book in the U.S. and 75¢ per book in Canada.* I understand that accepting the 2 free books and gifts places me under no obligation to buy anything. I can always return a shipment and cancel at any time. Even if I never buy another book, the two free books and gifts are mine to keep forever.

102/302 IDN FEHF

Name	(PLEASE PRINT)	
Address		Apt. #
City	State/Prov.	Zip/Postal Code

Signature (if under 18, a parent or guardian must sign)

Mail to the **Reader Service:**
IN U.S.A.: P.O. Box 1867, Buffalo, NY 14240-1867
IN CANADA: P.O. Box 609, Fort Erie, Ontario L2A 5X3
Not valid for current subscribers to Love Inspired Historical books.

Want to try two free books from another series?
Call 1-800-873-8635 or visit www.ReaderService.com.

* Terms and prices subject to change without notice. Prices do not include applicable taxes. Sales tax applicable in N.Y. Canadian residents will be charged applicable taxes. Offer not valid in Quebec. This offer is limited to one order per household. All orders subject to credit approval. Credit or debit balances in a customer's account(s) may be offset by any other outstanding balance owed by or to the customer. Please allow 4 to 6 weeks for delivery. Offer available while quantities last.

Your Privacy—The Reader Service is committed to protecting your privacy. Our Privacy Policy is available online at www.ReaderService.com or upon request from the Reader Service.

We make a portion of our mailing list available to reputable third parties that offer products we believe may interest you. If you prefer that we not exchange your name with third parties, or if you wish to clarify or modify your communication preferences, please visit us at www.ReaderService.com/consumerschoice or write to us at Reader Service Preference Service, P.O. Box 9062, Buffalo, NY 14269. Include your complete name and address.

LIH11B

Love Inspired HISTORICAL

celebrating
15
YEARS

Author
WINNIE GRIGGS

brings you another story from

Irish Brides

For two months, Nora Murphy cared for an abandoned infant she found while on her voyage from Ireland to Boston. Now settled in Faith Glen, Nora tells herself she's happy with little Grace and a good job as housekeeper to Sheriff Cameron Long. A traumatic childhood closed Cam off to any dreams of family life. Yet somehow his lovely housekeeper and her child have opened his heart again. When the unthinkable occurs, it will take all their faith to reach a new future together.

A Baby Between Them

Available June 2012 wherever books are sold.

www.LoveInspiredBooks.com

LIH82919

celebrating
15 YEARS

Get swept away with author

Carolyne Aarsen

Saving lives is what E.R. nurse Shannon Deacon excels at. It also distracts her from painful romantic memories and the fact that her ex-fiancé's brother, Dr. Ben Brouwer, just moved in next door. She doesn't want anything to do with him, but Ben is also hurting from a failed marriage…and two determined matchmakers think Ben and Shannon can help each other heal. Will they take a second chance at love?

Healing the Doctor's Heart

Home to
Hartley Creek

Available June 2012 wherever books are sold.

www.LoveInspiredBooks.com